Praise for First Edition (
Stanley G. West's *Amos*

". . . a first novel of extraordinary impact . . . a work of literature. This novel will warm your heart, lift your spirits and make you feel a certain goodness that we're prone to lose . . . [it is] about life, love, and being close to another person. About mistakes and petty human foolishness, and the senseless hurts we inflict upon those we care for most."
—Paul Bach, *Desert Sentinel*

"West has penned an unusual, well-written novel . . . The book features some marvelous descriptive passages that will be remembered long after the last page has been turned. The skillful plotting and the warm human relationships make it exciting, first-rate reading."
—Judy Schuster, *Minneapolis Star Tribune*

"This is a remarkable story . . . West shows himself to be a seasoned storyteller, offering the reader a variety of emotions . . . Suspense is built layer upon layer . . . And holding the story together is a theology that elevates the human spirit to heroic heights."
—Clark Morphew, *St. Paul Dispatch*

"This very good first novel . . . is an off-beat tale that features good characterization . . . solid background detail, and a strong sense of the value of human life. Highly recommended."
—James B. Hemesath, *Library Journal*

"The least likely protagonist of the year has to be Aaron Lasher, a resident of a seedy country poor farm called Sunset Home . . . Yet West has created a hero in prose that lives up to the promise of the novel's first sentence: 'He was an old man, clinging fiercely to the tattered garment that had once been his dignity.' Comparisons to *One Flew Over the Cuckoo's Nest* and even the film *Cool Hand Luke* are inevitable. In all three stories one man's invincible spirit overcomes the blindness of society and the brutality of its representatives."
—Sally Bright, *The Tulsa World*

Acclaim for Stanley G. West's
Until They Bring the Streetcars Back

"Stanley West, an extraordinary novelist and storyteller who writes with searing beauty and truth, has written a lyrical and moving novel . . . a story that pierces to the core of life . . . compelling reading for people of all times and places . . . "
—Richard Wheeler, Golden Spur Award

"It's great storytelling. Reminded me of *The Last Picture Show*. A wonderful way of life was dying, and nobody could stop it."
—Steve Thayer, author of *Weatherman* and *Silent Snow*

". . . the story is so universal, so honest in its challenges and themes, so compelling, that readers anywhere can relate to and feel for the protagonist . . . "
—Sue Hart, Prof. of English, Montana State University-Billings

"It's a charming and engaging book."
—John Moore, retired President, Columbia University Press

"One of the most gripping books I read all year."
—Marjorie Smith, *Bozeman Daily Chronicle*

"West has again captured an often untold yet important part of the human story . . . encouraging for all who may feel it's too late to make a change . . . "
—Brad Walton, The Brad Walton Show, wcco Radio

Acclaim for Stanley G. West's
Finding Laura Buggs

"Powerful storytelling . . . with a twist that Edgar Allen Poe would have enjoyed . . . one of those rare, haunting scenes that will stick in my mind for years. Stanley West is becoming one of my favorite writers . . . I recommend him to everybody."
—Steve Thayer, author of *Weatherman* and *Silent Snow*

"A story that reaffirms the miracle and wonder of life, and ultimately its preciousness . . . a terrific, uplifting read, written with great insight and compassion."
—Harvey Mackay, *New York Times* best-selling author of *How To Swim With the Sharks* and *Pushing the Envelope*

AMOS

To Ride A Dead Horse

Stanley Gordon West

LEXINGTON-MARSHALL PUBLISHING

SHAKOPEE, MINNESOTA

This Revised Edition Published in the United States by Lexington-Marshall Publishing, P.O. Box 388, Shakopee, Minnesota 55379

The poem quoted by Rainer Maria Rilke, translated by J. B. Leishman, from *Selected Works,* copyright © 1960 by The Hogarth Press. Reprinted by permission of New Directions Publishing Corporation.

Library of Congress Control Number: 00-133482

ISBN 0-9656247-0-6

Book design by Richard Krogstad
Book production by Peregrine Graphics Services
Cover photograph © Patsi Peterson
Author photograph © Rebecca Mulligan
Printed by McNaughton & Gunn, Inc.

7 9 10 8 6

First Revised Edition: September 2000
Sixth Printing: August 2012

Also By Stanley G. West

Until They Bring the Streetcars Back
Finding Laura Buggs
Growing An Inch
Blind Your Ponies
Sweet Shattered Dreams

With love for

*Karen and Julie and
Linda and Rebecca*

*delightful little girls who
grew up to be
extraordinary women*

In the midst of winter, I found there was within me
an invincible summer.
—Albert Camus

AMOS

To Ride A Dead Horse

CHAPTER 1

HE WAS AN OLD MAN, clinging fiercely to the tattered garment that had once been his dignity. He rode in the back of the converted hearse, lying on a gurney, lifting his head to see what he could of the world they passed. His gray eyes reflected a zest for life, though they struggled now from drowning in some recent pain. He joked with the two attendants and he knew this wasn't funny.

The old man guessed the two men were casualties from the railroad's recent layoffs. They'd probably picked up the hearse in some used car lot in Billings and went into business for themselves. By the way their graying-white uniforms fit, he figured they'd found them in some Salvation Army thrift store. They were all second-hand now.

The creaking Cadillac jostled them out the old road, once paved, now graveled to cover the broken asphalt and potholes. Like the old man, it had simply seen its day. It curved slowly past the town dump where crows and magpies swarmed over the heaps of refuse, scattering the lesser birds looking for a free lunch.

"You aren't taking me to the dump are you?" The old man laughed as best he could; the glass partition protecting the living from the dead stood open.

The man riding shotgun turned and made a sorry attempt at smiling. "No, it's a nice place," he said.

"It's kind of you to say."

The old man swallowed hard, a sudden panic seizing his chest. He had never been wealthy, but in his most pessimistic moods he never believed it would come to this. The road straightened out and he knew they were close. He saw the weathered post of the arch as they rumbled over the cattle guard, and he could visualize the tilted sign, if it was still there, hanging cockeyed in the sky. SUNSET HOME. The makeshift ambulance rolled to a stop, the engine coughed twice and died, the doors complained as they opened. His journey had ended, catching him surprisingly unprepared with its brevity, yet expected from years of hidden apprehension.

The building sat in the foothills seven or eight miles from town on a road that didn't go anywhere now, cut off by the freeway a mile further up, no ranch houses or other buildings in sight. Only the dump and the Home, a Spanish-style, flat-roofed structure that had once been a swank private clinic. Its white stucco had bleached in the western sun like an unburied bone from Folsom times, an artifact from another age. The once red trim was mostly faded and in places peeled down to the weatherbeaten wood. There was a small wind- and sun-tortured barn and one wobbly shed to stand with the lone cottonwood in the yard, the only sentinels rising higher than the profusion of sagebrush that danced across the deserted land. The foothills, like great shoulder muscles, swept up and away from the scrubby buildings with a magnificent announcement of the soaring snow-glazed mountains beyond.

"You sure this isn't a cathouse?" the old man said, trying to smile as they opened the back door.

"We wanted to surprise you, you're going to heaven," the driver said, taking hold of the gurney.

"Huh, for a man in my shape it would be more like hell."

They lifted him out into the mountain wind. In the wild grass it sang a whispered song that the old man heard.

They carried him up several steps, fumbling with a screen door while the old man clung to a last glimpse of the leaning cottonwood. Through the ornate woodwork of a narrow foyer they rolled him into a large inner room and waited. Faces stared. No one spoke. The attendants lost their humor and turned quiet and uneasy. The old man thought it reminiscent of a railroad station in the '30's, patiently waiting for a train that no longer ran. Some showed a mild curiosity, others were stoically uninterested, but one fragile lady in a faded gingham dress danced over to him, did a slow unsteady pirouette, and threw a little shower of confetti on him.

"Welcome," she said from deep inside her scrawny body, her mouth pinched in an oval.

Bewildered for a moment, the old man was about to speak when a nurse bristled into the room and started them on their journey again.

"You're early," she informed them, motioning for them to follow.

The old man wondered why anyone would arrive at this place *early*. He also wondered if everyone was welcomed by that brief ceremony in the gingham dress or if it had been something special. They turned down a dingy hallway, interrupted only by bare light bulbs hanging from the peeling ceiling and the bare heads of old men with peeling faces, peering at him from doorways along the passage. She led them into a room with two beds and they carefully lifted the old man onto one of them. He stiffened with the pain and whispered to the man near his head.

"I'll be waiting by the cottonwood at midnight. Big money in it if you're there."

The attendant backed away and gestured helplessly with a childlike shrug.

"That's just fine," the nurse said as she stepped in and pulled the covers up to his neck. "I'll bet we're tired from the trip."

Her voice was motherly and artificially sweetened. The two men left his baggage and vanished like smoke. A roommate, kiln dried in the sun, squinted with restrained interest from the folds of his rumpled bedding. They had no choice about those they would spend their last days with, just as they had had no choice about their first.

"You must be Amos Lasher," the nurse said, smiling with straight white teeth.

"Well if I'm not, my whole life has been one helluva mistake."

The gnarled little man in the other bed hooted once and began coughing as if he'd die on the spot. She ignored the hoot and put up with the little joke as a monotonous ingredient of her unenviable routine.

"I'm Miss Daws, Daisy Daws. I'm in charge of our little home, and I know we're going to be real happy here."

She was a correct, handsome woman with a classic figure, insanely out of place in this shabby end-of-the-road flophouse.

3

"How long were you in the hospital?" she said, smoothing out his bedding.

"Long enough to be cleaned out lock, stock, and barrel," Amos said, glancing over at his gagging neighbor.

"This is Johnny Sumers."

She swept her hand toward the little man, his body twisted like sagebrush, wind and blizzard bent, skin so rough it looked as if it were patched. He had a sly smile that crunched up his corrugated face and was its punch line. Though he hadn't been in the sun for years, there was a hat line across his forehead like a shadow; pale above, leather-skinned below, indelibly darkened by years under the sky. He squinted out of his stubborn face as though he were looking into a glaring sun, unable or unwilling to break the habit.

"Hullo," he said with a voice of gravel, peering out of his gaunt face as from a cell.

Amos struggled to get a grip on himself, suddenly overcome with this idiotic ritual and this stark room where he would surely die. He caught a sob like a cup falling from a shelf and turned to the wall, which was certainly no stranger to the reflections of old men choking on their despair. He could hear water running on the other side, a bath, a flushing toilet, impervious to whatever was happening to him on this side. This was his life, and he was watching its images on the worn plaster wall.

"Amos is just tired, Johnny." She was making excuses for his laconic attitude. "Do you have any family in town, Amos?"

She went about unpacking his belongings.

"Nope." He turned slowly. "Mildred was the last."

A vase with plastic flowers sat on the chipped dresser, and he recalled how Mildred hated such cheap pretense. A few homey little touches tried to give some sense of warmth but utterly failed in their attempt, only pointing out more starkly the bleakness of that little room: a pallid blue with cracks and patches, accumulated unmatched furniture, and an aroma he couldn't identify—a blend of human waste, disinfectant, and discarded dreams.

"We're never alone here at Sunset, Amos," she said. "You'll feel much better in a day or two."

She placed his things in the drawers and hung some clothing in a corner wardrobe. The last item, a cigar box tied snugly with a cord, she started to put in the dresser.

"I want that here," he said, holding out his hand.

"Of course," she said, "we have some important things in here, don't we?"

Amos took the box without answering. She shoved his empty suitcase under the bed with her foot and straightened her bright uniform.

"If there is anything you need, just let us know," she said and she was gone.

"Haw!" Johnny coughed and spit into a Hills Brothers coffee can on his bed table. "You from around these parts?"

"Nope . . . spent a good many years down west of Undine Falls."

"Never been in that country," Johnny said and he tuned his radio.

Amos mentally grit his teeth. Why couldn't he have died in the accident with Mildred? He attempted to quell the rage within him by giving thanks that she was spared this mortifying madness. Killed instantly they told him, though he suspected otherwise from the whispers in the corridors, the look on the faces of well-meaning nurses. He hoped she didn't survive that goddamn crash for one second.

A bizarre procession of old men moved up and down the hall like illusions: shuffling, wandering, loitering, convincing Amos beyond his worst premonitions that he didn't belong here. He would ignore them, denying any kinship with the likes of these. None of them seemed to notice Amos as anything out of the ordinary, and that suited him just fine. If any of them showed signs of getting friendly he would turn to the wall and imitate slumber.

"Here you go, Johnny," a short figureless woman said as she set a tray on Johnny's bed table and rolled it into place.

With the slightly-retarded look she wore like a mask, it was hard to guess her age. A long white apron hung over her faded institutional dress. She started out of the room and was bewildered to see Amos.

"Oh!" She stopped in her tracks. "I thought you was gone. You want lunch?" she said with a puzzled expression.

"Nope," Amos said, indifferent to the oversight.

"That's good. I ain't got none made up for you anyways."

In black socks and scuffed brown oxfords, she went out and pushed a squeaking tray cart past the door.

"She meant Harold," Johnny said. "He was in yer bed." Johnny picked up his fork and rummaged through his food. "Or you're in his."

Johnny ate in sucks and slurps with some sloshing. When he chewed he rotated his lower jaw like a Hereford cow.

"Rode Steamboat once."

"Where was that?" Amos forced himself.

"Livingston," Johnny said.

He seemed short on teeth, his mouth caved in and pleated.

"On the Yellowstone?" Amos said.

He didn't think the river was deep enough for a steamboat at Livingston.

"No, Steamboat," Johnny said.

"Over on the Missouri?" Amos tried to understand.

"In Livingston . . . are ya deef?"

"Oh, on the Yellowstone."

It was the only water near Livingston. Maybe the old man was confused.

"I rode Steamboat," Johnny said. "Stayed on the critter fer better'n eight seconds. Won me a hundred and thirty dollars that day."

"Oh, a horse. I thought you were talking about a boat."

"A boat? What the hell would I be doin' on a boat? You never hear of Steamboat? Damnedest buckin' horse I ever seen. Hell, I don't even know how to swim."

Johnny muttered to himself, and Amos shut his eyes and attempted to sleep. Certain he could feel the pin—his hip had its usual dull ache—he tried to hush the complaints coming from every part of his nervous system with the same message, reminding him that all flesh is grass.

He dozed and dreamed through the afternoon, scrambling what was real and what imaginary. Nell came for Johnny's tray, Mildred was talking to him about one of the children's birthdays, strange voices in the dark and toilets flushing; he's driving again, past the shufflers in the hall, the same stretch of highway, and no matter how he turns the wheel, he heads straight for the truck.

When he woke he was in a sweat, and he pushed the blanket down. Johnny's radio chattered nonsense, and Amos realized from the light fading through the smudged window that the afternoon was gone. Rage seethed in his bones. He had been a normal, competent human being, lived a good life, contributed to those around him, never done anything terrible or lawless. It was a divine joke to make him carry on here, and by god he'd refuse.

CHAPTER 2

"Here's your supper, Harold," Nell said, standing by the bed with a tray, startling Amos out of a catnap.

"His name's Amos," Johnny said with an edge to his voice.

"Here's your supper, Amos," Nell said, watching Amos blankly from her blotched face. "Want to sit up?"

She helped him with the pillow and swung the bed stand and tray in place.

"What we havin'?" Johnny said.

He squinted across the no man's land between them, trying to identify the food he had coming.

"It might be better if you don't see this," Amos said. "It looks like leftover hot dish from what we used to call *cleaning out the icebox.*"

Nell brought Johnny his portion while Amos tasted a mouthful of the food and found it as tasteless as his life.

"It's the salt," Johnny said. "Some can't have none so they leave it outta ever'thing."

Johnny tried to mangle a raw carrot with his remnant teeth.

"It doesn't matter," Amos said.

He moved the food around on his plate with his fork and ate little. Johnny ate the unidentifiable hot dish with the resolution of his words.

"If we don't eat it in this dish, it'll show up tomorrow in another."

Daisy swooped into the room.

"And how are we doing tonight?" She surveyed Amos's plate. "Aren't we hungry after our long day? We have to keep up our strength."

Amos wondered why.

"Your hospital report says you should begin using your hip, start walking. Then you can come to the dayroom, watch TV, play bingo, and meet the ladies."

She patted his leg as if it were a friendly retriever. An attractive woman, she had some quality that awakened slumbering lyrics within him. Did she ever realize a man of his age still felt those chords?

"I know this is your first day," she said, "but you'll get used to it, and your appetite will come back."

She turned abruptly and took a paper from her pocket. She unfolded it and presented it to Johnny like a summons.

"Would you like to sign this now, Johnny?"

Her voice was warmly persuasive.

"Nope. I'm leavin' it the way it was."

"We want our tobacco, don't we," she said, "some hard candy and licorice? We can't have them if there isn't enough money, now can we?"

Her voice lost some of its melody and flattened out.

"Why not just sign it and we'll put it in the mail."

"Nope."

Johnny looked at her stubbornly, his hardpan face and almost hairless head resolute. Daisy returned his stare for a moment, a brief, silent struggle of wills, and then she smiled.

"All right, you just think about it."

She walked gracefully into the hall on her crepe-soled shoes as soundlessly as a cat.

Nell cleared Amos's half-eaten meal and Johnny tuned the radio. The radio reminded Amos of the people in town, going about their living as though everything remained the same: the traffic, the noise, the laughter, buying and selling, couples making love, all continuing uninterruptedly as if he'd never been there. Its ruthlessness goaded him.

"Do you have to have that damn thing blaring all day?" Amos said.

Johnny ignored him, and Amos felt as if he were coming unglued. He shut his eyes and silently repeated the words he knew so well. *Lamb of God, who takes away the sins of the world, have mercy on us,* reciting them over and over with a frantic bewilderment, fearing he would go mad.

Some time later Amos woke when a large man in a grubby white uniform took over the room. He wore a jovial expression on his corpulent face, and Amos suspected a ringer. His black hair was retreating on a balding head, a large paunchy body sported a beer belly that bulged over his straining belt, and his hairy arms hung from his frame like hams in a cooler. Amos thought: zoo keeper. The keeper picked up Johnny's coffee can and turned to Amos.

"You're the new one, huh? I'm Roland."

"Can't find work?" Amos said with a wary smile.

"I wanted something out of the wind." He looked at Amos with a tired expression. "So what're *you* going to be?"

"I don't know what you mean."

"Well we've got bed-wetters, strippers, feelers, finger-painters, furniture-movers, pack rats, wheelers, yellers, sleepers. What's your story?"

"What's a finger-painter?"

"Someone who shits and then draws on the wall with it. Don't pick that one, please."

Roland held up his hands in a playful gesture.

"Can I be more than one thing at a time?" Amos said.

"Oh, hell yes. We have all possible combinations. A bed-wetter, feeler, pack rat. We've got a wheeler, sleeper, finger-painter who sometimes hollers a lot. Surprise me."

"Have you any exiles?" Amos said.

"Any what?"

The big man shifted his weight to his other leg.

"Put me down as an escapee," Amos said.

"Can't . . . ain't none of them out here. Only one way outta this place. In a bag. You want to be a baggee?"

"Do I have to decide right off?" Amos said.

"Hell no, take your time, see if I can figure you out."

"I'd like to look around, find out who's having the most fun. There must be a combination that will restore my interest in life, inspire me to accomplish great feats."

"Just keep your blinking eyes open," Roland said. "You'll have plenty of good ideas in this freak show."

"What would you advise?"

Amos sensed both a genuine humor and something to fear in this man. Roland lost his smirk and stared out the darkened window. He was quiet for a moment.

"You want my advice? Be a forgetter. Try to forget you was ever born."

He set the Hills Brothers on the table next to the urinal that Amos had used an hour before—secretly, under his blankets—his lack of privacy still deeply disturbing. The urinal was dented and corroded, and Amos hoped it was halfway sanitary.

"Now, when do you shit?"

Roland seemed to regain his frivolity.

"Only when I remember the horse Waldo MacGregor sold me," Amos shot back, irked by this crudeness.

He wanted to tell this moron it was none of his goddamn business and he'd shit whenever he felt like it. He might even take up finger-painting. The keeper stooped down with a grunt and pulled a bedpan from under the bed.

"I don't have to go right now," Amos said.

"Well, think of MacGregor's horse for a while. I'm not sitting here all night until you get the urge."

Roland whipped back the bedding, lifted Amos with one arm, and slipped the cold metal pan under his bare rump. Leaving Amos with his bony legs and ass exposed to the world, Roland left with the odious cargo from the table. Amos tried to reach the covers, but the bulky orderly had thrown them clear over the foot of the bed.

"When will he be back?" Amos said.

"Soon," Johnny said, "he's gittin' us ta bed early. Wants ta git done and git outta here. He puts the slow ones on first."

A short, stocky man stood in the doorway, casually watching Amos, sucking a smokeless pipe. With a gray scrub-brush mustache and small wire-rimmed glasses, he looked like an old Teddy Roosevelt. Amos was painfully self-conscious, feeling the blood rising in his face. This man was stopping by for a neighborly chat while Amos squatted on a bedpan like a two year old being potty trained. He made one more try for the blanket but couldn't reach it, only to notice a second man standing there watching him. Tall and thin, with a baggy sweatshirt that read PEPSI GENERATION, he gazed out of a long droopy face that reminded Amos of a bloodhound. The accumulated anger of the day overwhelmed him. He couldn't escape their relentless stare, a mannequin in a store window promoting a sale on bedpans. He turned on them viciously.

"What in the hell are you idiots looking at? Haven't you ever seen a man shit before?"

The two men blinked lazily at his outburst, watched a minute longer, then drifted down the hall. Roland swung through, set Johnny on his bedpan, and urged Amos to get on with the task. Old men passed the doorway in various stages of undress, and Amos tried the best he could, but it was no use. He couldn't perform on stage and the whole scene was absurdly degrading. His rear end was numb when Roland returned, first pulling Johnny's bedpan from under the crippled little man and complaining.

"Damn, Johnny, you must be dead inside."

Roland then pulled the metal from under Amos and threw the covers back over him. Thankfully, Amos found relief in the mattress and privacy under the bedding.

"Couldn't crap, huh? Well, you'll have to hold it till morning now. Try like hell not to dream of MacGregor's horse."

Roland roared at his own humor, riding it out into the hall, totally oblivious to the fact that his coarse manner was devastating to Amos.

"When do we wash?" Amos said without glancing at his roommate.

"Sometimes. Don't rile 'im, he can be mean. If ya mess the bed he'll hurt ya."

Johnny fiddled with the radio. Amos felt sick, thinking he should laugh but couldn't, trapped by the terrible depression incubating in the room. A thick, deep voice startled Amos.

"She at you again?"

The old Teddy Roosevelt with his pipe in his hand stood at the foot of Johnny's bed.

"The new man's Amos," Johnny said. He coughed and spit into his can. "This here's Emil."

Johnny waved a hand from Amos to Emil as a guide to introduction. Amos studied the other man for a moment. From a blockish head with thinning gray hair, his joyless face was so rigidly set against a smile that the smile no longer seemed possible. From behind small round spectacles, his eyes stood distant, unyielding, observing with an impassive intelligence, holing up behind his great gray hedgerow of a mustache. Amos turned quickly to the wall at a total disadvantage. This man had just watched him fumbling on a bedpan like the feebleminded.

"You got any tobac?" Johnny asked the man.

"No . . . she says she'll get some on the next shopping trip." Emil's accent was mild, Amos guessed German.

"Will ya sneak me some when ya git it?" Johnny whispered. "Don't dare."

Emil sucked his empty pipe, savoring the taste of flavored air passing over old tobacco stains like memories.

Roland thundered down the hall.

"Lights out. Let's go, you baboons, hit the sack. In your bed, Winston. Mick, let's shake it. No walking around tonight, or we'll have to tie you down."

He clapped his hands as he spoke, his menacing hulk carrying the unspoken threat of violence. Up the corridor his voice trailed off; voices muttered, a drawer banged shut, a toilet flushed. Then the lights in the room went out, leaving the hall dimly lit, night-lights for those who wandered after dark. Amos rolled over slowly and looked across to Johnny, now only a silhouette under the bedding in the shadows.

"Is it always like this?" Amos said quietly.

"Mostly . . . can be worse."

The radiator under the window hissed and sputtered, carrying heat to this cold cold room that spurned all forms of warmth.

"How long have you been here?" Amos whispered.

"How's that?"

Amos raised his voice. "How long have you been here?"

"Goin' on five years, I guess, or maybe six. I used ta keep close track, but I don't no more. Ya git used to it."

"I sure as hell don't intend to get used to it," Amos said, recognizing the fear caught in his throat. "Not hardly."

"Never say die," Johnny said.

Amos turned back to the wall. What difference did it make where any of them had been if they ended up here, an unpredictable gathering of souls? What they had done, where they had been, all seemed unimportant and meaningless in the shattering reality of this place. None of them would ever go home again.

They were here, the sun had set, and the door was closed for the long night ahead.

CHAPTER 3

AFTER A RESTLESS NIGHT, Amos opened his eyes to a gray morning and fought against the truth that this was now his life—the last ride at the fair. Muffled noises came out of the dawn sporadically, cobwebs in his mind. A mirthful, happy laughter danced down the hall, catching Amos off guard. Someone was cracking up and the hilarity seemed as out of place as a brain tumor in a child. He closed his eyes in the vain hope that what was happening here wasn't true. Escaping back into sleep, maybe he could rid himself of that living nightmare. In the arsenal of dreams, he could surely come up with something better than this: a welfare case dumped at the county poor farm with an aggregate of society's leftovers.

Sounding like a horse peeing in a pail, Johnny wouldn't allow him to escape the reality of it.

"You still here?" Johnny asked with a froggy voice.

"Hell, yes, you can't get rid of me. I've been waiting too long for reservations in this soup kitchen."

Amos forced the sarcasm, as if shoving a hara-kiri knife into his belly. He'd wondered sometimes if he'd get caught like this before death, falling through the cracks and losing control of his destiny in the fickle crosswinds of chance. Like a foul-smelling fog drifting in from the sea, it took several minutes for Johnny's odor to reach him. In self-defense—with his body aching and his hip sore and stiff—he relieved himself and set the urinal carefully on the bed stand. It stank. Johnny turned on the radio, and Amos caught himself listening with interest until it struck him that that information from the outside world was beside the point in the useless state he'd fallen into. What did it matter, the price of wheat or the weather or that a Senator from Massachusetts named Kennedy had been elected President?

The Home came alive lethargically. Johnny coughed up the night's accumulation and deposited what he could with the Hills Brothers. They lay quietly waiting for another hour, their urine flavoring the room like a bittersweet memory. The squeaking cart proclaimed the coming of breakfast, serving up another bland day with the overcooked oatmeal.

Nell plodded in with his tray, her tattered apron hanging to her ankles, decorated with multi-colored smears of food.

"Here's your breakfast, Harold."

"His name's Amos, ya dingbat!" Johnny said.

"Would you empty that?" Amos nodded sheepishly at the urinal.

He resented having to rely on others just to take care of his natural functions, needing their cooperation and blessing.

"I can't," she said woodenly. "Daisy'd tan my hide."

The expression on her face remained constant, somewhere between a grin and surprise, and it seemed she could never quite make up her mind.

"I can only touch the dishes. Daisy'd hide me good."

The warm oatmeal carried Amos back to a winter morning on the ranch. It was early, Mildred set the steaming oatmeal in front of him, the children were scampering to make the school bus, the kitchen cozy with a warmth far beyond material things. He was wrenched from the past by a plaintive voice in the hall.

"Here, Ginger, come on, girl, good girl."

"Will they let you have a dog in here?" Amos said.

"Naw." Johnny spit. "Thas jes Winston. He's always callin' his dog. Ain't no dog."

The tall thin man with the droopy bloodhound face appeared in the doorway. He wore brown suspenders over his PEPSI GENERATION sweatshirt, had a tennis racket in one hand and patted his thigh with the other.

"Here, girl, come, girl. Have you seen my dog?"

"No, but if you can get a court this afternoon, I'll play some tennis with you," Amos said.

"Git outta here, ya dumb coot!" Johnny said as he threw a wad of toilet paper and missed Winston completely. Winston backed a step and swung the racket at the missile several seconds after it had hit the floor. He gawked at Johnny for a moment and then ambled after Daisy when she hurried past the door. Amos ate half the oatmeal before Nell collected the trays.

"I won't put up with anymore of this, Elroy. We'll tie you in bed at night," Daisy said while marching a slightly hunchbacked old man up the hallway. His nightshirt was covered with dried blood.

"What happened to *him?*" Amos said.

"Pickin' his nose. Tries ta bleed ta death at night. She keeps tellin' him it won't work, an' he keeps tryin'."

"Killing himself?" Amos said.

"He don't have the brains or the guts ta try somethin' that'd work."

"That's terrible." Amos shook his head.

"It's a sure as shootin' way outta here," Johnny said with a snarl.

"It's wrong, suicide is always wrong," Amos said.

"You some kinda Catholic or somethin'?" Johnny said.

"No, Lutheran."

"You could change yer relig'n 'fore yer outta here," Johnny said just as Roland strode into the room.

"You boys got dry beds this morning?"

He ran his hand under Johnny's bedding.

"Good. That damn Marvin unloaded last night like he'd been out on a weekend beer bust."

He picked up the fermenting urinals and carried them casually to the lavatory, still griping when he returned.

"Well, by god, he can just sleep in those stinkin' sheets for a few nights. We have to change yours, Johnny, they're getting ripe."

He banged the urinals in their places and blustered out of the room.

The morning traffic plodded the passageway, an endless dance of unnumbered steps that somewhere in time had lost track of the beat and gone on without the music. Amos tried to shut them all out but couldn't avoid noticing a short brawny woman who seemed lost in the men's ward, a linebacker. And the half-wit Bloodhound.

Daisy appeared in the room as brightly as a morning sun. The contradiction of her sparkling presence—out of place in this cemetery—wounded Amos with remembrances he fled to avoid.

"Did we have a good night?"

"I don't belong here," Amos said with a frightened plea in his voice. "I want to get out of here."

"There, there, Amos, you'll feel more at home in a few days. That's only natural."

She fussed with his pillow and bedding while Amos searched behind the makeup on her appealing face, thinking he detected a scar on her right cheek. He worried that his smell still lingered around the bed like a damp curse, making him just one more old man smelling of piss. She smelled fresh, like a newly opened box of laundry soap. Her uniform was immaculate, except for one small smudge of blood over her left breast, evidence of another of Elroy's desperate failures.

She turned on Johnny again with her paper and pen, trying to coerce him to sign it with various threats, some of which Amos thought ridiculous. Johnny stonewalled from his soiled bastion of bedding.

"I guess we'll have to take the radio. Electricity costs money."

She unplugged the radio and snatched it from his table.

"Not the radio," Johnny said.

He tried to reach out and prevent her, hanging on for a brief moment with his fragile strength. She paused.

"Just sign it, and we'll have plenty of tobacco and electricity and everything you want."

She spread the paper on his table and held out the pen. Johnny hesitated, casting an expeditious glance toward Amos, who was avoiding any eye contact during the confrontation.

"Nope," the old cowboy said, "leave it the way it is."

Johnny put a hand over his eyes and Daisy strutted out with the plunder but without the victory.

"Goddamn witch," Johnny said with a snarl.

"What's the paper she wants you to sign?"

"Insurance. A paper makin' her the one who'll git it. It ain't a whole lot."

Johnny rubbed his head, as he thought about someone or something in the past.

"I want ta leave it ta someone who did me kind once."

"She can't make you do that. It's illegal," Amos said.

"Ain't no legal or illegal in here."

Amos didn't understand, but it frightened him.

Roland thundered into their room.

"OK, Johnny, let's clean your cage."

Roland carried several clean sheets over one arm and Amos thought he could smell him.

"You must work twelve hours a day," Amos said.

Roland rolled Johnny around in the bed as he maneuvered the bottom sheet off and a clean one on.

"I work a split shift." He grunted with the work, his forehead glistening with sweat. "And every shift out here is the graveyard shift. Haw! Get it? That's what I tell them at Rosy's. I work the graveyard shift."

Johnny's bony legs were yellowed like a chicken's, an ugly sore spread on his hollow, meatless rump. Amos wondered when they'd be bathed, used to the daily washing and clean sheets at the hospital. He realized he'd checked out of first class and checked in down around fourth or fifth.

"You got any tobac?" Johnny asked Roland in a hushed plea.

"No tobacco, Daisy's orders," Roland said, "you know that."

He snapped a clean sheet over the bed and tucked it in with the blanket.

"She don't need ta know. It can be just between us men," Johnny said.

"How much money have you?"

"I don't have any right now, but I'll be gittin' some."

"When you do, just whistle."

Roland gathered up the dirty bedding and headed out of the room.

"I could owe ya."

"Ha! I can't be a stinking loan department on this death row; I'd be trying to collect my money at the cemetery."

"Horse's ass," Johnny said as if he knew he'd come up dry.

The day outside looked sullen and blustery, fall with the suspicion of winter. The radiator knocked, and Amos shut his eyes, drifting away. He saw them together in their apartment, he and Mildred and their black Labrador, Bandit, enjoying each other. He hadn't been negligent or stupid, saved and accumulated enough for them to live like that for years. They had the car, taking trips into the country, exploring, returning to favorite fishing holes, Mildred packed delicious picnics. God Almighty, what *happened.*

They said the accident was his fault. With Mildred's funeral and the lawsuit and the long stay in the hospital it cleaned him out, running through his wallet and savings like a grass fire in August. Goddamn insurance, they tell you it covers every-thing—any possible tragedy—until the calamity you're in comes up *uncovered,* the circumstances don't fit the fine print on the policy. You'd be covered if a bee stung you in the ass and you kicked an old woman to death with the reflex, but in your insured car on a magnificent spring day, you fall through a loop-hole into that zoo.

His wrath would find some satisfaction if he could just get his hands on the smiling insurance salesman who explained it all to them so politely. Mildred had even fed the liar. Amos was glad he hadn't seen Mildred afterward, battling not to allow his mind to visualize what that smashed and twisted metal had done to her tender body. She was chattering happily, then she was gone. It gave him an aching satisfaction that she'd been able to fly away free and clear.

"Do they ever give you any pills around here so you can sleep?" Amos said.

He pulled his hip around, rubbing the stubborn wound.

"Nope. Only if you're a little wacky like Winston or Sadie," Johnny said. "They keep the others outta the beds during the day so's they'll sleep at night. You got pain?"

"Some."

"Never say die," Johnny said flatly.

Amos craned his neck to see his little roommate.

"What did you do before they stuck you in here?" Amos said.

"Mostly cowboyin', 'fore I got sick. I spent so many years with cows an' horses I started thinkin' like 'em. Only trouble was, the cows always belonged ta someone else." He laughed.

"Any children?"

"Hell," Johnny paused, "probably, somewhere in Montana or Wyoming, but none I knows of. When I's young and full a piss an' vinegar I never held still long enough ta git hitched. When I's older I was smarter. I knew I'd be by myself when I's old, always been alone. But I never thought it'd be like this."

Amos had no reply, not to Johnny, not to God, not to this idiotic comedy. He gave in to an irrepressible despondency and shut his eyes against it all. Nell with her lithium trays, the salt-less food, the unseasoned faces in the corridor, the cheap electric razor, the inane conversation, and Roland serving the evening humiliation. Then the lights were out, the Home quiet, except for the night noises.

The room seemed smaller in the night-light, the air stifling. Down the hall someone laughed boisterously, giggling, finding something in that wasteland hilarious. Amos feared he would go mad. He felt a strong compulsion against all reason to escape, to get up and get out of there right then or he knew it would for-ever be too late. In flushed panic he threw aside the covers and slid to the floor. The agony and weakness gripped him, laughed in his face, and quickly informed him to abort the ridiculous attempt. He was fainting. With his last measure of strength he pulled himself back into the bed, exhausted, refusing to recog-nize that he was utterly helpless. He had denied for as long as possible that devastating reality, until it finally washed over him, a surf battering him onto the rocks on that alien shore.

He took the cigar box out and sorted through the contents, carefully handling each object: pieces of his life, tattered rem-nants of the lives of others, evidences that he had not always been here. He took a photograph and held it up to the obscure light. It was of him and Mildred in Los Angeles, a trip he'd won for selling the most John Deere equipment in his region. They were happy in the picture. He could remember the hotel, how they made love like youngsters, how they ate dinner at ten o'clock at night and slept until ten in the morning. God, they were young even then. He held the photograph closer and real-ized that one of these experiences wasn't real. That strong, healthy man in the picture couldn't be the broken, shriveled old man in this bed. Either one was a pipe dream, or he was insane.

As he put the box away, he heard Winston whispering a mournful plea in the dark.

"Here, Ginger. Come back, girl."

"Shut up! Yer goddamn dog is dead!" someone shouted.

Winston's dog was dead. So was Amos's dog. Mildred was gone, and his children, Marilyn and Greg. Now he had to get the job done. He'd always figured he'd be the first to go, never dreaming he'd be the last. Always, he'd believed that life was precious, beautiful, something to cherish and fight for. But there had to be a purpose to give it meaning. In the furthest corners of his mind he could no longer find any sane reason to carry on. It was as dimwitted as Winston calling for a dead dog. He knew he could never be a forgetter.

He'd be a baggee.

CHAPTER 4

D<small>AYS BLURRED WITH A BLEAK SAMENESS</small>, out of focus in a numbing regularity. Amos no longer kept track of time, trying to shut it all out and slip quietly away. But he noticed the cord on his cigar box tied strangely and quickly examined the familiar contents.

"Damn it, Johnny, someone took my money and my twenty-dollar gold piece. Did you see anyone in here last night?"

"Nope. Did you have any tobac?"

Johnny raised his brows.

"No, damn it! Are you deaf? There's a thief in this place."

"Sure as hell is," Johnny said without concern.

Amos was livid by the time Roland showed up, half awake. He set a wash basin on the bed stand and plugged Amos's razor in.

"Chop off them whiskers and pretty yourself up," Roland said.

"I was robbed last night, Roland, over a hundred dollars, right while I slept."

"That much, huh?" Roland yawned. "Too bad. Let's change this bed."

Roland roughly manhandled Amos as he changed the sheets, and his aroma crowded Amos. The coarse hair of his arms against Amos's bare skin seemed crudely intimate, violating Amos's last private space.

"Aren't you going to do something about it?" Amos said.

"Probably one of the pack rats. They're always making off with something." Roland snapped on the top sheet. "Finish them whiskers."

"I want to see Miss Daws."

"She'll be around," Roland said.

He emptied the urinals and the Hills Brothers, checked over the room, and took a flannel shirt out of the lower drawer. He pulled it right over Amos's hospital gown and buttoned it.

"I can do it," Amos said with fire in his nostrils.

Roland found a shirt for Johnny and helped him into it.

"Now don't spill your lunch all over your shirts and clean beds, damn it."

Amos finished shaving and Roland moved on with the dirty bedding and his body odor.

"What's going on?" Amos said.

"It's Sunday, visitin' day." Johnny hacked and tried to clear his throat. "You got any visit'rs?"

"Afraid not, everyone's gone. Don't know any folks up here. A grandson in Ohio, my daughter's boy. Haven't seen Scott since her funeral. Cancer got her. Never did get to know the boy."

"You ever been close to a grizzly?" Johnny said.

"No, not close." Amos rubbed his chin for stubble.

"That's what he smells like. A goddamn grizzly."

"Who?" Amos said.

"Roland, like a musty ol' grizzly."

His words sprang an avalanche in Amos's mind, bombarding him with memory shards long underground. The aroma of lodge pole pine and Douglas fir in the sun-warmed forest, a rush of cool air off the snow-melted water, mica and feldspar reflecting the sun on the path. A Clark's nutcracker calling from high in the trees, rusted pine needles, moose and elk scats in neat little piles along the trail, wild columbine, fireweed, mountain bluebells dancing among the grass and rock, a marmot scurrying into his burrow, leaving his shrieking whistle behind in the air. They were fishing the Slough Creek drainage, excellent trout, but one of the better natural grizzly habitats in the country. Amos was always on the watch for a sow, especially in early summer. They were walking single file when young Gregory expressed his anxiety.

"Do you think a grizzly will get us?" he said solemnly.

Amos explained, as they hiked further into the wilderness, that the grizzly seemed more likely to attack a single person or small group. Gregory had his friend John with them and Marilyn had a girlfriend. With Mildred and grandpa there were seven of them.

"How can a grizzly tell how many people there are?" Greg said, puffing along with his fishing pole and knickers.

Amos told him it was a bear's fine sense of smell, that it could detect humans a long way off without ever seeing them. Most likely, the bear could tell if it was one person or many.

"With all of us along today, we probably don't have to worry about it. Any grizzly around will catch our scent and run."

Amos tried to relieve Greg's mind to enjoy the day's fishing, but Amos worried about it some, making sure they yelled back and forth and made plenty of noise.

Greg hiked silently for several minutes, contemplating this new information. Then he said, "Dad, what if it's just one huge fat kid?"

Amos got to laughing so hard he had to sit down on a deadfall. Since that time the family had used this child's question as their lighthearted way of telling each other to watch out, be careful. *Take a fat kid with you* was a prayer that all forms of the grizzly, the danger secretly hidden in every moment, would be warded off, thinking there was a greater force of Lashers on the trail than there actually was.

Daisy followed in the wake of the retreating lunch cart, herding men up the hall like reluctant strays in a procession that could only be laughable to anyone who still possessed any shred of a sense of humor: a tie hanging to the crotch, a shirt straining unbuttoned over a potbelly, pants whose wearer must expect high water, unzipped fly, unmatched socks, all color coordinated by the color blind. A small dark-skinned man stepped into the doorway and squinted at Amos. Daisy prodded him to keep moving.

"Let's go, gentlemen, up front."

Amos tried to catch her attention, but she sailed on unheeding.

"That's Carlos," Johnny said.

The gnarled cowboy watched the parade with the apathy of one who'd grown up in the circus.

"He's blind in the right eye, can't see good outta the left. Creosote. He used ta visit Harold all the time. Both railroadin' men. Harold drove 'em, Carlos laid track. Carlos was always arguin' that the damn engineers drove 'em too fast, tearin' up the bed."

"Where are they all going?" Amos said.

"Dayroom. They's s'posed to watch the TV and play games and look happy for visitin' hours."

"A big day on the farm, huh?" Amos said.

"Yep. No one will come."

"No one will come?" Amos said.

"Nope. Never do. Maybe a preacher. Robert gets visitors. No one else."

"Why the circus then?"

"So no one will come," Johnny said.

"*So no one will come?* You don't make any sense."

"It's Daisy's way. If we git all spruced up, no one will come," Johnny said. "If we leave things as bad as they is, someone will show up sure as shootin', a relative Daisy don't know about or some local yokel doin' a good deed. So we put on the dog and then no one comes."

Amos thought they were all lunatics.

But he couldn't avoid thinking about his own response to this type of place whenever he had inadvertently been confronted with one. You were uneasy, haunted, you felt helpless, so you ducked out, made excuses, stayed away. Amos thought about his father. Grandpa lived with them until Greg found him dead one morning on the bathroom floor. With a blink of an eye he made a clean getaway.

Daisy appeared in the room like color, a light blue sweater over her uniform, her hair held back with a matching blue ribbon, captivating.

"Are we all ready in here?" she said with melody in her voice.

"Someone robbed me last night," Amos said.

"Oh, Amos, that's a shame. Some of the men will walk off with things, I'm sorry to say. But it will show up."

She calmly pushed his bedpan further under the bed with a foot.

"Maybe we've just misplaced some things."

"Maybe you misplace things, but I don't," Amos said, letting the anger color his voice. "It was right in this goddamn drawer when I went to sleep, and now it's gone."

"Calm down, Amos, no need for that kind of language. We want a pleasant Sunday. Let's not mention it anymore today. Daisy will take care of it."

She patted his leg and hurried on her inspection of the barracks.

"Haw!" Johnny laughed, like gravel rolling down a metal chute. "Daisy'll take care of it all right."

Amos thought it strange that she hadn't even asked what was missing.

"Well, if she thinks I'm some doddering old fool, she's in for a helluva surprise," Amos said. "I'll get the police in here."

Amos sat up in the bed, shaking.

"Would Roland make a phone call for me?"

"Huh!" Johnny slapped his leg and laughed.

"Would Nell?"

"Nell!" Johnny hooted and started to choke with the hilarity of it. "Hell, you'd have ta write down every word'n then she'd screw it all up anyhow. Probably can't even read."

"I'll write a letter, to the sheriff," Amos said. "This is a county home, there are laws."

Amos searched Johnny's windswept face for some glimmer of hope. He came up empty.

"Don't let it get ta ya, that's jes the penny ante stuff anyway." Johnny sighed softly, running his hand across his furrowed head, leaving it over his eyes. "Never say die."

Amos lay back, his pulse slowing. Of course Johnny was right. What difference did it make? Let them have the money, anything, everything. He was getting all the juices flowing for nothing, forgetting he was only in the waiting room of the morgue, no longer here to care about law or justice or anything else. So the head nurse is trying to fleece Johnny out of his insurance money, and maybe Roland will be showing off a twenty-dollar gold piece at Rosy's tonight. He wouldn't allow himself to care. Anyway, they couldn't be that cut off out here, that isolated. Johnny had just been here too long. It was Sunday, visiting day, the men were up in the dayroom, people would be coming from the real world. Amos told himself he had to keep his perspective. But he was still damn mad.

The afternoon evaporated slowly, and Johnny was proved wrong. They had three visitors. Around midafternoon a squat woman wandered into their room, confused, disoriented, searching with her dark vacant eyes. It was the linebacker. Her head sat squarely on her powerful masculine frame with no neck, no breasts, no hips. Her black hair resembled a nest, some of it sprouting from her face.

"I'm going home today," she said, gazing at Amos with a look as distant and frigid as the Arctic Ocean.

Amos felt a devastating sadness and refused to admit any affinity with those outcasts, guarding his own sanity by denial.

"Where are you from?" Amos said, unable to ignore her.

She shuffled to their narrow window and gazed blankly into the afternoon sky, dressed in high institutional fashion: a flowered cotton dress reminiscent of a flour sack, her underwear exposed in the partially buttoned gaps, one support stocking slumped down over her tennis shoe.

"That's Sadie," Johnny said. "She don't understand nothin'. Scatterbrained. Got family south a here, but they don't visit 'er no more. Heard tell they run a big spread."

"I'm going home today," Sadie said, "they're coming for me."

She looked at Amos but he could find no response to offer her.

"Sure ya are, Sadie, they's comin' fer ya," Johnny said.

She drifted off, muttering to herself, the visit over.

Amos had no more than resolved to banish all of them from his mind after Sadie's assault on his emotional balance when Emil blustered in, grumbling bitterly to Johnny.

"They turn off the football for some preacher who shows up. Who needs that drool. The morons sit there and lap it up. They'd be better off with the football than the God lies, the fairy tales."

The Teddy Roosevelt look-alike raved and bitched for several minutes and turned for his room. Amos tried to stay on top of it, thinking first Linebacker and now Grouch.

"What's Emil's problem?" Amos said.

"Aw, he was born pissed. If you gave him a good sound horse, it'd be the wrong color. He's probably a commie."

Amos gave in to the hilarity with visitor number three.

"SKIP, SKIP, SKIP TO MY LOU, FLIES IN THE BUTTERMILK, SHOO, FLY, SHOO."

Winston stepped to the foot of Johnny's bed, delivering the words in a rhythmic monotone, and timidly marched in place in cadence with the song. He moved like a character in a silent movie.

"Get outta here, ya yahoo."

Johnny wheezed.

"CAT IN THE CREAM JAR, WHAT'LL I DO?" Winston chanted, his weight shifting from one foot to the other, seeming to taunt Johnny.

Johnny picked up a bar of soap. "I'll show ya what ta do."

He raised his arm as if to throw it. Winston never stopped his litany, stepping backward into the hall like a windup mechanical soldier and away.

"CAT IN THE CREAM JAR, WHAT'LL I DO?"

Visiting hours were over and the men slogged down the hall to their quarters like a sluggish incoming tide, carrying all sorts of emotional flotsam. Amos hardened himself against the tide, against the insanity, turning to the wall, beckoning death to carry him out of this godforsaken menagerie forever. Nell brought supper, Roland had the night off, and Daisy went through the nightly chores. She intimidated Johnny both subtly and blatantly to sign the paper, bringing him no wash water and

Amos tried to find sleep, quelling his thoughts unsuccessfully. God! A cowboy. If Johnny could've seen how he'd end up, it would've ruined his whole life. Then he came up with the odd and alarming thought that Sadie might have been voted the Girl Most Likely To Succeed by her graduating class, if she ever had one. Someone was laughing quietly in the dark, blending with the snoring, gently hooting and howling with a subdued hilarity, as if he knew something none of the rest of them did.

Amos listened to the wind humming around the building, the window rattling in its frame, and he couldn't duck the agony of it. That promising spring day, how he felt enthusiastic, optimistic that there was life in front of them still. He packed with some pleasure and anticipation. Then the God-awful accident. In their hurry to pack and gather up all their things, they had forgotten the most important.

They hadn't taken a fat kid with them.

CHAPTER 5

"A MOS, YOU HAVE SOME MAIL."

Daisy brought the cheery news in the form of two light green envelopes.

"Mail, for me?" Amos said with a shudder of hope.

"They're checks," Daisy said, quickly dashing his expectations.

Amos took them with silent disappointment and read the return address.

"Insurance company. I figured these would run out when I left the hospital. They can't last much longer."

"Why don't you open them?"

Daisy's blue eyes danced a happy jig. Amos struggled with the heavy envelope and with some difficulty released the impersonal printed check, his only message from the outside world.

"One hundred and twenty-three dollars," he said.

He opened the other. It was the same.

"If you'll endorse them, I'll get them cashed. Some of the money can be used to make your stay more pleasant and if you want, I'll put the rest in the bank for you."

When she handed Amos a pen, he glanced at Johnny, who was conspicuously examining the ceiling. Daisy had badgered Johnny relentlessly with the pen and paper, and Amos thought Johnny was stupid to go on with it. They had taken his coffee can and forced him to spit in his urinal, emptying it only when it threatened to overflow, withholding every trivial extra above the line of survival. He wished Johnny would give in, sign the damn paper, and permit Amos to die in peace. Amos signed the two checks with a shaky scrawl and handed them to her.

"That's just fine. I'll take care of these for you. Now, I've asked Roland to come in later and help you try the walker. You should be using your legs by now. You've been here over five weeks. It's time you got moving." She started for the door and turned. "Would you like some candy?"

"No, nothing."

He figured that was more for Johnny's treatment than his pleasure. When she was gone, Amos slid down into the bed and wondered why he was afraid to look at Johnny. He had to laugh inside, visualizing two hundred and forty-six dollars worth of jawbreakers and licorice whips.

"Haw! Daisy Daws, the gal with the quickest draw in the West," Johnny said. "Bet ya never saw 'er pull that pen."

"Why not sign, what difference does it make?" Amos avoided Johnny's eyes. "The checks are worthless to me."

"The hell ya say. Ya plan to lay in that stinkin' bed fer the resta yer life? You could save them checks an' have somethin' when ya git outta here." `

Emil, the Grouch, materialized in the doorway and listened, his pipe set rigidly in his jaw under his imposing scrub-brush mustache.

"I'm starting a new career as a county ward and invalid," Amos said, his own words leaving a bitter taste in his mind.

"Hell, there's nothin' wrong with ya, once ya git healed up a bit," Johnny said. "Ya can git clear a this stink hole, less'n ya don't want to."

"It's the cooking and company I can't leave."

"Emil," Johnny said, "he likes it here, by jiggers. He's found a home."

A coughing jag gripped Johnny. Emil held his stone-faced expression without batting an eye. Johnny spit into the urinal, caught his breath, and looked into Amos's eyes with fixed bayonet.

"I wouldn't sign if I know'd I was dyin' that minute."

Amos avoided his fellow residents as much as possible. He imitated sleep when they would visit with Johnny, turn to the wall if they gave any indication of friendliness or a desire to become acquainted. He wanted no fellowship with these outcasts, preferring the companionship of his memories during his deathwatch, unable or unwilling to lay aside his growing self-pity. But the small Mexican caught him unguarded, slipping in behind

Emil while Emil talked with Johnny. The man felt along Amos's bed until he was very close.

"You work on the railroad?" Carlos said, squinting at Amos.

"No." Amos started to turn his back.

"I worked the railroad, gandy dancing. Blinded me, the creosote. Still see some out of my left eye, right one's no good. You remind me of my straw boss."

Carlos leaned closer, spraying Amos with his rank breath. His skin was the color and texture of adobe and it appeared that life had troweled it on, layer after layer, in an attempt to cover the scars.

"He left our crew one day to go get married," Carlos said. "We had to blast some rock for a trestle. Clinker said he could do it, so we drilled the holes, and he set the dynamite. We blew the whole trestle to hell. The straw boss was only gone three days, and when he got back, he nearly died. We'd spent three months on that trestle. You look just like him. You ever worked the railroad?"

"No."

Amos turned to the wall. He could bear no more of this idiocy, would acknowledge no more of that ridiculous sideshow.

"Roland found my plant behind the shower this morning," Carlos said with the grief befitting a death in the family.

"A plant?" Amos twisted his head back toward Carlos.

"He don't let me grow no plants. Says it's too big a mess, so I have to hide 'em."

"I try ta git him ta grow some tobac while he's at it," Johnny said.

Amos made it to the wall, shutting out the railroader, and Carlos drifted off with Emil, something about checkers.

"He sez they hung his pappy," Johnny said. "Had to raise seven or eight brothers and sisters. When ya ask him why they hung his pappy, he just sez, Because he was Mex. Guess it could be."

Amos was about to shout that he didn't care, that he didn't want to hear about it, when Roland carried an aluminum walker into the room.

"Well, Amos old buddy, let's see if we can get out of that sack."

He smiled and smacked his hands together as if he were approaching a cord of wood that needed splitting. He lifted Amos's scrawny legs over the edge of the bed and Amos quickly pulled his nightshirt over his exposed genitals, wishing to put off or avoid this trial altogether. He could dredge up no motivation to walk, foreseeing his hip coming unglued and anticipating the resultant shattering pain.

"Just sit there for a minute, we'll take it slow," Roland said, steadying him with a hand on his shoulder.

"I don't want to walk," Amos said.

"Sure you do. You want to make Roland happy. If you walk you can go to the toilet on your own, no more bedpans for old Roland to haul, no more stink, and believe me, you won't be happy if Roland isn't happy."

He lifted Amos off the bed and slowly stood him up.

"Just the good leg to start," Roland said.

Amos put all his weight on his left leg. It wobbled like a yo-yo string. He seized the walking frame, dizzy, his strength running out on him.

"You OK?" Roland said.

He lifted Amos back onto the bed. Instantly covered in sweat, Amos felt faint. Roland waited a minute and then repeated the exercise several times until Amos was standing, supporting his body with the walker. He tested his right leg. It held him with little pain.

"That's it for today, old fella."

Roland hoisted him back into his bunk, and Amos wondered if that's what a grizzly really smelled like. Johnny seemed to know. Roland flung the covers over him and slapped the bed with his bear's paw.

"Next time we'll take a few steps. You'll be walking in no time, take a bath, clean up your act."

He left the walker at the foot of the bed on his way out.

Amos lay exhausted, surprised at the tingle of excitement he felt in his stomach, never having considered the possibility of walking again. But now that option seemed open, enticing him to get out of this foul nest, to exercise his aching bones, to take care of his own bodily functions again. He realized it might also prolong his life here until he failed enough to be bedridden once more, stretching this indignity into a protracted purgatory. He weighed the priorities of his life carefully, possessing this one last freedom in the matter. No one would be able to tell if he could walk or not. It was his undetectable choice.

Night faithfully filled the gap behind the day, and Johnny was grumbling on the bedpan. When he attempted to shift to a more comfortable position, he lost his balance and knocked over the urinal full of phlegm and urine. Like a flow of lava the nauseous mess moved slowly across the green and black linoleum toward Amos's bed.

"Holy balls, Roland will have my ass fer this," Johnny said with a note of fright in his voice.

Amos turned away from the advancing filth just as Roland stopped in his tracks in the doorway.

"Had a little accident, huh?"

Roland didn't seem upset. He fetched a mop and bucket and swabbed up the mess. When he finished, the great bear slid the bedpan from under Johnny and set it on the nightstand. He glanced toward Amos, and with the pretense of straightening Johnny's bedding, hit him quickly between the legs with the urinal.

"Oops, sorry," Roland said.

Johnny curled up in the bed, gasping, fighting the pain. Roland threw the covers over him and laughed.

"*You* have an accident, *I* have an accident."

Johnny was panting, choking on his own juices, trampled with the lingering agony long after Roland had finished. Amos shook with outrage, having witnessed the brutality through the window of terror.

The night traffic passed: a bent old man in denim cap, Winston with long exaggerated strides chanting some verse, the little gandy dancer feeling along the wall with creosote eyeballs and a face forever tanned by race.

"Come on, Winston," Daisy's voice carried along the hall, "time for your pill."

She passed with the bloodhound at heel. Then the commotion stilled, the lights went out. Amos, sweating with his fury, sat up as high as possible in an attempt to find Johnny's face in the rumpled bedding.

"Are you all right?" Amos said.

"Yeah, that son of a bitch." Johnny moaned quietly with the residue of pain lingering in his groin. "Never say die."

That same unseen man was laughing again, irritating Amos with the absurdity of his lightheartedness. What in hell was so funny!

"Who gets such a kick out of this hell hole?" Amos said.

"Thas jes Owen, never talks, jes laughs. No one knows at what, somethin' he remembers maybe. He's saddled to his bed like me, plumb crazy."

"Maybe he's the sanest one in here," Amos said.

They were quiet for a long time, thinking, listening. Someone snored; a voice called like haunted wind; Owen giggled; the Home gave an imperceptible sigh. The room seemed colder with winter lurking around the building, peering through the window with its frozen face. In spite of himself, Amos was intrigued by that stubborn, wiry little man, and he couldn't help admiring Johnny's grit, helpless in that old metal bed, hunkering down against Daisy with all he had left in him. Amos admitted he had resented Johnny when he arrived here, forced to share a room with a no-account, thinking he was in some way above Johnny. Amos was changing his mind.

"How old are you?" Amos said, reluctant to break his self-imposed isolation.

"Seventy-six," Johnny said.

"I'm seventy-eight."

Amos thought Johnny looked much older than that.

"Yer jes a spring chicken."

"Why don't you let her have what she wants?" Amos said. "It won't make any difference in the end."

Johnny lay like a corpse in the faint illumination from the hallway and spoke firmly to the ceiling.

"It does ta me. I ain't gonna let her git away with it."

"Well I sure as hell am, whatever it is she's getting away with. If you want to go on living in a bedpan, you're dumber than I thought."

Amos's anger spilled over, still boiling and poised near the surface of his elderly pretense. He turned it back on himself for adding another blow to Johnny's fragile frame, almost as cruel as Roland's.

"I'm sorry," Amos said, "do what you have to do."

Johnny didn't respond and Amos remained awake until Johnny was singing his slumber's song in garbled notes. Amos thought about the checks as Daisy passed with her flashlight on night rounds. Would it ever be possible for him to get out of here, even if only for a few months, or was that Johnny's nonsense? His life was over when they wheeled him into this room, and these last days were a bad joke in the fellowship of crazies and clowns and a dopey cowboy.

The wind knocked at the window, threatening to shake loose its panes and blitzkrieg the warmth within. Amos sensed an inner chill his blankets could not prevent. He knew he was soon to die, the cold reaching him ultimately, irrefutably. Creosote preserves the railroad ties forever, it seems, against the worms of time. Would it preserve Carlos against the devastation and annihilation to come? Having reached his eyes, did the creosote seep through to the regions of his soul, protecting it from the worms that breed with anticipation? Amos knew that the world's creosote wouldn't preserve him from the storm center of death. They were all railroading with laceless boots, sightless eyes, lost and naked souls.

And they were on the last spur into the wasteland.

CHAPTER 6

AMOS COULD STILL SEE THE TELEGRAM, the lettering, some of the words crooked, the spaces wrong.

WE REGRET TO INFORM YOU THAT SGT. GREGORY J. LASHER
HAS BEEN KILLED IN ACTION IN THE SOUTH PACIFIC STOP
THE WAR DEPARTMENT . . .

Amos could recall all of it: the windy spring day, Mildred coming into the kitchen from the backyard, calling in and asking who it was. How he searched the room, the furniture, the walls, for some way to break this to her without killing her. The telegram—stuffed frantically into his sweater pocket—felt like a cannonball, tipping him over with the horror of it, the world tilting off its axis.

Greg would never come home.

When Greg was boarding the train after his furlough and they knew he was going overseas, he laughed at Amos with his lusty young voice. *Don't worry, Dad, I'll take a fat kid with me.* Amos didn't think they had grizzlies in the South Pacific.

Mildred puttered in the kitchen, immune to the concussion of the blow, fussing with some insignificant detail of life. He thought of Angie, as he clung to his favorite chair, the beautiful country girl with the golden hair and the tanned limbs whom they loved as much as Greg. How could Amos ever tell her? She had lovingly cemented the foundation of her life on Greg. Now her bedrock had been washed away by the bloodied waters of the South Pacific and Amos feared she would crumble and wash away with it.

Mildred came into the living room and stood in front of him, trying to interpret the storm squall spreading over his face, knowing that something was terribly wrong.

"What is it, Amos, are you feeling all right?"

"Amos, Amos, wake up," Daisy said, "we can't be sleeping all day like this."

Daisy's pleasant voice tore him from the living room and saved him from telling Mildred all over again. Daisy was holding his wrist, taking his pulse, and Amos, only half awake, realized he was succeeding, unconsciously giving his body the correct signals to die. Eating little, sleeping more, he was leaving it all behind, withdrawing during the daylight hours by rummaging through the dusty trunks of his memory, his mind jumping the years erratically with no apparent pattern.

He would remember a particular recess during his school days, and then some microfilm, stored faithfully in his memory bank, would be touched off by a mystical electric charge and he would be on the ranch, stacking hay with Greg and Marilyn on a hot July day. He would be with his father, as a boy on the farm, smell that inviting aroma of man and tobacco and work that the aftershave industry could never quite capture, even though his father left it behind for them on all his clothing. He would recall a time when he made love with a woman, the touch of her, sure he could faintly hear their sounds, catch her scent, remember the taste of her.

"If we don't start using our legs we're going to just shrivel up," Daisy said. "Roland tells me you're not progressing, not eating. We have to forget about the accident, Amos, and get back to living."

Daisy took his blood pressure and jotted her findings in a notebook, genuine concern on her handsome face. Her hands were well cared for, manicured, soft, her complexion smooth, indicating a high priority to salvage what youthfulness remained. Did they all haunt her like a gigantic mirror, reflecting her certain future?

"I have a check for you to sign, Amos, want to sit up?"

She handed him the check and pen matter-of-factly, opening them herself to save him the trouble. Amos shoved himself up and neglected to glance toward his roommate. Johnny wasn't judging any longer, enjoying a cigarette as evidence of his capitulation. Though Amos no longer had a clear conception of the passage of time, he knew Johnny had taken down his flag and

surrendered— signed the form that made Daisy Daws the beneficiary—back there somewhere when Amos was selling farm
machinery or running for the school board. It all merged in that
timeless vapor drifting around his bed and through his mind.

Johnny sucked the cigarette while the radiator pumped
heat into the room against a winter that had come to the
mountains with an arctic indifference. Johnny was living
again; his radio playing, candy in his drawer, and the Hills
Brothers back on the stand. He nursed the butt down to his
fingertips, savoring every drag, only allowed a cigarette when
Roland or Daisy worked in the area. The air in the room was
oppressive, stale, the cigarette smoke blending with the
resident odors, making an unpleasant soup.

"Dunk the butt, Johnny," Daisy said.

She scurried off on her nurse's charge and Johnny dropped
the scant remains of his pleasure into the juicy can. He'd told
Amos that Daisy would try to keep Amos alive as long as possible, not because of her kindheartedness but because of the faith-
fully-arriving checks. Johnny could be wrong; she could be a
good soul at heart, yet Amos was growing to respect the insights
of his gnarled mate who bore a striking resemblance to the
barbed wire he'd spent so much of his life with. Amos hadn't
conversed with Johnny much in the past weeks, at least not since
Johnny's surrender, ignoring even that final signing at the
summit.

"It's a goddamn blizzard," Johnny said. "Glad I'm not feedin'
cows in that ball-frostin' blow. Poor critters."

Johnny watched the snow flatten up against the window and
almost seal it off from the daylight. One of the ranchers he'd
worked for told him the cows didn't mind the cold and wind as
much as people thought—as if to appease his conscience—but
Johnny had never heard a cow say that.

"Why did you quit?" Amos said as he studied his wrinkled
conscience.

"Hell, it was your idea."

"What happened to 'Never say die?'" Amos said.

"I'm givin' it ta you," the old rider said after some thought.
"I'm not as strong as you."

How could Johnny say that? Amos didn't understand, knowing he had signed everything Daisy stuck under his nose. He'd admired Johnny's courage—though not always his good sense—in the face of the cruel pressure they put on him, rooting for Johnny in his heart of hearts to hold out. Even now, it was Amos's terrible disappointment that drove him to know why.

"Good afternoon, gentlemen," an elderly woman said, "what can I do for you today?"

She stood in the doorway, stout, white-haired, adorned with a Gray Lady uniform. She stepped in tentatively. Johnny propped himself up and looked in wonder. Amos watched silently from his pillow, the two of them staring at the poor paralyzed woman as if she wore her underware on the outside of her starched gray uniform. She was starting to melt into the scarred linoleum when Johnny saved her.

"Have ya got any tobac?"

Johnny reflected his surprise with a leathered squint. It was all he could think of to say. Someone out there cared about them, dumbfounding both. The woman was thankful for Johnny's request, even though she couldn't decipher it.

"Toe back?" she pronounced the words slowly.

"Smokes, cigarettes, snuff, you know," Johnny said as his face lit up.

"Ooooh, my." She laughed warmly at herself. "Daisy says we aren't to give anything like that without her permission. Your special diets and medications, you know. I'm Clara Channing."

She beamed from her starched dress.

Johnny turned off the radio. He stole a peek at Amos, and they exchanged a silent hope.

"I'm Johnny and that there's Amos." He nodded, a smile slowly creeping over the warp of his dogged face. "What are you doin' here?"

"Oh, I'm here to make your time a little more pleasant."

She was enchanted with her mission, swooning slightly as she spoke, her face as homey and plain as warm pie crust.

"Can you write letters for us?" Johnny said, glancing furtively at Amos.

"Ooooh, yes." She sang the words. "That's one of the things I *can* do for you. I have the stationery right here."

She opened her embroidered satchel and proudly produced paper, envelopes, and pen.

"Who would like to write a letter?"

Amos didn't blink, having written off the stolen money and his outrage. Johnny jumped in.

"I want to write a letter."

He sat up, eager. Clara pulled the chair up to his bed and arranged the stationery on a magazine she'd brought, ecstatic with her task.

"Who would you like to write?"

"One a them county commissioners," Johnny said.

"Are you going to mail the letter?" Amos said calmly.

"Oh, nooo, Miss Daws says all mail must go to her office. She will provide the postage, and she wants to know who is receiving mail and who is sending mail, for her records. She's so afraid that some of you might be left out."

"Haw!" Amos said, purposely imitating Johnny's skepticism.

Clara punched the button on top of her ball-point and waited excitedly for Johnny's first word. It never came. Johnny felt like an old fool, swindled out of his horse and saddle by some slicker. In the wake of Clara's stunning appearance he stupidly forgot that Daisy covers every base and he, better than any of them, should have known. Amos didn't look over and rub it in with his eyes.

"I'm tired, lady, ah, Clara. Maybe some other time," Johnny said to their newly acquired fairy godmother with her false promise. "I think I'll jes sleep some."

He slid his bantam frame into the covers and bedded down with his devastating disappointment. Amos shut his eyes, feigning sleep, discouraging even that simple woman from stirring up false hope. Clara folded up her things and contemplated the two old men in their vintage beds.

"I'll come again when it's not your nap time."

She tiptoed from the room as if reluctant to wake a sleeping child, observed by both from half-raised lids.

"Son of a bitch! You son of a bitch!" The man who attempted suicidal nosebleeds scrambled by, tracked closely by a taller, toothless fellow jabbering something about a story.

"You didn't tell it right, you didn't tell it right!"

They were two Olympic athletes, trapped on the instant replay by some fluke of technology, running in slow motion until they were old men. Emil stepped into the room with the manner of an undertaker.

"Marvin poured a urinal on Elroy's bed to make him stop teasing him about the Gypsy story," Emil said.

"They'll wish they hadn't brung Daisy into it," Johnny said. "Those two ain't playin' with a full deck."

"Seen the lady?" Emil said with a brooding stoicism.

"Yep."

"It won't work," Emil said.

"Nope. She had me jiggered fer a minute there, by cracky."

Amos ran their conversation through his mind while Emil watched up the hall to see what hellfire and brimstone would belch forth. What was going on in this warehouse of strays? The undercurrent in their dialogue intrigued Amos, became a burr under his saddle when he wanted a smooth ride into the grave. It was like an underground movement, a word here, a nod there. Amos's interest was awakening, and that he couldn't allow. It must be like this in every old folks home, a geriatric version of *Stalag 17*. The Gray Lady, wandering freely all over the building, proved it. They couldn't really be in captivity the way Johnny would have him believe.

Daisy prodded the old men toward their chambers like naughty children on their way to the woodshed for a whaling. Roland stormed past seconds later, and Daisy returned with Clara Channing, visiting, diverting her out of the war zone. Everyone listened tensely, held their breath, that end of the building deathly silent. Amos could hear Roland's voice without the meaning, then a grunt and a shrill outcry of pain carried up through the rafters and out into the mountain winds. The tension crackled along the corridor like electricity and subsided slowly with the sounds of a man whimpering. Amos was up on his elbows, showing emotion for the first time in many weeks, his face covered in sweat, enraged.

"This is a nuthouse! They just stand around all day and drive each other crazy."

Amos attempted to calm himself, slowing his breathing.

"Never say die," Johnny said.

Winston paced the hall like a frantic bird, reciting nervously, "RINGS ON HER FINGERS AND BELLS ON HER TOES, SHE SHALL HAVE MUSIC WHEREVER SHE GOES."

Marvin, the battered man, sobbed, while Elroy, his roommate, taunted him, mimicking his sounds of suffering. Amos thought they were like fish in an aquarium, nowhere to go, nothing to do with themselves, swimming round and round all day over the same marbles and colored rocks, all because they committed the crime of living too long. Roland sashayed up the hall like a brash bully, and Amos tried to quell the infuriating scandal of it all, escaping in the only manner he had left. He grit his teeth and shut his eyes and raced back to the ranch in his mind.

Greg is running toward him across the pasture, shouting frantically. Amos runs to meet him, alarmed, and the ten year old talks excitedly, his bleached hair tangled in the sunlight. The tarp in the main ditch had washed out, sending an avalanche of water into the barley, a field with too much slope; the water flooding over it would tear a terrible swath in very little time.

The two of them jump into the Ford truck. It cranks over slowly, finally starting with a jolt. Amos heads right across the pasture, hitting the many smaller irrigation ditches without slowing down, sending him and Gregory ricocheting off the seat into the cab roof at each ditch. At the top of the pasture they can see the field, the glossy sheen a widening wedge of gushing water, spreading rapidly across the infant grain shoots. Amos can see Mildred, in the water up to her waist, diverting much of it into the big ditch. Kneeling there in the gap, clinging to the tarp, fighting to keep from being washed away, she has saved the field from horrendous erosion.

Amos runs toward her. He can see her muddied face, the determination, the spirit there, as she matches her strength against the unremitting force of the icy current. He remembers he wanted to kiss her before he repaired the breach, step down into the water beside her and kiss her, he was so drawn to her courage and heart.

When he thought about it—with no little suffering and agony—he wished he had. That one kiss was worth more than the barley field. They lost the ranch anyway, and now he couldn't kiss her. She was swept away by the waters of time. The memory of that unfulfilled longing to kiss her was sharp, tormenting. He tried to move on in his mind, mulling over the accident. He opened his eyes and observed the disinherited around him, but even the reality of that company couldn't carry it away. He'd have to stay with it until it chose to release him. He could see her, kneeling in the swirling water, waiting for him to come into the current and kiss her.

He never did.

Like the color in his blue jeans, the romance and excitement in their marriage had washed out and faded. Mildred had the children, he his work, and in the end they were congenial companions. They started out in love and stuck it out as fellow travelers with the same itinerary.

He knew there were other things he ought to have done and never did. He couldn't recall them just now, but he could taste their aching regret. It was part of life; the haunting melody of lost moments, like missed kisses, floating away forever on the muddied waters, down to the salty seas of the South Pacific.

CHAPTER 7

LIKE FACES PRESSED ON A MONKEY CAGE, they peered into the room, and Amos thought there wasn't that much difference. A group from a local church brought their Christmas carols to the zoo. Daisy had put a few pine boughs on the bureau, a tree in the dayroom, and tiny Santas on some of the windowpanes. There was little anticipation for the big day among the boarders. Maybe it was the most painful day of the year for them, when memories of other Christmases—hidden in the crusted dust of their past and kept out of sight—were stirred up.

"Joy to the world, the Lord is come," they sang in something other than perfect harmony. This was the yearly pilgrimage to the Home, bringing generic gifts marked MALE and FEMALE and depositing them under the tree: combs, toothbrushes, toothpaste, razors, soap, magazines, candy, perfume, deodorant. They meant well, throwing popcorn and Cracker Jack through the bars: depersonalized coins of charity, harvesting some satisfaction in their hearts for having been there, although none of them ever came back to visit.

While Johnny pondered the ceiling and Amos faked a nap, they finished the carol, some with happy faces, some indifferent, a few searching the beds for some sign of human likeness. A young boy, high school age, stepped into the room one pace: the appointed spokesman. He wore a letterman's sweater.

"Merry Christmas, men, and a Happy New Year."

His words trailed off quietly when he looked at the two old men, recognizing the irony of his words and finding them stuck in his throat. He attempted to swallow them, but they kept bobbing back up with his Adam's apple. The choir moved uneasily down the hall and he turned to escape.

"Hey, sonny, want ta do me a favor?" Johnny said.

The boy paused, sensing he was on sinking sand, a vacillating smile on his innocent face.

"Sure, mister, what can I do?"

His eyebrows were raised in eager anticipation of his good deed to come.

"Go back into town and tell the people that we's prisoners out here," Johnny said. "All our belongings is stolen, and they hurt us bad if we don't do like they say."

The singing athlete had the smile plastered on his face and he couldn't get rid of it without faltering. He took a step straight backward, searching the corners of his eyes for the door. The strange old-timer raved on.

"She's gettin' rich off'n us, she's a mean bastard, you tell 'em."

Johnny started coughing and the boy took advantage of the pause.

"I will, sir, I'll tell them."

He rearranged his face and escaped, joining the unorganized choir a few rooms down, already singing "Silent night, holy night." Daisy stood in the doorway, something menacing about her nursely bearing, and embraced Johnny with a riveting glare, her expression in stark contrast to the Christmas lyrics. He returned her cold recognition for a moment and then had to turn away, defeated. When he glanced back, she was gone.

It was just another day for Amos. He tried not to disturb those lovely poignant memories he kept delicately out of mind. Their trays came with little decorations, colored napkins, a wrapped gift from under the tree and a "Merry Christmas" from Nell with all three meals. Amos looked at the red and silver paper around the small gift that was marked MALE. He picked at the food. Winston skipped past the door singing "Jingle Bells" and would seem saner to an outsider than Johnny, after the way the old wrangler had talked to the young caroler. Roland did his chores earlier than usual, wanting to be somewhere else on Christmas Eve. Except for the congestion of the Methodists and the digestion of the saltless turkey, nothing was different.

"You're still pissed at me fer signin' the paper ain't ya?" Johnny said as he chewed on the turkey with tooth and gum.

"Isn't any of my business," Amos said.

"Ya haven't said two words ta me in a month."

"I've been busy."

"It's a stinkin' lipstick," Johnny said.

He cackled and held up the precious gift. Someone had marked it wrong.

"I'll use it on my piles, hee, hee. Can ya see the look on Daisy's face the next time she takes my temperature."

He giggled in delight.

The lights went out and the frail children of Sunset were tucked in prematurely in hopes that St. Nick would soon be there. Settled in a dull stupor, Amos opened his eyes when Emil bumped against his bed. The Grouch pressed his face on the window glass and squinted out into the moonless night.

"The Buick's here," he said as he shuffled into the hall.

"What's that supposed to mean," Amos said, irritated at being left out.

"If you's ever awake you'd know what it means," Johnny said. "Daisy's boyfriend's here. The boys can do whatever they like fer a time. She'll be busy."

A card game formed just inside Emil's room, taking advantage of the night-light from the hall. No one had ever caught more than a glimpse of Daisy's boyfriend, but they knew that when the Buick was parked by the cottonwood, Daisy would be occupied and they could play. Like mischievous kids, it seemed more fun when they were supposed to be in bed.

After awhile, Johnny propped himself up on one elbow. When he found Amos awake, he spoke hoarsely, softly, words he couldn't restrain.

"It's the hardest day of all fer me ta git through. I jes can't fergit that Christmas back in '09. I was in love like I never thought possible. Jane Marie."

He pronounced the name with reverence, pausing a moment at the sound of it.

"I was twenty-two, she about the same, married off to a preacher by 'er parents when she's sixteen. He was about forty, forty-five, a big, round man. He had a congregation in a town in Wyoming I was workin' near. I'd see her when I'd git ta town, started goin' ta church, got saved an' ever'thing. She'd look at me an' I'd look at her. I know'd she wasn't happy with that ol' fart, but he kept a close string on 'er. Once, in the store, she took hold a my finger and held it fer a bit. I nearly exploded right there in the dry goods. I can tell ya this for sure, my pants wasn't no longer dry goods."

Johnny hacked, struggling to clear his throat. Amos didn't want to pay any attention to Johnny's rambling nostalgia, but he was hooked. He nodded for Johnny to go on.

"Anaways, one day she sneaks me a note when I's in church. It said I's ta come ta the house on Christmas Day. I was scared and excited, couldn't sleep, couldn't eat, couldn't work straight. Wal, Christmas come, an' I headed fer town. I nearly froze ta death takin' a bath that mornin'. I put my horse by the stockyard and walked up the street toward the house. I had a story all fixed up in case the preacher come ta the door. I knocked on the back door, scared ta hell, an'—"

Johnny wheezed and fought for breath. Now Amos was up on an elbow, wanting him to go on, completely absorbed in that bygone Wyoming Christmas. Johnny spit.

"She come ta the door an' I wasn't even breathin' with the fright of it. She waved me in and latched the door. The preacher is way off somewhere doin' Christmas services for the country folk, bless his soul. She told 'im she was sick. He wouldn't be back fer *two whole days!* She takes my hand an' leads me inta the front room, all the shades is pulled, the room smellin' all womanlike. I was so steamed up I coulda flown through the roof. I never seen a more beautiful creature in all my born days. She was so young and full and bloomin' it would have been a sin to have her go to waste."

Johnny sucked air, wheezing.

"Go on, what happened?" Amos said.

"We didn't say nothin'. I kissed her as careful as I could, then I went kinda wild, squeezin' her against me, kissin' her hard and she was doin' it right back at me. I knew right then that'd never be the end of it. I loved that girl more'n anything on God's earth. She took my hand an' led me upstairs to a bedroom. I sat on a big featherbed and she stood in front of me. I jes started unbuttoning her dress. It was blue, like her eyes. I remember she took off my hat, I'd fergot to, and she kissed my head. I unbuttoned down to her waist, fumblin' and shakin', and she helped me slip it over her arms. God, she was so ripe and lush I couldn't breathe, my heart's a poundin' right outta my chest."

Johnny was overcome by a spasm of coughing, the remembered erotic moment taking its toll. Amos was back there with him in that bedroom. Johnny hurried on.

"Wal, we got our clothes off, and someone's poundin' on the front door. I was scared ta hell. I didn't know what ta do. I jumped up and grabbed fer my hat and boots when she stops me, calm as ever. She tells me to stay in the bed, puts on a robe, and goes down to the door."

Johnny gasped, unable to breath for so long that Amos sat up in fear. Johnny was choking on his own phlegm, straining to cough it up. Finally he gurgled a string into the Hills Brothers can and sucked air, exhausted. He waved a hand at Amos.

"Finish tomorrow."

Johnny slid slowly out of sight in the folds of his rumpled bedding. He could dream of Jane Marie and whatever happened in the big featherbed, but Amos was left hanging, tantalized more than he would have believed and flustered, as if the last pages in a novel he was reading were missing. He turned to the wall with the bankrupt hope that he might dream too, of the good Christmas times past and of the woman he never found.

Was it real or just the muddle of dreams flowing through his unconsciousness? He saw Daisy, or so he thought. And through half-opened eyes he caught the hypodermic glint reflected in the night-light, for just an instant, maybe a dream. A woman was standing by Johnny's bed in a fur-trimmed·robe and slippers. Could it be Jane Marie coming back to her young cowboy? It was Daisy he focused through hazed vision. Johnny wheezed regularly. She bent over him, her flashlight on for a moment, then out. Johnny continued sleeping, unaware that she was so close. Daisy stood upright in the dusky shadows, and Amos froze. Johnny had stopped wheezing, stopped rattling, stopped breathing.

Johnny had stopped altogether.

Amos held his breath, not moving, then quickly began breathing regularly, loudly, trying in terror to imitate slumber. Daisy turned and came to his bedside, bending low, brushing his face with a scented breath. If she took his pulse she'd know he saw her. She remained there in frozen time, a tree taking root, never moving. He almost peeked to see if she had silently stolen away without his realizing it, but he didn't dare. Finally satisfied, she hurried up the hall to slip into bed with the Buick driver and claim she never left him.

Amos cautiously opened his eyes and tried to sort out his dreams from what he'd just seen, if in fact he had seen. He waited for immeasurable weighted stretches of time, listening for Johnny, outwaiting Daisy if she were standing just outside in the hall, lurking to trap him.

She killed him!

Could that be true or had he dreamed it? He pushed off his covers, slid stiffly to the floor, and crawled to Johnny's bed. He pulled himself up alongside the bed, his legs wobbling, and leaned close to Johnny's face. He placed his hand over Johnny's mouth and nose. Not a breath, nothing. Amos felt faint, all strength evaporated swiftly. He touched Johnny's still face for a moment and then crawled back to his bed.

Amos lost his practiced denial and control. He thrashed in his bed, his thoughts unfocused, ragged, impulsive, his heart fluttering. Who could he trust enough to tell? How will she get away with it with the medical reports and all of that? Amos remembered the paper, how Daisy would get the money from Johnny's life insurance, still stealing from him after he's dead. Amos could hear Johnny's voice, *I'm not as strong as you,* and he muddled over what he meant. Did Johnny realize that once he signed the beneficiary change it would become his personal death warrant and he would live each day by the grace of Daisy?

Amos felt shame for the way he'd treated that wrinkled warrior. While he was feeding on self-pity and trying to run away from it all, Johnny was alone, waging war with this impeccable serpent in nurse's disguise. He tried to visualize Johnny, a young drover aching with love, waiting in a featherbed for Jane Marie to come up the stairs. Amos wondered if she ever did. He hoped so, hoped Johnny had that much to take with him. God knows he didn't have much else. Amos wiped his eyes and looked over at the twisted old horseman, lying in his bed without the girl he loved. Jane Marie would never get back to him now.

Amos gazed out into the murky hallway, contemplating where he found himself at this strange moment in his life; looked down his own history, where he'd been, *who* he'd been. The wind had been at his back for many years now, since those years of pain, but lately it had turned and come straight in his face, an arctic blast from the ice fields. He was going against the wind, and he'd given up, retreated for shelter. He tried to look into his heart, see into the hidden places of his soul. When he spoke out loud, he startled himself.

"I'm not going to die, by God, and *I'm not going to let her get away with it!*"

His words sounded feeble and impotent in the quiet night, fragile birds in a violent storm, floating hollow down the hall. They were brave words, noble, uttered by an old man who doubted he could ever back them up. He lay awake all night with his thoughts, keeping vigil over Johnny's fallen body.

He could see Johnny, running a white horse across the Wyoming prairie, smiling and waving to a girl in a blue dress.

CHAPTER 8

Dawn materialized around them, and Amos suspected he had only dreamed the night's shadowed horror. He watched Johnny's shrouded form intently, expecting him to move, to wake up and spit. But Amos knew it wasn't Santa who had paid them a visit and she didn't leave their stockings full. She didn't leave a trace.

The Home awoke sluggishly, normally. Emil stopped at the door, figured Johnny was still asleep, and carried his sour disposition toward the latrine. Amos's pulse quickened with his terrifying secret, desperately wanting to tell the other men but panic-stricken they would give him away. One slip and Daisy would know he had seen her. Bloodhound, Gandy Dancer, even Linebacker floated the corridor, attired only in her wool under-wear. None of them bothered to stop for a visit until Johnny was stirring. Except one, an extremely stooped man wearing a denim engineer's cap pulled down to his ears and a soiled red bandana around his scrawny neck. He rapped Johnny's bed with a cane.

"You going to sleep all day?" he said to Johnny.

"Yes, I think he is," Amos said.

"You don't talk much, do you?" the man said and grinned. He was so bent over he found it difficult to look in Amos's face.

"I'm Amos Lasher. I've been sick lately."

"I'm Mick. Been a hobo all my life. Johnny'd better wake up and see what Santa brung him." He chuckled on his way out.

"He already knows," Amos said without humor.

"How are we doing this morning, gentlemen?" Daisy sang the words in her normal voice, doing Roland's rounds for him like an angel on Christmas morn.

She went about her task calmly, finding Johnny's urinal empty with genuine surprise. Amos watched with amazement.

"Come on, Johnny," she said, "it's time to pass our water."

It sounded as though they had a common bladder. Amos thought he detected a slight hesitation as she rolled Johnny's lifeless body toward her.

"Oh no, poor Johnny has left us, Amos."

Amos could think of no reply that wouldn't give him away.

Without a hitch in her serene confidence, she made a cursory examination of his left arm and then covered death's face with the sheet. She was used to finding men dead in their beds at Sunset; it was more amazing to find them alive.

She turned to Amos.

"Did you see or hear anything last night?"

Her eyes were piercing, inescapable flames from the carved face of a Halloween pumpkin in the dark. Amos's voice faltered and he feared it would stumble over his secret.

"No . . . nothing, he never said a thing," Amos said.

She took his wrist, found his pulse—a goddamn built-in lie detector. Could she tell by his heartbeat that he knew? She could, but in her overconfidence she read it wrong.

"Well, don't let it frighten you. He lived a long life. I knew he wouldn't be with us much longer. It's best for him."

It's best for who, you murdering bitch, so damn clean, so well groomed and always in control.

Who would ever believe him if he told?

Amos ate breakfast in the company of the sheeted cadaver, and the coroner arrived shortly after. He examined Johnny superficially and made out the proper papers with a flamboyant scrawl. Middle-aged, sincere, efficient, he said little. Daisy hovered close in case he needed anything, or to distract him if he wandered near the mark. Amos wondered what the man would find if he told him to look for a needle hole, if it would even show, one tiny tooth mark from the lovely Dracula standing at the foot of the bed in her antiseptic reputation. Amos struggled for courage to speak.

"Are you a doctor?" Amos said, all he could muster under the burden of Daisy's presence.

The man didn't look up, scribbling on the paper.

"No, mortician."

"Doesn't a doctor have to look at him?" Amos said, avoiding Daisy's eyes.

"Not necessary. The man just died, probably his heart," he said dryly and returned to his form.

Look closer, damn it! A man is murdered in his bed and this county sleepwalker writes it off as death by natural causes. What kind of a public servant is he? But hell, who is ever suspicious when an old bedridden man dies in his sleep at a county home? No insurance investigator would come snooping around or even raise a routine eyebrow. She really had something going for her, watching the mortician with a glowing satisfaction that everything was going smoothly under society's lazy eye of indifference. Amos couldn't help but wonder how many others there had been.

"Are you finished, Harry?" Daisy said.

"All done."

He packed his leather bag and left with Daisy and the official papers that would forever legally explain Johnny away to whoever might inquire about his passing. *No one.*

Winston appeared in his baggy pants and floppy shoes, a dark growth of stubble on his face, staring at the little mound Johnny created. The bloodhound chanted, "HE WENT TO BED AND BUMPED HIS HEAD AND NEVER GOT UP IN THE MORNING." Winston had outlived his opponent, longevity's reward. Daisy ushered two men into the funereal climate of their Christmas morning, the same two who had brought Amos in the fall. Apparently they didn't remember Amos as they flipped a large black bag alongside Johnny and unzipped it. They were taking a man who had stayed on Steamboat for over eight seconds to the dump in an economy-size garbage bag. Not in the room three minutes, they absconded with Johnny and whatever feelings of distaste they accepted with the job. Daisy bustled back with clean bedding, stripped and remade the bed, and began dumping Johnny's few personal belongings into a garbage bag.

"You'll have a room all to yourself for a while, Amos. Won't that be nice?"

She grabbed Johnny's few hanging clothes from the wardrobe and with them sent a small plant in a paper cup cascading to the floor.

"That damn Carlos. Have you seen him coming in here, Amos?"

"No." He wouldn't rat on Gandy Dancer if he had.

"No, you wouldn't with your sleeping night and day."

She cleaned up the mess, dumping it into the coffee can, straightened that corner of the room and carted off any trace of the old cowman. When she finished, you'd never know that Johnny had ever been there. Even the Hills Brothers were gone, all of his memories, all of the events of his long singular life, dusted from the earth, obliterated in half an hour. The days working cows seen from his squinted eyes, the fencing, the branding, the calving, the sleet hitting his cheeks, the long, silent hours under the solitary sky, the drinking and jabbering in the glow of friendship, or the buttoning of his jacket against a friendless night. Even Jane Marie was gone with him.

Amos could hear Johnny vowing *I ain't gonna let 'er get away with it.* But she had, gotten away with it clean. In a few weeks or a month an envelope would arrive in Daisy's mailbox with an insurance check, the last shred of Johnny's life, rewarding the one who murdered him. Amos winced from the outrage that ganged up on him, and he was struck by this question: Why would a single cowboy buy life insurance in the first place? Who was there in Johnny's past that he wanted to provide for if he should die? That too was gone in the zippered bag.

Roland punched in the following morning for his customary ritual of slopping out the place.

"Did Santa come to see you?" he said to Amos.

"Yes. Will you help me walk?"

Amos stopped him short as he foraged bearishly around the room. Roland frowned with curiosity.

"Old Johnny kicking off scared you a little, huh?" He smiled.

"Yeah, I don't want to end up like him."

Amos picked up on Roland's theme, guarding his real thoughts with a benign expression.

"OK, but you'll have to get the hang of it fast. I already spent too much time on you."

Roland helped Amos slide down and steady himself against the dusty aluminum frame. He resembled a scarecrow and felt as strong, gripping the cold metal and forcing himself to shift his weight onto his right leg. Jell-O. He wanted to quit immediately, but looked at Johnny's empty bed and commanded his body into obedience when it was threatening to flee under enemy fire. Suspecting he would collapse, he shoved one obstinate foot several inches forward and followed the same grueling distance with the other, neither ever leaving the linoleum. He hurt, sweat seeped from his face and body, but Amos refused to relent, shoving first one foot, then the other, shuffling snail against hammering surf.

"Hey, that's great," Roland said, holding him from crumbling onto the floor, "but you look terrible. We'll do more tomorrow."

He deposited Amos back into the bed, drained of all strength, already excitedly forming a plan in his mind. He would start eating, build up his stamina, train for the conflict he had— to his own astonishment—gladly accepted as his personal quest.

Amos swayed on the walker, having reached the doorway, skeptical that he could make it back to his chair before his sand ran out. The days had passed rapidly and Amos sensed an electricity in them, an excitement in the meanest of humdrum routines, generated by the secret lying undetected just under his rib cage. He ate all his saltless food, gained strength, shoved himself a step further each day, until he could scan the length of the hall and measure the dimensions of his captivity.

"You getting the hang of it?" Marvin, the tall toothless man, said, stopping to visit. He assaulted Amos's nostrils with the stink of urine.

"Yes, thank you," Amos said with a smile. "I'm learning over."

The men accepted him back among the living, ignoring his long rebuff, and their tokens of kinship fortified him for the journey. He pushed himself to the limits of his pluck and will and made it to the chair, dropping into the arms of the comfortably worn frame, completely spent. He restored himself there in pants and shirt, no longer wearing the hospital gown of dying men.

As though impersonating an old down-and-out Teddy Roosevelt, Emil appeared with a wooden box and stool.

"Want to play checkers?"

"Yes, if I have the mustard to move the pieces," Amos said, still catching his breath.

Amos sat with the walker at his side like a young cowhand with new holster and gun, overcome by the first muzzle blast. Emil methodically set up the game: the weathered box, then the stool from which the Grouch would guide his pieces in combat, and finally a careful placement of the board and checkers. Emil nodded for Amos to make the first move and the game began.

"You fish?" Amos said as he slid a red checker forward.

"Used to . . . the Yellowstone, the Shields, Spring Creek."

Emil studied the board with a keen eye, plucking at his bristling mustache, then made up his mind and moved a black.

"I took some fine rainbow from the Yellowstone," Amos said as he moved another red.

A neat-appearing old man came erectly to watch the contest.

"Who's got the advantage?" he asked politely.

"Don't know yet, Robert," Emil said loudly, almost a shout.

They played, and Robert watched through thick lenses that distorted his eyes and cheeks, the skin on his face and bald head shedding scales. He stood back a pace, not to impose.

"You a fly fisherman?" Emil said, sitting back with hands on hips.

"At the end I was. Started out a meat hunter." Amos chuckled.

"Where's Johnny?" Robert said.

"He's dead, remember?" Emil shouted.

The man was obviously hard of hearing. His head gently shook as he thought about it.

"Did I ever tell you about the time President Roosevelt visited my classroom?" Robert said.

"Yes, you did," Emil said without looking up.

"He said education was the backbone of the nation," Robert said and fell silent. Then, as the checker game went on, he slipped silently up the hall.

"Which Roosevelt?" Amos said.

"It doesn't matter," Emil said. "We call Robert the Professor. Can't hear much, doesn't remember. He's Daisy's decoy: nice room, family that visits from time to time. Trouble is, he can't remember where his prick is ten seconds after he's peed."

Emil jumped a man and removed it from the board with a sullen satisfaction. While Emil reset the pipe in his mouth, Amos tried to look into the squat German's evasive eyes.

"What did you do for a living?" Amos said.

"A carpenter," he said with a subdued pride, removing the pipe from his mouth and gazing through the window. "There's a lot of houses that I built out there, standing solid in this damn country. That's my immortality, huh?" He grunted cynically. "I built anything made of wood: houses, barns, elevators, furniture. I built a fine home for my family, five bedrooms, big porch . . ." His voice trailed off, a shadow of pain fled across his face.

"Did you have a large family?"

"Yes, a good family."

Emil appeared to be searching for their faces on the checkerboard. "How do you think my *English* is? Do I speak correctly?" Sarcasm laced his careful pronunciation.

"Sounds fine to me." Amos knew he was getting into something.

"In 1944 we were living in the house I had built in the breaks, nine miles from town. We had lived there for more than fifteen years, worked and bought and schooled and worshiped. We had a nice place, a few animals, big garden. I was a carpenter. Then there was the war, far away some place, and we could not hear the guns or smell the smoke. After a time some of the town people lost their sons in the war. They were angry. They knew I was German, I had always been German. They started making insults, talking, warning people not to hire the Nazi. I stayed home much of the time, even the children didn't want to go to school. We got by."

Amos squirmed, sensing the room was filling with sorrow.

"A rancher down the valley hired me to build a barn. Said that my nationality was 'A damn good carpenter.' One night my truck won't start. I work on the truck for two hours, but I get it running. It's already dark. I'm almost home when two trucks come racing towards me, almost ran me into the barrow pit. In my heart I already know. I can see the glow in the sky, then the flames in that black night."

Emil's voice quickened, the checkers forgotten.

"The house is half gone when I get there. I tried to get inside, but it is impossible. I shout for them, all of them, running around the house, again and again, running around and shouting. No one answers. No one. My wife, my five good children are all inside. They used dynamite. I waited all night for the fire to burn out. By dawn there are only ashes, my beautiful family only ashes."

His voice broke, trembled, he shook with rekindled anguish and rage.

"I told the authorities about the trucks. The incident was looked into. The paper hardly mentioned it. No one was ever arrested." Emil turned and spit toward the floor, mostly a gesture. "That's what I think of your 'Home of the brave.'"

Amos didn't know what to say, there were no words.

"I've always wondered if they thought they were killing me," Emil said softly, "or if they were so devious they knew I was gone and wanted me to know how it felt to lose your children in the war. My mistake was I didn't realize that I *was* at war!"

Emil struggled against the flood of emotion gathering behind his eyes like stored gravity. He held it all back, swallowed it in the manner he'd mastered through the years.

"Damn! I swore I'd never tell anyone. Didn't want to give one more goddamn American the satisfaction."

"I got no satisfaction," Amos whispered.

"I left everything, never went back . . ."

Emil could no longer continue. He wiped one eye quickly with the back of his thick hand and focused on the forgotten board. Tears slowly slid down his weathered cheeks like children who hid their faces in his grand gray mustache. Amos wondered if Emil had been alone all the years since the night he watched his family being cremated. He didn't dare ask, already weighted with Emil's heartache.

"It's your move," Amos said softly, hoping it would turn him away from the ashes that had seeped into the closets of his soul.

Emil studied the partially played game, figured a move, and left his memory. They played three games and talked of fishing.

"Play tomorrow?" Emil said.

He picked up the pieces with his unabsolved wrath and walked heavily out of the room, leaving his sadness over Amos like a sticky cobweb.

Amos fought it off. He turned and looked out the wire-meshed window. The sun was falling rapidly in the thin winter sky, sagebrush poked out of the snow from a midwinter thaw, and a magpie skipped across the lifeless ground in search of a morsel. An unexplainable surge of joy welled up in Amos's breast, bringing tears to his eyes. He just noticed how beautiful it all was, surprising him that it had always been, and as he absorbed the shimmering creation through the unwashed glass, he found a new feeling of belonging. He crawled wearily into his bed and knew he was going to live, and he was looking forward to the evening meal.

As the traffic picked up in the hall, Amos closed his eyes to avoid being disturbed, a nap respected by most. He thought of Emil, racing down that dark road to his roasting family, standing helplessly in the yard as they were swallowed up by the predatory flames, just because of his nationality and the accent in his speech. Amos wondered what became of those who did it. Had the dynamite exploded in their minds, rearranging their consciences and telling them it was an act of patriotism and bravery? Could they go on living without noticing the bits and pieces of five children and their mother lying on the windowsill with the rest of the world's dust?

That bloody war cost Emil much more than it cost Amos. He thought of Greg, his only son, and felt tears welling in his closed eyes. He couldn't sort them out. Were they for Gregory or for Emil, or were they for Johnny? He could do nothing about that kamikaze or those two trucks full of fleeing arsonists, but he was getting stronger, and he wouldn't let Johnny go with only the shedding of a tear. Unlike Emil, Amos knew full well he was at war with Daisy. She was certainly intelligent and would have plugged the most obvious leaks in her stronghold.

But there is always one, like an unnoticed rat hole, and he would find it.

CHAPTER 9

IT WAS A MILESTONE IN HIS LIFE instead of a tombstone, to reach the toilet on his own again. Amos had taken back a portion of occupied territory: that land of privacy where a human can take care of his own bodily functions without the consent or help of anyone else. He sat there with his trousers down around his ankles, glowing with self-satisfaction and a growing elation. He noticed that the shower had handles in the stall, rusting and staining down the sides as though it were slowly bleeding to death. *A shower.*

He stood carefully and shuffled over to the metal compartment, kicking off his slippers and stepping out of his pants along the way. He worked off his shirt and turned on the water, testing its temperature with one hand until it was right. Into the water, he felt its clean rushing flow embrace him like the arms of a forgiving lover, laughing on him, singing him a happy song, slapping his shriveled rump with a playful hand.

On second thought, the shower was more like an affectionate mother, engulfing him in her hot moist bosom and whispering to him that everything was all right. Down the drain went the hopelessness accumulated on his body and soul, the stench of his self-pity and resignation to die, breaking off him like barnacles, the grime and blood of the accident, the guilt and despair. He turned his face up into the flying water and felt a renewal surge through his being, a strange joy flowing in his veins. He wanted to sing. He soaped his body several times and hummed a broken tune, washing the crud from his life.

Instead of a door, the men's bathroom had a curtain hanging across the entrance, affording easy access but less privacy. Emil stood halfway in, watching Amos, apparently reluctant to impose on his ceremony. Amos noticed him and called, "I'd forgotten how good it feels."

Emil moved over to the porcelain urinal, chipped in several places, the wounds turned black. Amos turned off the shower and stood dripping.

"Haven't got a towel?" the Grouch said indifferently.

"I never thought about it."

"You should have."

Emil left through the curtained door. Amos stepped out of the shower and thought it would be nice to soak in the large antiquated tub that stood on four squat legs against the wall, if one could have some privacy. He steadied himself on the walker and realized Daisy was standing in the doorway, silent for a moment, her eyes fondling his nakedness. Amos felt utterly vulnerable, as if her eyes were fingering his skeletal body for the secret that was burning in his chest. Then she grinned out of her pleasing face.

"I'm proud of you, Amos, you're doing so well. It's nice we can wash ourselves again, but we mustn't use too much hot water."

Her stare never wavered, and he had to turn away. Emil saved him, arriving with a towel, and Daisy quit the men's room. Her appearance had sobered Amos's exhilaration and redirected it, reminding him of where he was. He accepted the towel from Emil.

"Thank you. I think it's time we bust out of this hoosegow."

"Humph," Emil said. "Big talk for a cripple."

Amos dried himself the best he could; his hip still bore some numbness. He was learning the floor plan of the building with each sortie into new territory. There was a door to the outside at the far end of the hall.

"Is the hall door ever open?" Amos said as he toweled his thin gray hair.

"Sometimes in the summer," Emil said, "when they're watching, we can go outside for a while."

Emil handed him his shirt.

"Anyone ever run away?" Amos said.

"A few." Emil stroked his bristling mustache. "Fern did last summer. Roland drove out in the sage and hauled her back."

"Any others?" Amos sat on the toilet to pull on his pants.

"Old Jens Jenson, last winter. Wandered out and froze to death in the foothills." Emil toned down his voice and glanced at the half-drawn curtain. "Never did know why that door was open. Maybe they wanted him out there."

Amos stepped into his slippers.

"How did the guy before me die . . . ah, Harold?"

"In his sleep. Always hoped he'd die in his sleep."

Amos gripped the walker, ready for the journey back to his room. Exhausted and bone weary, he also felt rejuvenated. Emil shuffled along behind him, a convoy through enemy waters. Amos filed the information Emil had given him, knowing all of it was easily explained. You're always reading about some old person wandering away from an institution: incoherent, lost, freezing to death. Who would give it a second thought? It was an old person's task to die. He knew the real question was What had they bequeathed in their dying and to whom?

It had been exactly one month since Johnny's bed was empty. Daisy led the man into the room, a lovable-looking fellow, gnomelike, wearing little round wire-rimmed spectacles, white hair topping his round face, punctuated with a small cherry nose. His body was slightly rotund, a pronounced potbelly with little arms and legs coming along for the ride.

"This is Amos Lasher," Daisy said. "Amos, this is Spencer Pace. He's going to be your new roommate. Won't that be nice?"

Daisy set an overflowing cardboard carton on the dresser, and a young woman followed with a second box and suitcase.

"Hello," Amos said from his chair.

The man looked like Santa Claus without the whiskers.

"Hello, Amos," the quaint man said, preoccupied with this devastating thing that was happening to him. He began finding a place for his belongings around the room, laying a large Bible on the bed table. A young timid man appeared with a rocking chair—set it in the room as if old age were a communicable disease—and fled. On an unused nail above the dresser, Spencer hung a K-Mart picture of Jesus holding a lamb in his arms. Daisy and the woman talked about him as though he weren't present, departing in idle chatter. Spencer, meanwhile, was as busy as a chipmunk who feels winter coming on and knows he's wasted the summer.

"Now you just tell me if I do anything wrong. It'll take me a day or two to get used to this place."

Amos remembered the annihilating desperation of this experience: out the old road past the dump, dropped off at the poor farm, your last scraps of hope crushed, and how he had retreated in his anguish. It seemed that this jolly old-timer was doing the opposite—attacking with every shred of courage he could lay hands on. Amos hoped Santa Claus wouldn't discover what captives they were until he had grown some callus against this animal farm.

Nell marked out another chunk of time with her faithful deliveries, her multi-flavored apron, and her inflexible expression.

"Here's your supper, Johnny." She set it before Spencer.

"His name is Spencer, Nell," Amos said. "Johnny died, remember?" She paused a moment, her tongue worked at the side of her mouth, but nothing seemed to register.

The men sat side by side with their supper trays. Spencer bowed his head in silent prayer and Amos waited awkwardly until he finished.

"Why don't we eat with the other folks?" Spencer said as he dug right in.

"There isn't any space for tables and chairs, they say."

Amos began eating. Spencer ate with undivided resolve, a hearing aid in his left ear.

"I thought we'd be able to socialize and visit while we ate."

Disappointment crept into Spencer's voice.

"Maybe things will change," Amos said.

He reviewed the letter to the sheriff he'd composed in his mind for days, contemplating the joy and terror of sharing his secret.

"I've been taking care of myself, cooked, cleaned, got around," Spencer said, glancing over his little round glasses. "Now they don't think I can be alone, just because the hot plate caught fire. It wasn't much of a fire, didn't hurt anyone, but they said I'd best be where they could look after me, for my own good. The fella who rents the rooms booted me out, said I was dangerous. I looked, but there was nowhere else to go."

Spencer started to choke up, holding a forkful of potatoes to his mouth without eating.

"I get a little money each month. I told them I could . . ."

He put the potatoes in his mouth and sat silently, unable to swallow.

"If you're wondering about the food," Amos said, "it's the salt. There isn't any."

They finished the meal in silence and Amos anticipated the coming challenge. Tomorrow was Sunday.

The Sabbath arrived and Amos felt strong. He worked the walker past the bathroom and paused at Owen's door. Owen lay bedridden, never talked, but with his sporadic laughing he cheered the place up or—depending on your point of view— haunted the night like an unseen hyena in the African veld. He lived on like one of Carlos's plants, a fruitcake for Daisy to discourage any do-gooder citizens who wanted to visit the folks at the Home.

"Hello in there," Amos called, "I'm Amos Lasher."

There was no response. Amos pushed on a few paces and looked into Robert's well-furnished room across the hall, flabbergasted by the contrast. Curtains, rugs, nice furniture, books, right at the head of the hall with high visibility from the dayroom, a showcase for the occasional visitor. Johnny had called it Daisy's decoy.

Amos moved on to the edge of the dayroom and was immediately overcome by the gathered inhabitants, so fresh from his self-imposed solitary confinement. The room was a patchwork of faces and clothing where neither heeded any recognizable fashion or pattern; a collage of children turned old, carrying all they had left on earth in their worn-out pockets, in their fading memories, in their creviced, weathered, toothless faces. They carried on with the scars and crippled limbs and warp of their pinched bodies, the twinkle dying in their eyes, the luster in their laugh, the bravery in their voices. A university of experience in the human passage; the drama, the tragedy, the comedy, a million million steps before the footlights, a panoply of the emotions known to humans, etched with the brush of time, not a hue or note missing; a symphony played on the heartstrings of these kids who found one another at the far end of the playground at nightfall. Who ever heard this music, who saw this play, who came to this university to learn?

Amos suffered an unbearable anguish as he joined that throng, pushing the walker amid chairs and benches, old sofas, secondhand lamps, and tables stacked with soiled games, puzzles, and frayed *National Geographic* magazines. He thought it was a dead ringer for a Goodwill outlet, these people grubbing for a bargain. In fact, all of them could be from the Goodwill, like objects that no longer belonged to anyone. Some could no longer see, no longer hear, some could no longer think clearly or remember. Some could no longer chew or walk or always control their bladders. But these people who had survived everything else in their lives now carried on in the face of this monstrous degradation with a threadbare courage that overwhelmed him. He moved as quickly as he could to the double window and tried to gulp control of his filling throat and wetting face.

He distracted himself by tracing the building's form, revealed from the window in the drifted snow. A narrow courtyard separated the men's wing from the women's, and they connected to this central part of the Home. He glanced down at a *Reader's Digest* atop a pile of magazines. It was dated June 1960, over four years old. He tried to remember what his life was like when that magazine came out. He was in control again.

He wove through the clutter to a bench in the middle of the room and lowered himself, fighting back the demon within who urged him to give up. A thin, pleasant-looking woman in a nearby chair took him in immediately.

"You must be Amos. We were wondering when we'd get to meet you." She smiled warmly.

"Yes, Amos Lasher. I broke my hip in a car accident. Couldn't walk for a spell." Amos returned the smile, feeling lost inside.

"I'm Fern Knutson. I've been here just over three years."

She was mending a dress as she spoke, the skin loose and wrinkled on slender hands that moved quickly and adeptly at the work they seemed to know well.

Sadie interrupted their conversation by meandering between them. "I'm going home today." She reminded Amos of a baseball player, the sleeves of her underwear longer than the short sleeves of her dress. He wondered if she could throw a curve.

"You've met Sadie I take it," Fern said, glancing up from her mending.

"Yes, she strays our way now and then."

Amos had the urge to tell Fern that Sadie's nickname was Linebacker, but refrained.

"Poor dear, she doesn't realize where she is."

"Maybe none of us does," Amos said and then laughed.

"You having trouble with Daisy?" Fern said with narrowed eyes.

"No, no trouble."

Amos was unsure of the channels of communication in this museum, yet his instincts told him he could trust Fern from the beginning. Fern seemed to sense his dishonesty, and she fell silent with her work.

Amos watched a grizzled old woman in a wheelchair prattling ceaselessly with no one, blending with the television noise. Some watched the set without enthusiasm, some dozed, a few men played cards, and everyone seemed to know who could carry on a rational conversation and who couldn't. A woman with exploding white hair and open mouth walked unsteadily toward the new boy on the street. Amos turned to greet her when she swooped a birdlike hand in the air and sprinkled him with a little cloud of confetti, the woman who had done the same thing when he arrived months ago.

"This is Grace," Fern said. She showed no surprise at the shower of paper. "Grace, this is Amos Lasher."

"Hello, Grace," Amos said, uncertain what he should do about the scraps of paper on his clothes and in his hair. "What are we celebrating?"

"Celebrating?" the wispy hollow-cheeked lady said. "Why *you*. You've come to live with us. We've been waiting for you."

"Grace! I've warned you about that paper throwing," a husky woman said while shaking a finger. "You pick up every speck."

Grace's blank response seemed unperturbed, but she bent her knees slowly, snapping branches, and knelt to pick up the scattered scraps.

"That's Mae," Fern said. "She cleans and takes care of the women, like Roland over on your side."

Amos thought, grizzly sow.

"She lives here," Grace said, "like the rest of us. Guess she doesn't have anyone."

Grace picked a shred of paper off Amos's lap, and he unconsciously began helping her collect the fragments of her unspoken words.

"Are you chewing your food thoroughly?" Grace said to Amos.

"When?" Amos said.

"Always," Grace said. "You must chew your food well or you could choke, you know. It's very easy to choke."

Amos didn't know how to respond. Fern raised her eyebrows and rolled her eyes.

"You must remember to chew your food very well," Grace said as she gathered the pieces of paper.

Daisy entered the room with a tall young man.

"Pastor Harper has a devotion for us, folks, isn't that wonderful."

Daisy smiled and snapped off the TV in the middle of the program. The minister stood uneasily in front of the set, gripping his black Bible with unnecessary tenacity. He waited a moment, then realized he'd never have any more attention than he had at the moment. He read a portion where Jesus heals a blind man and then commented on what that meant for them. Amos wondered if the preacher, so engrossed in his own words, could *see them*, this present audience he embraced. Grace picked confetti from the floor, the woman in the wheelchair entertained herself in conversation, Sadie wandered, others slept with dangling heads or open mouths. The preacher could give a few communion by just going by and dropping it in and they'd never know unless they came up gagging on the Body of Christ.

Daisy roamed in and out, like the assistant manager at a kiddies' matinee, watching for rowdy kids throwing popcorn. Robert had a visitor in his room, and that was it, except for the clergyman, the professional visitor who expounded on human blindness to one another's needs. He finished with a free prayer, getting stuck in the middle and stammering his way to the amen.

Emil turned the TV on and tried to find football to the protests of several others. The Reverend Harper worked his way through the folks with perfunctory salutations and ducked out the door. Daisy announced that visiting hours were over and slipped through a door on the far wall. Amos guessed it was her private quarters. With reluctance, the room emptied. Amos paused to let the traffic move out.

"Nice to meet you, Amos," Fern said. "Have a nice week."

She gathered her mending and followed the women's procession. Amos wanted to scream, unable to comprehend why they weren't all shrieking. He stood, and like the rest, followed in this savage march, only sustaining his sanity by reciting the letter in his mind over and over in hope. Spencer passed him, commenting on the fine devotion. Carlos felt his way along the wall, a grubby trail of human narrative, left by the touch of the uncounted halt and blind who once dwelled here, fingerprints on the wailing wall, silently telling their tale that no one would read. Amos loathed his identity with this parade.

"It's awfully early, isn't it?" Spencer said when the lights went out.

"You get plenty of sleep at Sunset," Amos said, though he didn't plan to sleep.

Emil cautiously stole into the room and went to the window, cupping his hands around his face and pressing them against the glass.

"He's here," Emil said, watching a moment.

"Who's here?" Spencer said. He sat up in bed.

"The Buick driver," Amos said, "Daisy's boyfriend."

Carlos sneaked into their room, inching his way toward Amos.

"If you don't use the bedpan anymore, can I use it?" Carlos said.

"What for?" Amos was puzzled.

"I have another plant started." Carlos leaned close to Amos and whispered. "Roland'll never look in your pan."

"A plant?" Amos said and caught himself laughing.

"Philodendron. It won't cause you no harm," Carlos said.

"Sure, be my guest," Amos said. "We can stand some greenery around here."

Carlos moved away stealthily to relocate his smuggled alien.

"He collects mud and dirt off Roland's shoes," Emil said, "anything he can scrape up to bed his plants. Roland keeps throwing them out and providing the soil for the next one. Sometimes a preacher leaves a chunk of mud."

Carlos returned, gently cradling a paper cup with a green stem and several leaves sprouting from its soil. Emil guarded the hall while Carlos tucked his plant into the bedpan and slid Amos's suitcase in front of it. He stood with a grunt, nodded his thanks, and blended into the shadows.

"Why won't they allow the poor man to have a plant?" Spencer said, trying to keep tabs on the madness around him.

"Roland says they clutter up the room, make cleaning a lot harder," the Teddy Roosevelt look-alike said. "Truth is, Carlos makes a mess when he waters them. He's so blind he misses half the time."

Emil went downstream to inform those who were able that they could play for a while.

They lay quietly as the night noises of the Home came like crickets in the spring, the snoring reminiscent of frogs and locomotives and wood saws. Some of the men were visiting in hushed voices and playing cards by the night-light. Before long, Spencer snored, his hearing aid atop the Bible beside his bed. Amos waited impatiently for another few minutes and then slid out of bed, found his slippers with his feet, and took the walker to the shower stall, concealing it behind the curtain. He walked without support up the hall and into the darkness of the dayroom, his solo flight.

He knew it was imperative that Daisy remain ignorant of his ability to walk and he was confident she was preoccupied at the moment with the enthusiasm of the Buick driver. He stood very still at the center of the dayroom and listened, the sounds from the two wings echoes of the same labored sleep, sighs of a common sorrow, neither male nor female. Amos walked to Daisy's door and listened, thinking he could hear muffled conversation but unwilling to bet it wasn't his imagination. He moved to the east end where Mae's door was shut, probably locked against the night wanderers. He crossed to the outside door on the west and found it locked with several keyed bolts, causing him to question what would happen in this trap if fire broke out. It was enough, his energy quickly sapped, and he retraced his steps, flopping into his bed's cozy embrace.

His mind reeled. Daisy in bed with a lover, Roland gone, Mae barricaded against the horde. Was this a moment the beast's jugular was exposed? Would he settle for escape or try to tear down her kingdom? No choice. With paper and a stubby pencil as his weapons he would broadcast his perilous secret to the government's officials who were elected to speak for and protect those who could not speak nor protect themselves.

He wanted to believe in the law of the land.

CHAPTER 10

Amos THOUGHT IT WOULD BE EASY, but as he sat on the flowered davenport a week later and tried to act nonchalant, his bones threatened to explode with the tension of a steel-spring trap. The residents were gathered for the fabricated visiting hours and just knowing the letter was in his pocket made Amos tremble. Effie, a small blind woman, sat next to him, and Fern sat facing them, flipping through a magazine.

"If the Depression hadn't come for another few years," Amos said, attempting to visit, "I think we could have made it on the ranch."

"I think I would have liked a ranch," Fern said, noting Amos's nervousness. "I've always loved animals."

"I love animals," Effie said. "I love to hold them."

Effie held onto Amos's arm—which she was in the habit of doing when visiting with someone—to be sure he was still there and she wouldn't be thought a fool talking to herself. Amos guessed she was very old, or she'd soaked too long in the tub of heartache and disappointment. Her skin looked like dried up leather and her eyes darted around at the top of their sockets as if they were trying to fly free.

"Well, I got into selling farm machinery eventually," Amos said, "and when the war came on I stayed in it. I always laughed the way they gave F.D.R. the credit for pulling the country out of the Depression. Hitler did that, and Tojo."

Amos tried to keep track of Daisy and carry on a normal conversation.

"I used to have cats at home," Effie said. "I love cats."

She looked out into her personal blackness for the image of those cats. Maybe she didn't even notice the darkness in the Home after her long personal tyranny. She had never been taught or trained in any way, left like a mushroom on a stump until her life had dried up in the sun. Amos noticed one of the visitors in Robert's room move near the door. He swallowed hard with a cotton mouth, wiped his damp hands on his pants, and edged forward on the lumpy couch.

"I saw a cat out back last summer," Fern said. "I think it was a farm cat gone wild. I called it, but it ran off."

Fern was unconsciously watching Robert's doorway with Amos. Amos felt in his pocket. The letter hadn't dissolved but he was sure his drumming heart would be visible through his shirt.

"I wouldn't take all the cats in the country for one good dog," Amos said and managed a hollow laugh. "For one *lousy* dog as far as that goes."

Effie clung to his arm as she spoke.

"My folks sez they was gonna get me a dog once, one that could take me around so's I could go off by myself. But it cost too much. The dogs we always had couldn't lead me nowhere 'cept through the hogpen or chasin' a chicken."

When she talked, Effie gave the impression she was watching a tennis match on the ceiling. Grace worked her way over to them.

"You folks be sure to chew your food real good," Grace said.

"Yes, dear," Fern said, "we will."

Robert's visitors were leaving. Amos stood, quickly, breaking Effie's fragile grip. Daisy had hurried down the women's wing minutes before and he saw no sign of her return.

"Where you goin'?" Effie said as she felt for a shadow of Amos. Fern reached over and touched Effie's knee, reassuring her.

"Shhh, Amos will be right back."

Amos pushed the walker as swiftly as he could through his fellow boarders, angrily chasing Winston when he briefly blocked Amos's passage. There were two of them, a young man and a middle-aged woman. They had turned the corner of the dayroom and were heading for the exit, exactly where Amos hoped to catch them. They made no pretense at loitering on their way out, and Amos had to call to stall their retreat.

"Pardon me, I'm Amos Lasher, a good friend of Robert's."

Hesitating, they turned to see if the old man was addressing them.

"I have a letter I'd like mailed and Daisy said she wouldn't be going in tomorrow. She thought you might not mind taking it for me."

Amos spoke calmly, trying to conceal his raging excitement with the canvas of old age. Nell peered from the kitchen, an observer of life, her tongue at the corner of her mouth. Amos hadn't produced the letter yet, not until he was sure.

"Oh, it's nice to meet you, Mr. Lasher, but Daisy has strictly forbidden us to take any mail."

Amos guessed the woman was Robert's daughter or maybe a niece, and he knew the next few moments would decide. He took a deep breath and plunged ahead.

"Oh, it's okay with Daisy," Amos said. "If you can wait a minute, I'm sure she'll be along. One of the women threw up all over herself and Daisy's cleaning her up."

Amos smiled like a nice old man. The woman paused, deliberating.

"Go ahead, what'll it hurt. I have to get home," the young man said, having spent enough time in this haunting zone.

That-a-boy, kid.

"All right," the woman said, "I suppose it won't hurt."

She relaxed like someone who had just given in to sin. Amos pulled the letter from his pocket and casually handed it to her, sensing Daisy's hand on the back of his neck any second. The woman took the envelope without reading it.

"How do you think Robert is doing lately? Do you think he's failing some?"

"I think he's doing very well." Amos tried to terminate the friendly chat. "We discuss the books he lends me. He's fine."

Amos hoped for more help from the boy. He got it.

"Come on, Mom, let's go."

The woman noticed the addressee when she started to slip the letter into her purse.

"Wait a minute, this is to the sheriff."

She attempted to hand it back just as Amos caught a glimpse of Daisy emerging from the women's ward. Hair on the back of his neck electrified.

"Yes, we're related in some distant connection. My mother's family, the Thomases. Fine man, the sheriff, we used to fish together."

Amos smiled placidly while he was coming unglued inside. Fern intercepted Daisy and distracted her in conversation while the woman deposited his desperate testimony into her handbag.

"It's been nice meeting you, Amos," the woman said, "we'll mail this on the way home."

They disappeared through the narrow portico and Mae stepped out of the kitchen, monitoring the exit. Amos turned quickly and plowed down the hall with an exhilarating relief. He shouted a hello in to Owen and hoped that Daisy hadn't noticed him talking with Robert's family. The tension broke, a water balloon hitting the pavement, and he wanted to jump and dance and hoot. His body wouldn't comply with the first two, but he managed the hoot. He'd done it. His spirit skipped and soared through the empty corridor. The sheriff would be out to see him in a few days, and then he would tear down this house of death.

Mick startled Amos in the failing light of the afternoon, weeping quietly in Amos's chair with his head in his hands. Amos reined up abruptly from his celebration, hesitating uncomfortably. Mick looked up with burning eyes from under his denim engineer's cap. His extreme curvature of the spine gave the impression he was carrying every burden known to the human race on his back.

"What's wrong, Mick?" Amos eased into Spencer's rocker, frazzled by the strain of his smuggling activities. "Are you in pain?"

"I don't know what's wrong, I just can't help it." He appealed to Amos for an explanation. Then he lowered his head into his hands and spoke to the floor. "I told my father to go to hell."

"Why don't you go and watch TV," Amos said. "There's still time. You like to watch TV, Mick."

"She won't let me. I want to, but she won't let me."

"Why not?" Amos said.

"I can't remember." Mick lifted his head out of his hands. "I think it was 'cuz I turned on the TV when I wasn't s'posed to be in there."

"Would you like to play checkers?" Amos said, attempting to steer away from the chuckholes of depression.

"Do you think there's a hell?" Mick said with a seasoned despair.

"Hell?" Amos laughed. "Yes . . . we're in it."

"I told my father to go to hell. Right to his face," Mick said. "We'd fought. I left home, found a place, was eighteen. I had a job cleanin' out bins in the grain elevators in Minneapolis. Shoveled a lot of dust and rat shit. My mother came right to the elevator. I knew something was haywire. She had a look I'd never seen before, I'll never forget it. All she said was, *You got your wish.* I didn't know what she meant. I told my boss I had to leave and ran home, but she beat me there. My father worked the yards. He was crushed between two boxcars, switchin'. My mother never let me see him. Said I killed him. I watched the funeral from across the street. Never saw my family after that day. Hopped a freight west."

Mick left it at that, and Amos found it difficult visualizing this crippled-up old man riding the boxcars west like so many rootless youngsters who followed the sun. Yet, as he slumped in that chair in this isolated building on the foothills of the Rockies, Mick still carried the same feelings that had overwhelmed him the day his father died. Amos knew that. When he looked in the mirror, sometimes he perceived that the mask of an old man only hid the thoughts and feelings within him that were always there, still very young and alive. Who would guess? Just every other kid who had seen sixty birthday cakes or more. According to Mick's story, he just kept riding the freights for the rest of his life.

"That's not the kind of hell I mean," Amos said. "You can't believe your words had anything to do with your father's accident."

"It happened so soon. Two days after I said it. Maybe he was thinkin' about it and not payin' no mind to the switchin'."

That stunned Amos. Mick wasn't talking about curses or voodoo or a warped interpretation of divine wrath. He was talking about how humans wound each other and try to limp on with their lives. Mick could be right. He had thought about it all these years, carried it around on his back like a dead skunk, rotting and festering and weighing him down until his stooped posture became the symbol of his certainty that he had killed his father as surely as if he had pushed him between the crushing tonnage of those boxcars with his own hands.

"I had planned to go home in a few days," Mick said so softly Amos barely caught the words. "My father and I was real close. If I'd just gone home, if I'd just . . ."

A sweaty silence wedged its way into the sparse room, and Amos wrestled to turn it back, grasping for words to shatter it, but he didn't want them to be sentimental and cheap. He struggled in vain, his vocabulary bankrupt, finding no offering for the altar of Mick's tormenting grief.

"Visiting hours are already over," Spencer said, huffing and puffing into the room. "I always thought visiting hours was when visitors came out to see the people in a home, not when the people in the home got to visit each other."

Amos welcomed the reprieve from coming up with adequate words, like the offering plate miraculously missing your pew when your wallet is empty; but he was frustrated, not willing to leave it at that. Mick stood without certainty, took up his cane and dead skunk, dragging his feet for the door.

"Maybe you can watch TV next week, Mick."

Amos did it. His last words were cheap, demeaning what Mick had shared with him. Don't worry about killing your father, Mick, after all, next week you can watch *Gunsmoke.* Amos hated it when he did that and he seemed to do it all his life. He moved to his own chair.

"She told me I'd have to miss the dayroom privileges for a while," Spencer said, "just because I complained about so little time in there. She said something about spreading colds and flu around and I told her that was ridiculous."

Santa clung to his rocker, sighing another small surrender and pouting helplessly at the world. Amos warmed with exasperation, recognizing that this submission permeated the fiber of their existence. Had they all rebelled at first, stood up to her for some morsel of dignity or privilege, or had they settled into this oppression tamely? Most disheartening to Amos, they had given up, feeling this was all they could expect now that their lives were over, prematurely entombed in her graveyard. He could see her walking the halls at night, confident in her fur-lined slippers that all the animals were domesticated and she could put them to death when it best suited her. She imagined herself as the warden on a death row for those who had unconditionally surrendered.

Well, by God, she was walking in a combat zone, a mine field, and her charm and wit would not prevent the detonation from one false step. His heartbeat quickened and his outrage turned to exhilaration when he remembered what he had already set in motion: the letter traveling its benign journey through the monotonous channels of the U.S. Postal Service like a ticking bomb. He told the sheriff that he had evidence about several crimes committed in this county, and that he would talk to him alone if he would come out to Sunset. He asked the sheriff to keep this in strictest confidence. He had her, and he wanted to share his euphoria with his roommate.

"Don't worry about dayroom privileges," Amos said, "there's going to be a change around here real soon."

"I've heard that before," Spencer said.

The squeak of Nell's cart preceded her down the hallway.

"Here's your supper, Amos," Nell said.

Spencer dug into his meal, the first time he forgot to pray.

"No dayroom," he grumbled with a mouthful. "Does she think I'm a little child or a lame-brain or something?"

"Never say die," Amos said.

He tried to swallow his excitement with the macaroni and cheese, wanting to let Spencer in on the intrigue in the worst way, but knowing he couldn't. In his anger, Spencer might give it away, like a kid on the playground warning the bully that word is on the way to the teacher. Spencer would have to endure awhile longer, like the rest of them—the poverty of her rule—and Amos would have to endure with his pent-up exuberance.

Amos felt something strange in the middle of the macaroni, and Spencer watched him remove a tooth from his mouth and contemplate it mournfully. Root and all, it had just given up and let go.

"Damn it, I just spit out a tooth."

Amos tried to laugh. He was disintegrating, falling apart before his own eyes, momentarily shocked by the evidence of his mortality.

"Saves going to the dentist," Spencer said without sympathy.

Amos wiped the tooth dry with his napkin and thought about all it had gone through with him, this one solid chunk of Amos Lasher. When he kissed Alice Cromwell in eighth grade, when he sat all night with Marilyn on the cancer ward, when he bit through the leader on his fly line standing in the middle of the Lamar, when he vowed he'd love Mildred until death do us part, when he laughed and cried and worked and shuddered in orgasm; it was part of him. He took out his cigar box and carefully placed the tooth in with his other tokens of life. Then he turned to his meal, openly admitting to himself that he was senile.

Nell retrieved the trays. "You didn't finish, Spencer," Nell said with her deadpan expression.

"I'm not hungry." He dropped his fork on the tray with a clatter.

Amos could envision a patrol car moving out the old road past the dump, and it fortified him when Daisy appeared with the ball-point.

"I have a check for you to sign, Amos. I'll be going to the bank tomorrow." She sprightly delivered the pen and check.

"How much do I have in the bank?" he said calmly.

"Oh, I wouldn't know exactly, but it's adding up."

She held out the check and pen. Amos held onto one of Robert's books unflinchingly.

"Well, I want to see the balance."

"Right now?" She lowered her hand, irritation in her voice.

"Right now," Amos said and he looked directly into her strong blue eyes. She met him, eye for an eye, a fury kindling in her fetching face.

"I'll be right back."

When she was gone, Spencer regarded Amos with a bit of awe and Amos waited nervously, wondering what she'd come up with. It was a bankbook from the West Stover State Bank, his name on the first page, along with hers, the deposits regular, every month, totaling four hundred and eighty-six dollars and six cents. She stood triumphant, everything in order.

"I used some of it for the things you needed: toothpaste, lotion, toothbrush, electric razor."

She held out the check and he signed it, something still unsettled at the back of his mind. She packed the loot away cheerfully and Spencer lost some of his awe.

Amos was in the lavatory when the invitation came. It took him a while to respond. He was dumbstruck by the carnival atmosphere, the splash of frivolity lapping over him at the edge of the dayroom, as if the headmaster of an orphanage had gone for the evening and the children were all at play. But the astonishing thing was that Daisy sat right in the middle of the action, egging Mick on, slapping him on the back and almost knocking him out of his chair. Mae was calling the numbers while the rest of the gang were covering bingo cards with pennies: grumbling, hooting, cheating, laughing, squinting at their cards for the right combination to win. Amos stood a moment. Leaning on his walker, he reflected on the faces so engrossed in the game.

"Hold it! Hold it!" Carlos shouted, scrambling to keep abreast with his creosoted eyes. Elroy, the man with a slight hump on his back, was stealing pennies from the gandy dancer, one at a time.

"Did you say B-8 or B-18?" Emil said, working two cards grimly.

"You missed N-11," Daisy said, pointing out a square to Grace.

"We've got four in a row," Fern excitedly informed her blind companion and Effie cooed like a mourning dove, enjoying the entertainment she couldn't see.

"G-7," Mae hollered with a lethargic voice.

"Bingo!" Marvin, the bed-wetter, shouted with his flapping, toothless mouth, hooting and laughing.

"Atta boy, Marv," Daisy said.

Mae, with some air of importance, checked his card and paid him off with a pile of pennies. Marvin grinned ear to ear in victory while his fellow gamblers murmured and readied their cards for another round. Carlos was at the refreshment table, which looked as if a fraternity had had a food fight: leftover desserts, pudding, tapioca, cake, cookies, Kool-Aid, coffee, milk, the choices confounding the Mexican.

"Come on, Mick, you son of a gun," Daisy said, "let's win one."

The little hobo with the red bandanna settled in for another game, forgetting his mangled father for a while. Amos broke the spell and slid his walker to a bench and flopped next to Emil.

"Give Amos a couple cards," Daisy said. "And his fifty pennies. Win some big money now, Amos."

Amos didn't do well on the first round because he realized with her words that she'd only showed him the bankbook the depositor keeps, not the bank. Those were Daisy's neat entries. He'd have to see the deposit slips to know the truth. She opened an account all right, and there was probably ten dollars in it. His face flushed with anger. She figured when he died, she'd let the county take care of his bank account, but she'd have all his money. He intended to fly free of this pit and he wanted his money when he was out. She'd flimflammed him pure and simple. He vowed never to endorse another check.

Winston ambled around the room calling out bingo numbers, and sometimes the players would cover one he manufactured.

"Pipe down, Winston," Daisy said with a laugh, "or I'll tie you in bed."

Grace knocked her card and pennies to the floor.

"How often does this go on?" Amos whispered to Emil, who was posing as Teddy Roosevelt come back from the grave.

"Whenever she has the notion."

The Grouch tugged at his mustache and scrutinized his cards. Amos wondered if they were all putting on one grand act on this makeshift stage, or if they were genuinely enjoying themselves with a heroic effort of forgetfulness. He had to admit he was taken back by this side of Daisy, frivolous, joyful, childlike.

"Bingo!" Grace shouted, after rearranging her spilled coins.

"You can't have a bingo, dear," Daisy said, "we've only had three numbers."

"She listens to Winston's numbers," Elroy said. "Run the nitwit outta here."

Sadie watched from the women's corridor, seemingly baffled by the hullabaloo, and Carlos stuffed his pockets with peanut butter cookies. Amos wondered, plant food?

They played long past bedtime, Mick and Grace falling asleep in their chairs. Then they ate treats and collected their pennies, if they had any left, and marched off to bed buzzing about their fortune at the gaming table. Amos pushed toward his room somewhat bewildered, wanting to tell them they were soon to be free of her terrible clutch, but somehow it didn't make sense at the moment. Daisy had been more like one of them, playing and eating and joking, thrilled like a young girl when she won and almost equally happy for them when they beat her to the punch. Once Carlos called bingo and he didn't have a correct number. Daisy checked it and declared him a winner. Only Amos and Mae noticed the error.

Amos lay disturbed in the shadows, listening to Daisy still tucking some of the men in with a caring voice. They had played together like youngsters at the carnival, all of them. He knew he should no longer be bushwhacked by the absurdity of life, but he was.

Several hours later, unable to sleep, Amos stood gazing through the window into a black winter sky. His heart ached. Oh, Mick, Oh, Emil, Oh, God! Who can bear the sorrow of this life, this loss, this beautiful promise gone to ruin. Mick, tell me there was a freedom and joy in riding the rails; Emil, tell me there was a fulfillment raising your children; tell me, someone, that the beauty outweighs the anguish, that the lion *will* lie down with the lamb. Sadie in her lostness, Effie in her blindness, Winston in his madness, who had been careless with this abundance of life?

It was carelessness he knew, identifying the sorrow that had been his lifelong companion.

CHAPTER 11

Monday dragged by and Amos noticed every sound, every footstep in the hall, all the usual sighs of the building and the unusual. Emil beat him easily at checkers and bitched because Amos wasn't working at it. He ate without realizing what he ate, answered people without remembering what they asked. Spencer was succumbing to the surroundings, turning despondent. Amos tried to uphold him, recalling how Johnny had prodded him through the first days, but as with Johnny's effort, it did little good. All in all, it was a depressing day, a wasteland, colored with boredom, uselessness and squandered hours. Amos kept reminding himself that the mail was on its way through rain, hail, and fire, or whatever the damn slogan said. Then the barren routines came to their conclusions in the shadows of the night-light.

Tuesday the tension was as visible as the frost on the window. He felt that Daisy looked at him with a growing suspicion. Very soon she would know what he had been up to, and it sent tremors through his vitals. He lay on his bed during the day to remain as invisible as possible. He was reading when Daisy came to the door in the afternoon.

"Amos, would you come with me? There's someone here to see you."

Her voice was matter-of-fact as she delivered a thunder clap into the placid atmosphere and the smile she wore clashed with the storm gathering on her brow.

When the moment did come, it caught him off balance, a dream becoming real. He shut the book too quickly and sat up, knowing his guilt was embroidered on his face in many colors. She appeared unruffled, coolly camouflaging any fear she carried under her lovely complexion. Amos found it difficult to breathe, hauling his vacillating gallantry toward the dayroom with alarm.

A large man in a brown uniform stood with his trooper hat in hand. He appeared friendly behind his brass star and he smiled out of a handsome squarely-set face.

"This is Amos Lasher, John. This is Sheriff Thomas, Amos. The sheriff would like to talk with you. I'll just leave you two gentlemen alone."

Daisy sailed gracefully into the kitchen, seemingly unperturbed. The sheriff's eyes tracked her going. Amos took refuge in an old upholstered chair, frayed until the stuffing was exposed. How strange it was that he should wonder, at a time like that, what happy times that chair had seen in some family home, before it was donated to the county or had come with one of the residents and outlasted him. He sat facing the sheriff and guessed that he could be risking his life.

"Amos, I got your letter, and I figured I'd better come out and hear what you had to say."

Sheriff Thomas was around six three, well over two hundred pounds, filling out his brown uniform smartly and making the .38 Smith & Wesson on his hip seem small in its squeaky black leather holster. He was probably close to fifty and looked as if he could be a local rancher moonlighting. He still had most of his dark brown hair, neatly trimmed. His face was kind, yet not one you'd take lightly, and Amos figured if he was selling this man some farm machinery, he wouldn't beat around the bush. The sheriff seemed in good humor and Amos was happy to see him, to be alone with him. But at the same time, as the sheriff sat down, Amos felt something in the air that disturbed him, something he couldn't put his finger on. He checked quickly to see if anyone could hear them. Only Sadie, prowling the women's wing, showed up at the entrance to the dayroom from time to time. There was no one else.

Amos looked the sheriff in the eye and spoke as self-assuredly as he was able, trying to appear as normal and reasonable as possible. He was shaking, trying to keep the tremors out of his voice. A cold void moved into his stomach; a feeling of doom came over him, like a change in the weather.

"I'm Amos Lasher, I'm a retired rancher and businessman. I'm perfectly sane and I'm not unintelligent. My memory is excellent. I'm only in this place because of a freakish twist of fate. What I'm about to tell you will seem very hard to believe, I realize, actually incredible."

"Try me." The sheriff looked at him intently, sizing him up.

"This Home is far from what it appears. Miss Daws runs a stockade. No one dares speak up because they're scared to death. She steals our valuables, forces us to sign checks over to her, and punishes us for the smallest rebellion. She censors all mail, and we can never use a phone."

Amos tried to stay calm, to speak slowly, but he kept hurrying, racing on under the whip of his emotions.

"Have you any evidence, Amos?" The sheriff wasn't showing the interest that Amos had hoped for, too relaxed in the old sofa. "Can you prove any of these allegations?"

"You can, if you'd talk to other people here, check with the bank, look into her finances."

Amos's voice rose with his sense of failure. He glanced around to see if Daisy could hear him. Winston came into the dayroom and stared out the window. Amos leaned toward the lawman and played his trump card.

"On Christmas Eve I saw Daisy *kill* a man, Johnny Sumers," Amos said, finding his outrage. "*I'm* your evidence!"

"What do you mean, Amos. How did she kill him?"

The big man spoke casually, with little reaction to Amos's deadly secret. His expression never changed, almost giving the impression of boredom.

What's the matter, you need gunplay or a bank robbery to excite you? Some cattle rustling? Just killing helpless old men in their beds is too tame for you?

Amos was frightened. He was way out on a limb, hanging by a twig, and the sheriff's nonchalance was shaking the tree.

"She came into our room late at night. She had a hypodermic needle, I think. She bent over his bed and did something to him, stuck him with that needle, and he died. He quit breathing right then and there. She killed him! I crawled over and checked. He was dead. She came back in the morning and pretended to find him."

Amos couldn't think of anything more to say.

"These are serious charges, Amos, you've probably seen something that can be explained. You suppose you could have had a bad dream?"

"It wasn't a dream. I crawled over and *touched him.*"

"Daisy's told me that the men steal from each other. I can't do much about that. She says it doesn't amount to much because none of you have much. I'm sorry."

Amos felt panic gathering under his ribs while the arm of justice was ignoring Johnny's death and trifling with the penny ante stuff. His evidence seemed so thin now, so intangible.

"She does it for the insurance. You can check on that. Harold died the same way. What would it hurt for you to look into it?"

"Daisy!" The sheriff called toward the kitchen. "Daisy, could you come in here for a minute?"

Daisy was coming on her silent crepe-soled way.

"Listen to me, please." Amos gripped the officer's arm. "She'll kill me! Is that what it will take for you to believe me?"

Daisy came gliding into the room on a smile as if she were modeling uniforms in a fashion show.

"What can I do for you, John?"

The question suggested few limits the way she looked at the man, ignoring Amos.

"I hate to trouble you," the sheriff said, "but do you keep records of the medication you give your patients?"

He liked her, Amos could see it. She exuded an earthy sexual aura, an exciting danger.

"Of course, everything, it's the law."

She sounded sincere when she spoke about the law.

"Would you look up for me, and Amos here, what you gave Johnny, ah . . ."

"Sumers," Amos said, knowing the fat was in the fire.

"Yeah, Johnny Sumers, on, ah . . . December twenty-fourth."

Daisy was ruffled now, for an instant. Amos hoped the sheriff caught that skip of a heartbeat, but he only looked at her apologetically for putting her through this farce. She recovered smoothly.

"I'm sure I can find that."

She opened the door on the north wall and went in. It was a small infirmary, everything white and stainless steel. Amos couldn't see her, but he heard a file drawer slide open. She came out with a manila folder, opened it, and thumbed through it calmly.

"Let's see, on the twenty-fourth you said. Here, oh . . . yes, that was the night poor Johnny died. He was a sweet old gentleman. It's right here. I gave him a hypo at eleven fourteen, to help him sleep. I remember I'd been giving him one for several nights, he complained so about his legs. Yes, the two previous nights I gave him the same. It was a light dose. Here."

She handed the chart to the lawman and pointed out the notations, while she smiled at Amos. The smile said *You pathetic old man, how stupid do you think I am?* It cut through Amos like a razor, exposing the bone marrow of his mortality, and he felt as if his bowels would slither out onto the floor. He recognized the face of retaliation soon to come in that sensual grin. The sheriff showed him the medications on the chart, as though the marks of the pen were eternal truth, a record of the hypos Johnny never got with no mention of the air bubble he did.

"See, here. That's what you saw," the sheriff said to Amos. "It probably just put the old man to sleep, and that's why his breathing seemed different."

The Law was satisfied. Amos was paralyzed, struggling to come up with something more. She was far more cunning than he had ever imagined, had covered herself completely. He felt warm all over, dizzy.

"What does Amos think he saw, John?" she said pleasantly.

"The insurance, she got his insurance money. If you'd check on it you'd know she did it." Amos couldn't control his fright. He was shouting. "She was the beneficiary!"

"Now, now, Amos, we don't want another of your temper tantrums, do we?" Daisy said, intimating tantrums were a common occurrence with him.

The sheriff put his large hand on Amos's shoulder and held him back in the tacky chair. Winston watched from the corner of the dayroom.

"I'm sorry about this, Daisy, but the letter was well written," John Thomas said. "I just thought I'd better come out and satisfy the old gent."

"That's all right. A letter like this gets out now and then. I just hate to bother you people with our little insanities when you've got so many more important things to do."

Amos realized how attractive she was to this man. Maybe the sheriff was contemplating cutting in on the Buick driver one of these nights. Between Amos, a scraggly old man, and this appealing nurse, who would you believe? Amos knew the answer to that one.

"The insurance would be easy to check on, Sheriff."

Amos tried halfheartedly to interrupt, knowing he sounded hysterical.

"Did he say how he got the letter mailed?" Daisy said. "I try to screen this kind before they do any harm. They're always writing letters to the police and the President and to God."

It was over. They were ignoring him, talking in front of him as though he weren't there, like grownups do with little children.

"He didn't say." The lawman stood up, black leather creaking. "Thanks for your time and patience, Daisy. I feel a little foolish about the whole thing. I'll try not to bother you again with anything like this."

He looked at Amos with his big, kind face.

"You better not write any more letters, Amos. If you have any questions, just ask Miss Daws. She'll explain everything to you."

If the fly has any questions about being caught in the web, the sheriff's advice was to consult the spider. The lawman started across the room, a little sheepishly for so big a man.

"Stop in the kitchen, John. Bertha has some fresh pie and coffee."

John Thomas took to the kitchen while Daisy returned her folder to the infirmary.

"Check on it, the insurance money!" Amos shouted his last desperate hurrah at the hungry sheriff's back, but the warm pie held more interest.

Winston looked at Amos with his houndlike eyes, as though he understood everything, what Amos had risked, how much he had lost. Daisy came out and locked the door behind her, all but ignoring her beaten opponent, on her way to the kitchen to cement her victory with pastry.

"You may go back to your room now, Amos," she said in passing.

Amos remained for a few minutes, stunned, unable to think or move. He could hear Daisy and John Thomas laughing together in the kitchen. Winston tripped down the men's wing chanting "Jingle Bells."

Amos had thrown his punch too quickly, wildly, off balance, out of hate and anger. She was too experienced, too graceful for that amateurish swing. She had ducked it shrewdly, unmarked, ready to continue the fight she now knew was upon her. He had lost all advantage, the power balance swung dramatically to her. He knew in that instant he would have to be more intelligent, more cunning than he had ever been in his life. And braver. He shuddered to think of what might lie ahead and muttered aloud that he would need a fat kid with him. He got up and hung onto the walker, sensing the crushing weight of failure.

He felt very old, suddenly tired, crossing the room on rickety legs. He had to admit; she was sharp. She probably let the sheriff talk to Grace and Robert before she came and got Amos. Or maybe she allowed Sadie and Winston to be highly visible, to make him uneasy and confirm the sheriff's opinion that they were all a little wacky at Sunset Home. Add to this his own claims of captivity and murder, and anyone would go for the coffee and pie.

CHAPTER 12

EMIL AND CARLOS WERE PLAYING CHECKERS in the hall with Marvin lazily watching the plodding action. Spencer—looking like an unemployed and whiskerless Santa—stood in their doorway.

"Move," Emil said with impatience.

"Give me time, give me time," Carlos said as he scanned the board, his nose almost knocking the pieces askew.

Though it seemed they hadn't noticed Amos's approach, he sensed they expected a word from him.

"I just told the sheriff that I saw Daisy kill Johnny."

He caught their attention instantly, wide-eyed, unbelieving.

"She'll have yer *balls,*" Marvin whispered.

"Killed Johnny?" Spencer said. "What did the sheriff say? What's he going to do?"

Spencer turned ashen, trembling the questions through his teeth.

"Nothing, he thinks I'm crazy," Amos said. "The more I told the truth the crazier I sounded. She sets us up, prepares them for some cockeyed story, something so unthinkable it sounds like the babbling of an incoherent old fool."

Only Spencer seemed shocked with the information. Winston strode up and joined the wake.

"You shouldn't have done it," Emil said.

His tone made it clear that he regarded Amos's attempt as stupid rather than courageous.

"Someone has to fight her," Amos said.

"She's been fought," Emil said. "You don't know what she did to Johnny before you showed up. She had to let up or it would have killed him too soon."

"She blew out Winston's pilot light before that," Marvin said, gesturing a rawboned hand at the tall old man with the tennis racket. Winston nodded a happy agreement.

"So everyone quits," Amos said.

"Our day to ride a white horse is long past," Emil said. "We're worn-out old men—"

"No! Never! It's never past," Amos said. "As long as we're still breathing, as long as our hearts beat and our minds think."

Amos felt an exhilaration come over him, mining courage from his own words.

"What can we do?" Spencer said with a whine.

"We can stop her," Amos said.

"All right, you go ahead, if you're that thick-skulled." Emil spoke as a father to his son. "But I'll tell you this for sure. You'll be riding a dead horse."

"Maybe so," Amos said, "but at least I'll have climbed on and kicked it."

"You'll end up like the others," Emil said, "and she'll have the last laugh as well as your carcass."

Emil spoke with bitterness, hating the words as much as he believed them. Amos had no time to respond. Daisy came cruising down the corridor, scattering them like panicky partridge crossing a highway. Spencer backed into the room, Winston headed toward her singing, "RIDE A COCK-HORSE TO BANBURY CROSS," and Marvin scurried for his door. Amos turned and faced her, his jaw set for a blow.

"We mustn't be clogging up the hallway, gentlemen."

She waltzed through her normal tasks with an arrogant nonchalance. Amos vamoosed into his room, relieved for the moment's respite. Spencer regarded Amos gravely from his chair, signaling that he had nothing to offer, no life preserver to throw him in the choppy seas. Amos picked up a book and tried to read, but the words ran before his eyes without meaning. His depression was massive, shoving him down into the chair, into the flooring. He knew he was sitting in an electric chair, just waiting for her to throw the switch, but he suspected it would be a limited, painful current instead of a killing charge, and he also suspected that she would make the waiting a separate agony, a toying cat with wounded mouse.

She wouldn't dare kill him immediately; Sheriff Thomas might notice the coincidence. Amos had his time at bat and struck out. He was harmless, and he was also worth more to her alive than dead. The lawman would forget all about him unless he came up too soon a corpse. She wasn't stupid.

Amos couldn't believe it; some of his fear drained away. They were in bed, the lights were out, and she had done nothing. Maybe she didn't dare do anything to him after his interview with the peace officer, now that he was visible to someone in the outside world.

"You ever think about what your life was for?" Amos said to Spencer in the shadows.

"It seemed to go by before I knew it. I don't know what it was for." Spencer sounded bewildered, his hearing aid still in place.

"The book I'm reading says we're part of an evolutionary process to a much higher intelligent being," Amos said. "We're each a small part of the big act."

"You mean I'm just a step to something better, that's what my whole life was for?" Spencer's voice broke.

"Yes, well, it isn't much comfort at this point in life, or maybe at any point for that matter."

They both lay silent for several moments until Spencer spoke softly.

"When I think back about it sometimes, it doesn't seem like it ever happened, like it was just a dream."

"I never did anything with my life," Amos said.

"What's to do with it? Just getting through it is enough. We never asked to be born, Lord knows." Spencer sighed.

"Maybe so, but just getting through it is so damn unsatisfying," Amos said. "There was always something gnawing at me to throw caution to the wind and risk it."

"What do you mean, risk *what?*"

"I don't rightly know. Quit saving everything, quit being a tight-fisted miser with life and just let 'er rip," Amos said. "Spit in the devil's eye and kick-up-your-heels living."

"Sounds like living in sin to me."

"Maybe the way we hang on to it is the sin." Amos laughed.

"I don't know what you mean," Spencer said. Then he removed his hearing aid, placed it carefully on his Bible, and asked, "I wonder what the higher intelligent beings will do with their old people?"

Amos had no chance to reply before Daisy materialized in the doorway with a flashlight and her instruments. The night-light amplified her form with shadow, making her loom larger in Amos's frozen eyes.

"We forgot to take your blood pressure and temperature today, Amos."

She made it sound as if it were a daily routine. He tensed as she wrapped the pressure band around his arm, pumped it up, and listened through the stethoscope. She jotted the numbers in a notebook while Amos scrutinized her instruments for a hypodermic syringe. She behaved as if it were nothing out of the ordinary, but Amos was gagging on his fright.

"Roll over," she said, quietly, throwing back the covers.

"I can hold it in my mouth."

Amos remained rigidly on his back, his jaw set.

"Roll over, or I'll get Mae."

She said it so calmly that Amos dared to believe there was nothing to all of this. He rolled on his side, exposing his back to her. She quickly pulled his pajama bottom to his knees, tipped an open bottle into a cotton swab, and wiped the fluid over his anus. It felt cool, like alcohol, but with a different yet familiar odor. She reached between his legs and took his scrotum in her hand, pulling it back gently and liberally bathing it with the liquid.

"What are you doing?" Amos said.

He reached back and grabbed her wrist, his face only inches from her eerie reflection. She took one of his testicles between her thumb and fingers.

"How did you get the letter out?" she said with a voice of ice.

Amos struggled against her grip to no avail.

"Take your hands off my balls! No one believed me. Leave me alone, goddamn it."

He was terrified and he knew he had good reason.

"We have to find out how you did it, so Daisy can be more careful. How did you mail it?"

She pressed her thumb into his testicle with a viselike force. Amos screamed as if he'd been hit with high voltage and curled up in a womb of excruciating pain. The torment swelled around him, covering him, sucking away his breath until he thought he would die. She held on, clamping with unsuspected strength. He blacked out.

When he came back to the room and the gut-wrenching pain, she had released her hold, standing above him while the acute throbbing continued clawing at his pelvis, up his spine.

"How did you get the letter out?"

She leaned close to his perspiring face and he caught her perfumed scent in the midst of the fire. He tried to recover his senses, having actually seen stars at the height of the torture. He couldn't go through that again.

"I gave it to one of Robert's visitors. I told her you said it was all right."

"How clever," she said.

She gathered up her things and turned off the flashlight.

"Have a nice night."

She vanished from the darkened room, leaving him curled like a smashed worm. Spencer looked on with terror in his eyes, hearing much more than he wanted without his hearing aid. Amos lay gasping, small streamers of pain still running up and down his legs and belly, throwing ice-pick jabs unexpectedly. He thought about what he would give to have met this woman when he still had strength of muscle and how he would have dealt with her, this jackal bitch in a pen of the weak and helpless. God! He'd beat all those death traps that had wiped out most of his generation: cancer of the prostate, hardening of the arteries, stroke, heart attack, and he ends up running into *her.* He was afraid of her, horrified; but somehow he still retained Johnny's stubborn resolve. He couldn't get stronger, so he had to get smarter.

The gnawing was almost gone, leaving a dull ache in its place. He felt warm. The men in the wing lay awake, listening, waiting for the shouting to begin. Gradually he felt the smarting, the light burning sensation spreading over his crotch. He rubbed himself and to his dismay discovered that only intensified the burning. His genitals were on fire. Unable to stay in bed with it, he danced around the room, then fell to the floor and kicked aimlessly to quench the flames. Springing back up, he knocked everything off the bed table, howling like an animal with its foot in a trap. Spencer was frightened out of his wits.

Amos slammed and crashed his way out into the hall and up to the bathroom. He flung on the shower, cold, and stood under it. The water rushing over him and between his legs seemed to stay the searing torment, but he was freezing in the process, hardly able to breathe. While the torture kept its grip on his vital parts, he stumbled out of the shower and filled the ancient tub with cool water. He climbed in and sat, shivering violently from the many shocks of the night.

Almost an hour later he dragged himself out of the tub and crept back to his bed. He left his soaked pajamas in a puddle on the floor and crawled between the sheets naked. He huddled there trembling, completely spent, his teeth chattering wildly. The palpable tension on the wing had melted away, the residents searching for sleep in the sweaty folds of their blankets, trembling prey who were thankful the hunter had passed them by.

"Shhh, roll over," Emil said, standing by the bed in a flannel night shirt. "I have Vaseline. Take some, rub it on."

Amos took a smear and gently covered his raw flesh. He took another and winced with his own touch.

"What was it?"

"Turpentine," Emil said.

He held the jar until Amos had covered the scorched area of his body and then sneaked back to his room. Carlos stole into the room and kneeled by Amos's bed. He pulled out the bedpan, and Amos heard a small trickle hitting the metal, like a mouse urinating.

"You're missing the plant," Amos said.

"What?" Carlos whispered.

"You're missing the plant."

Amos couldn't prevent his own laughter. Carlos re-aimed, and the mouse went silent. The greenhouse madman stood and touched Amos's shoulder very gently.

"I'm sorry," Carlos said, "I prayed for you."

Gandy Dancer slipped back into the night and the throbbing pain subsided as Amos let the tension flow out of his body. He was tender and sore, but the immediate assault on his nerve endings had abated.

Remembering when he arrived at Sunset, how he was sure that his life was finished, he now found himself in the most brutal fight he'd ever faced. With the residue of her punishment lingering in his body, he knew his objectivity had been thoroughly shattered, but with the husk peeled away, he thought his life came down to this: Whether he would square off with Daisy Daws in this ugly ferocious battle or back down and quit. He felt a sudden liberation from all the rest; no more clinging to the past, no longer any concern for the future, finding himself for the first time completely alive to the present moment. It was a fresh ocean squall rushing across the treeless plain that was his life. And most surprising, he found within himself the energy, the hope, the will to try. He wanted to do this, an inbred longing, finally, to act in a way that would count for something.

At seventy-eight he climbed onto the horse.

CHAPTER 13

Daisy appeared serene in her immaculate white uniform. Amos calculated she must change them at least twice a day.

"You have some mail, Spencer," Daisy said.

All was well in her world. She'd filled Sheriff Thomas with pie and baloney and he'd gladly swallowed all of it like some pompous fish. Sitting in his rocker, Spencer took the envelope with the frantic hope that one of his offspring was inviting him to come and live with him. It was his pension check.

"Oh, a check, how nice," she said. "Now we can have some of the little extras that make life more enjoyable, can't we." She had the pen in his face. "Just endorse it and Daisy will put it in the bank for you."

Still terrified from observing the past night's events, Spencer glanced faintheartedly toward Amos and signed the check without batting an eye, taking no chance on flirting with whatever it was that Amos got.

"How often do you receive a check?" Daisy said.

"Every month, one hundred and eighty-six dollars."

"Do you have any life insurance?"

She straightened the bed, trying to give the impression this was only idle conversation.

"Yes," Spencer said, "an old policy for ten thousand dollars, paid up."

Amos looked at the picture of Jesus holding the lamb and tried to remember the words about leading the lamb to slaughter while that frightened gnomelike man danced recklessly on his own grave.

"I'll have to take the radio and these books, Amos," she said. "No more privileges for you until you straighten out. The men have been informed that you are off limits. They're not to visit with you until you mend your ways. We don't tolerate trouble-makers here. Have we had our bowel movement yet this morning?"

She sang her subtle warning of the agony to come and absconded with the morning's take: Amos's books, Johnny's radio, and Spencer's money, not to mention the ten-thousand-dollar price tag on Spencer's head. Amos thought of saying something about the money, but what could he say. Poor Spencer was so completely unnerved he would do anything she wanted.

Amos's tender parts healed slowly and life came on with a unrelenting oppression. He laughed in its face, though the laugh caught in his throat occasionally. He had every little privilege denied him and he chuckled to himself over the desserts, the radio—though he did admit it had helped him judge his sanity against the outside world—the candy. He could go forever if that's all it took to beat her. But she didn't allow him much contact with the other residents: no more dayroom, no games with Emil and Carlos, no bingo. Spencer was his only real companionship, and Spencer had become totally submissive to her. Amos fought the oppression by constantly concocting plans to bring Daisy to ruin. Then he would carefully pick them apart, finding their flaws and discarding a plan when the total went much beyond two or three. He was concocting on the toilet when Roland invaded the latrine. He growled like a bear.

"Daisy tells me you're trying to get me fired."

"It had nothing to do with you, just Daisy," Amos said.

"Horse shit!"

Roland kicked him viciously in the shin with the hard toe of his work shoe. The blow knocked Amos to the floor, yowling on the way and grabbing for his violated leg. Roland took hold of his skimpy hair and pulled his head to the toilet bowl. The great bear shoved Amos's face into the dirtied water. Amos flayed with his arms, gasping for air, sucking in his own waste. He struggled futilely to free himself against Roland's strength. Just when he knew he would drown in the sloshing porcelain slaughterhouse, Roland released him and stepped quickly to the sinks. Amos collapsed onto the floor, gagging for air. Winston pushed through the curtained doorway with his jerky stride and faltered in his tracks, sensing the outrage bristling in that yellowed lavatory. Roland made a pretense at wiping out the basins.

"Oh gosh, Amos fell again," Roland said.

He manhandled Amos onto the toilet, still choking, his eyes about to burst with the fear that he'd never get his body back to breathing in time. Winston danced to the urinal.

"RINGS ON HER FINGERS, BELLS ON HER TOES," he sang in a monotone, with one eye on Roland.

Amos coughed up the filth from his throat, wiped it from his face, trying to stay upright on the toilet. He knew he was all right when he felt his shin burn with the ruptured blood vessels. A chunk of his hair clung to the wet floor in silent witness to Roland's brutality. Amos hung his head between his knees, trying to breathe quietly and wait for the pain to soften its grip while Roland stalled around the sinks.

"You about finished there, ding-a-ling?" Roland said to Winston with a clear threat in his voice.

Winston stood singing and peeing, on and on, until he won. Threatening Amos with a clenched fist as he passed, Roland bulled his way out of the room. Amos took mental note of another rule for survival. *Never come into the bathroom unless another man is present.* But Amos didn't understand why Roland was reluctant to have Winston witness a blow. Winston was so daffy no one would take anything he said seriously. Amos wondered how much Roland knew. Maybe Daisy did tell him that Amos was complaining about him. Did he know about the money? The insurance? Murder? Probably not. Daisy wouldn't trust that to anyone. It could be she just paid him well to do what he's told and look the other way. The bastard. He enjoyed kicking helpless old men around.

The pain subsided, leaving a spongy, coloring welt over his dented bone. Marvin dragged his stench through the curtain, followed closely by his roommate Elroy, like an old married couple who stuck glumly together because all other options were gone. The more Amos saw of Elroy the more he reminded Amos of a great toad. With wide-set eyes and large nostrils on a wide flat face, Elroy had no neck, his head with several chins emerged out of his slightly hunched shoulders and lumpy body. Even his skin was blotched and lumpy and Amos wondered if anyone else saw that resemblance. Amos almost expected Elroy to hop.

"You're a moron, a stinking moron," Elroy said.

"I'm not a moron. I'm as smart as you. Right, Amos?" Marvin said, seeming to pay no attention to Amos's dripping face. "Tell him I ain't no moron."

Amos regarded them both—his pants still down around his ankles.

"We're all morons. Anyone who ends up in this cesspool is a full-fledged moron. But it's time we morons broke out of this smell hole, and by God we're going to."

"How?" Marvin said, grinning between his large ears.

"You're crazy as a coot," Elroy said. "Can't be done."

"Maybe not," Amos said, "but wouldn't it be fun trying?"

"Fun!" Elroy said. "You see some of Daisy's handiwork you don't say fun."

Amos couldn't argue with that.

"It's worth tryin'," Marvin said. "What you got up your sleeve?"

They watched Amos stand and hitch up his pants with trembling hands.

"Nonsense," Elroy said. "You avoid Daisy like D-Con."

With his belly resting on his skinny thighs, Elroy squatted on a toilet and spoke to the cracked tile floor.

"It's all nonsense . . . always was, in here, out there. In real life Superman doesn't show up; nobody comes and saves you. That bullshit is for the fairy tales, and Winston there. Nothing saves you from the utter nonsense."

Winston still stood at the urinal, listening. Marvin turned to Amos for some hope under the burden of Elroy's biting obituary. Amos was momentarily smitten by Elroy's vision. He had touched some inner place in Amos that met him eye to eye and nodded yes, swept aside a lifetime of pretense and exposed truth where Amos had unknowingly hidden it away. He refused to allow it to overwhelm him, still smarting from Roland's violence, and he concocted as he went.

"We'll hit Roland all together, take him out, and steal his pickup," Amos said.

"We can never take Roland," Elroy said with a mocking tone.

"Ever hear of Gulliver and what happened to *him?*" Amos said.

"That's another fairy tale," Elroy said. "Roland is muscle and gristle and he'll splatter the whole lot of us all over the wall."

"Not if we have a plan," Amos said. "There's strength in numbers."

He told them they'd have to work out every detail, catch Roland when he was the most vulnerable and quickly subdue him. Marvin was all for it and told Elroy it was better than picking his nose, and the two started arguing. Amos warned them they had to keep their plan secret, that they had to plan it with all the men, and work it out until it was foolproof.

When they left the lavatory Elroy said, "Where will we go?" giving away the fact that hope hadn't completely drowned in his great toad heart.

It had started by accident, but Amos had been looking for something like it for weeks. These men faced living without purpose, the severest test of one's sanity and happiness. With nothing to do but get on each other's nerves, crowding, annoying, picking on each other, they spent their last days in a bleak meaningless stupor. Operation Gulliver was conceived, and the men in whispered tones devised elaborate and completely impossible ways to bring it off. Marvin warned Amos that they shouldn't let Elroy in on the plans because Elroy would tell Daisy anything for a shot of booze and that she often gave him one to hear the scuttlebutt from the wing. Amos insisted that Elroy be in on the plot as well as Winston, who none of the men wanted in on it. Without running for the office, Amos had inadvertently become their leader.

Under Daisy's restriction of mingling with the men, Amos stayed in his room, much of the time in bed. The men didn't dare talk to him under the threat of Daisy's rod, and it angered him to see them cowering, submissive rabbits, afraid to speak as they passed. It appeared to Daisy that Amos had returned to his early despair, sleeping most of the day, showing little interest in what went on around him. Unknown to her, he got his exercise at night.

He would wait until Daisy made her late round, eleven, sometimes eleven-thirty. Then he'd puff up his bed to look as if his thin frame were still there and move around the building in the shadows. Seeing the walker at the foot of his bed, he hoped Daisy would never investigate further into his bedding. He checked doors, always finding them securely locked. Many of the windows were nailed shut, and the few that opened had a wire mesh across them that would be difficult and noisy to break through. He knew every corner of the building except for the portions that were locked off to him. He learned to move quietly, learned where the floor creaked, what noises were background and which were danger signals. He became a nocturnal animal, always alert for a loose brick in her stronghold.

Amos sneaked down the women's wing under cover of Ruth's uneven snore and arrived safely at Fern's bedside.

"Hello," he whispered, leaning close to her.

"Oh, hello. I've been waiting for you."

She'd dropped off listening to her roommate's sleeping song, but was happy to see him. Amos crept around to the wall side of the bed, finding just enough room to sit on the floor and be unseen from the doorway. He slid down against the wall, and Fern moved to the edge of the mattress. This way they could visit privately for hours. Mae had passed in the hall several times when he was hidden there without detecting him.

"How are you?" Fern said as she peered over the side of the bed, unable to see his face in the obscure light.

"I'm healing . . . if I can just keep avoiding Roland. Daisy thinks I've given up. When I first got here I just tried to die."

"I know that feeling. I miss seeing you in the daytime."

"How did you ever end up in this place?" Amos said.

"By mistake. I could take care of myself perfectly well. Still can, but there was just no place I could live down around Absarokee. They told me they had a nice Home up here so I let them bring me up. I tried to live a normal life at first, but she punished me. Land sakes, I don't like to talk about what she did to me. Said she had to take the starch out of me. I told a minister once. Wish I hadn't. He reported it, but he thought I was deranged and when it was all over I got it good. So I just accepted it. Nothing I could do."

Like autumn leaves her words drifted wistfully down to Amos. Ruth kept up a good cover with a whistling, choppy snore.

"I ran away that summer, old fool that I am. We were allowed out on the lawn. I just went back into the hills when no one was watching. I tuckered out pretty fast. Roland came out in a truck and just sat there, waiting for me to climb in. I couldn't go another step. I think they saw me leave and knew I wouldn't get far."

"That bastard," Amos said.

"You know, when I was walking out there I prayed that John Wayne would come along, or someone like him. I stood there, trying to be strong and not give in. It was devastating to have to climb into that truck. It felt like I was murdering my soul."

Fern hung her hand over the side and touched Amos. He took her wrinkled offering in both hands, held it to his face, and she felt his tears. He began weeping.

"Shhh, shhh, there, there, Amos, it's all right."

"No, I killed her." He sobbed. "Oh, God, I *killed* her. That goddamn bumblebee, I should've waited until I stopped the car. I should've waited. But no, I had to get it right then. She told me to wait, that she'd get it and I got mad and told her I could do it, thank you. A proud, stubborn bastard. I murdered her."

He shook with his bitter tears, gripping Fern's hand to his sopping face. She didn't speak. They remained like that while his tears gradually subsided. Amos whispered to no one.

"What do we do when we've killed those we love?" He paused. "What *do* we do?"

"We have to believe they forgive us, we have to believe they still love us or we go insane. It's the same for all of us who've lost loved ones."

Amos would have none of Fern's forgiveness.

"No, it isn't the same. I killed her with carelessness."

Ida filled the wing with an unearthly shriek, and Amos thought it was appropriate. Ida was bedridden, like Owen, in the room next to Fern's, often screaming and cursing during the night, tied securely in her bed. Ida couldn't seem to die. Fern had attempted talking with her, but she had yelled until Fern left the room. Ida must not have had any life insurance.

"She's the only sane one in here," Amos said. "We should all be screaming instead of pretending this life is normal and everything is hunky-dory. We should be banging our heads on the walls and shrieking."

"You know what the worst thing is?" Fern said, "the worst thing that can happen to a body?"

Fern moved her hand against his cheek.

"What's that?"

"With all the sickness and accidents and misfortune in the world, there's something much worse, something awful. *Not to be wanted.* Worse than anything else that can happen to you is not to be wanted by someone. It happens to some people real early in their lives. With us it's come at the end. That never happened to your wife."

Fern spoke with such poignancy it alarmed Amos.

"Listen, we're going to bust out of here. Don't you go giving up. You're going to be walking through stores again, by jingy, watching children, eating at a cafe`, strolling around town."

Amos's voice was buoyant and cheerful once again.

"You sure make me feel good when you talk like that."

Fern chuckled, even if she didn't believe him. She had learned to play tricks with her mind, erasing the blackness and enjoying the little happinesses no matter how frail and short-lived. Amos stood stiffly, pulling himself up along the bed and wall.

"I'm going now," he said. "You better get some sleep."

He bent and kissed her on the cheek, surprising himself. It seemed the only thing to do, and he sensed by her unspoken response that it meant a great deal to her. He almost apologized for his weeping, but thought better of it.

"I'll send you a note with Sadie." Fern clung to his hand.

"With Sadie?" Amos laughed.

"I'll slip it in her pocket. You just slip it out. She'll never even notice. I won't put any name on it, just in case."

Amos chuckled at the idea of Sadie running underground messages. He squeezed Fern's hand, and under the protection of Ruth's craggy shadow and rattling sleep, moved out into the hall.

He turned for the dayroom and almost jumped out of his skin, finding himself face to face with a soundless, shadowy hulk. He stood frozen in fear until he realized it was Sadie, the abandoned linebacker who'd been put out on waivers and no one picked up. He slid past her and headed for safe harbor. At the far side of the dayroom, he heard her call behind him, more like the wind than human words. It reminded Amos of a loon he had heard calling one night across a mountain lake; a solitary call for its mate or for its companions or because it was lost in this world, haunting, wild. He knew at the time he would never forget it, and now Sadie had taken up the same note, calling into the darkness of her banishment. It would be morning soon. Amos crawled into bed and fell asleep, the cry of the loon lapping over him by the shore.

"Hellooo, Amos, remember me?"

Clara Channing woke him from his afternoon's sleep. She stood expectant in her gray uniform with starched white trim, effervescent with sweetness and light. Damn, Amos thought, How can a woman live past sixty and still be innocent? Clara had done it. Amos smiled, happy to see her.

"What can I do for you today?" She sang the words.

"Does Daisy know that you're here with me?" Amos said, sitting on the edge of the bed, logy from his night life.

"Oh, my, of course. She's so happy when I come, bless her soul. I'd have been here sooner, but the cold weather keeps me to home."

Like the multifarious clattering parts on an old thrashing machine, Amos's mind whirred so obviously he thought Clara could hear it. A puzzle flew together in his head like running the film of an explosion backward on the screen until the scattered debris flew back together again. He saw it all in an instant and began.

"I'd like to write a letter to my grandson in Ohio, if you still have your stationery with you."

Amos moved stiffly to his chair.

"My, yes, I have it right here."

She sat in Spencer's rocker and readied the ball-point.

"I'm ready," she said, giddy with delight.

Amos wondered if she ever questioned why he didn't write his own letters, if this was still a free society. It was actually better this way for his purpose. He cringed to think that the whole thing would hinge on Clara, sweet, gullible, guileless Clara. But he could test it without harm. He dictated a short, simple letter, telling Scott he was at Sunset Home, everything was just fine, he was enjoying his retirement and hoped that Scott would write sometime, sending some pictures of the family. Amos had the address in his cigar box, and Clara addressed the envelope.

"I'm not supposed to seal this," Clara said. "Daisy wants to see it first. Said she may want to drop a note to your family and tell them how you are and things like that."

"That's fine, Clara. You give it to Daisy."

Feeling hypocritical with the phony praise, Amos thanked her for the wonderful help.

"I hope you'll be back real soon. You don't know how much it means to me to have you visit."

Clara blushed with all the gratitude and gathered her things under her wing like a flustered mother hen.

"Oh, I'll be back soon, don't you worry. God bless you."

She departed in a swoon over a mission well done. Daisy carefully read the letter three times. It was harmless. She mailed it.

"Lights out in five minutes, men, let's haul ass," Roland roared up and down the corridor, smacking his hands together.

"It's time for your medication, Winston," Daisy said as she pushed the reluctant bloodhound toward his room with his tennis racket in hand. Amos waited for Emil's pilgrimage to the men's room and hurried after him with his walking frame. In his denim cap and underwear, Mick was sitting on one of the toilets that stood bleakly along the tiled wall, offering neither privacy nor comfort. He clasped Amos's pants leg and whispered loudly,

"You gotta wait for me when you go in the pickup."

"Shhh, we will, don't worry," Amos said and pulled free.

"I don't walk too good anymore," Mick said with a note of panic.

"Come on, come on, get on with it," Roland said with just his head sticking through the curtain. "This isn't the Ladies Aid. I want to get home tonight. Shit or get off the pot."

The grizzly threw a threatening glance into Amos's face that made his shin hurt, even though he felt his fellow inmates protected him with a transitory safety. Roland left, and the men hurried their ancient rituals. Emil moved next to Amos at the urinal, a spark in his voice.

"That's the place to hit him."

"What do you mean?" Amos glanced back at the doorway.

"The curtain. We'll catch him when he passes the curtain. He won't be able to see what hit him," Teddy Roosevelt said and shook his fist.

Amos agreed it was a good idea, visualizing that bear sticking just his head into the lavatory, presenting all kinds of vulnerabilities.

The men were leaving. Amos hustled, taking no chance on being found there alone. He didn't get washed, but no matter. He followed Emil and Marvin in the corridor, and when he remembered Clara and what he had begun, he felt a stab of excitement deep inside, that tingling sensation he'd felt before in his life but couldn't recall when or why. They were a fellowship of unspoken words, dreams of freedom and goodness that they had never quite been capable of, sharing a hatred for cruelty and this convalescent tyranny, and Amos carried their banner by some quirk of fate, their simple flag.

It was furled now, hidden from the world in this obscure human warehouse. But he could see it held high, unfurled, visible even to the people who chose to ignore it. These worn-out old men and women—invisible to society, considered worthless and an inconvenience by the good citizens of the county—were fighting their own battle against the power that was grinding them like corn in their final hour because there was no one else to fight it for them. Johnny had slyly knighted Amos to take up the sword, and some of the men were finding small glimmers of hope to at least hope again. As they shuffled down the hall, their bare scrawny asses showing under their tattered nightshirts, who would guess they were warriors in the most soul-searching warfare of their lives?

Carlos crept into the room after lights-out. He checked his plant in Amos's bedpan and partially watered it. The mouse had returned. Then he stood and leaned on the bed, close to Amos.

"I can't see," Gandy Dancer said.

"So I hear," Amos said.

"Can I be in on it?"

"We can't do it without you."

"I'll pull my own weight," Carlos said happily.

He crossed the room cautiously and stopped at the door.

"Good night, amigo."

"You sleep well, friend."

The brave little kid who saw his father hanged headed for his bunk, and Amos saluted him with his spirit. Amos wasn't alone. After so much, Carlos hadn't given up either, keeping his small plants alive like hope. Their goddamn flag was a philodendron.

All of them were tough, durable plants, trying to survive in a bedpan.

CHAPTER 14

"MY BOY KILLED HIMSELF when he was twenty-one," Spencer said.

He and Amos had finished supper and Spencer rocked gently while the springlike sunshine took its last peek through their narrow window.

"I never knew why. Everyone thought it was his fear of going to war. They thought the boy was a coward. I knew that wasn't it. I've always had a hunch it had something to do with a girl he'd never talk about," Spencer said without looking at Amos. "He didn't talk much. I did what I thought I should as a father . . . took them to Mass, prayed at meals, gave them everything they needed, I thought. I just don't think Dana liked me. I liked *my* father." Spencer paused. "Do you think suicide is a mortal sin?"

Peering through his little round glasses, Spencer's eyes pleaded for mercy with the jury in Amos's face.

"I don't know," Amos said. "There are a lot of ways to commit suicide. Hell, just giving up on life is a form of suicide, settling for less than we could be, taking the easy path, spending our days on things that don't matter; everyone commits suicide somewhere along the way. Everything we do is mortal."

"Then why wouldn't they bury Dana in the church cemetery?"

The cart stopped at the door and Nell retrieved her trays. She bent close as she picked up Amos's.

"I'm sorry about the desserts, Amos. I just—"

"It's all right, Nell. I don't care about them, I'm on a diet."

Amos cracked a smile and winked and she beamed like a child who's been loved.

"They were all like Dana, a little," Spencer said. "They grew up and went off, and we hardly ever heard from them again."

Spencer rocked gently and gazed into the hall, afraid to give the appearance that he was visiting with Amos.

"How many children did you have?" Amos said, watching the sunset through the murky window glass.

"Four, counting Dana, God have mercy on his soul. I thought Rachel would be different, our only girl. She ran off with an Italian boy and we never heard from her. Not even Christmas or birthdays. Oh, she sent a few letters at first. Then nothing. I don't even know if she's alive." Spencer sighed. "We must have done something terribly wrong. I always thought children would be a joy. They were an agony. And here I sit, in this silly little room, abandoned."

Working his gums together like chewing cud, Marvin furtively stopped at the door, scanning the corridor for any sign of the keepers. His sunken mouth looked more and more like a puckered knothole.

"Where are your teeth?" Amos said.

"They don't fit no more. Daisy says I get new ones if I quit wettin' the bed." He glanced nervously up the hall. "I won two dollars and eighty-seven cents last night at bingo."

His mouth opened like a leather coin purse, smiling with satisfaction.

"That's quite a pile of pennies," Amos said and laughed.

"A blackjack," Emil said, stepping across the hall.

"A what?" Amos said, all of them risking reprisal for talking.

"Put them in a sock. Make a helluva blackjack when we hit Roland," Emil whispered and hurried away.

"Yeah," Marvin said, off to his room for a sock.

Disregarding the interruption, Spencer continued their conversation.

"I never thought I'd end up in a place like this, not with four kids. I don't even know where they are now, except for Dana. He's in the Woodhill Cemetery, or worse. I always wonder, if the others knew I was here, would they come and get me? I always hope that tomorrow I'll get a letter from one of them asking me to come and live with them."

Spencer fell silent. Amos knew what he meant about never expecting to find yourself in the county poor farm, but he also knew he was only hearing one side of the story, that a story is seen by many and each sees something different. And then there is God.

"I'm going home today," Sadie said. Linebacker stood solidly in their doorway, blankly gazing out the window. "Have you seen my folks?"

Caught off guard, Amos all but forgot. When it hit him, she was turning to search other places. He pushed himself out of his chair and hurried to her side without the walker.

"Hello, Sadie, how are you?"

With one hand on her brawny shoulder he slid the other into the pocket on her flour-sack dress. He found a small folded note. On his way back to the chair he could hear Roland roaring in the distance, a small eruption in the dust of the evening. He concealed the note in his hand, anxious to read it, when Emil showed up. The grouch stood in the doorway and gazed down the hall nonchalantly, taking his pipe from his mouth and never turning his head.

"Roland found one of Carlos's plants in Owen's room, growing in a shoe," Emil said from under his wide gray mustache. "Roland laughed, said one vegetable in that room was enough. Then he made Carlos eat the plant. I'm betting he'll shit it out and start it growing again."

Emil put his pipe back in his mouth and walked away as though he'd been talking to the wall.

"Why won't they just let the poor Mexican have his plants?" Spencer said glumly.

"That wouldn't be as much fun," Amos said.

Then he whooped with an unsuspected joy and gave in to a belly laugh.

"What's always so goddamn funny?" Spencer swore for the first time with Amos.

"We are, Spencer, all of us. This place is funny. I'm funny. You're funny. Here I am, pretending I'm this grownup old man, having lived my life successfully, wise, mature, fulfilled; and all along, I'm just a lost little boy who has no idea what's going on."

"Yeah, well what's so funny about that?" Spencer said.

"I guess I can't explain it. If you don't get it, you don't get to laugh."

With that Spencer threw in the sponge, and Amos opened the note. It stung him with bittersweet arrows from school days, a simple, smuggled, printed note.

I MISS YOU. TAKE CARE OF YOURSELF. YOU ARE NOT
UNWANTED.

He tucked the note in his shirt pocket and wondered how
he'd reply.

Elroy was groaning and thrashing in a tormented sleep when
Amos arrived in the predawn stillness, the light at this end of the
hall bleak and vacant. With his mouth going like an untied tent
flap in a mountain storm, Marvin slept in oblivion, his bed reeking of urine. Amos shook Elroy gently by the shoulder as if he
were waking a great toad.

"It's me, Amos, you all right?"

Elroy woke with a start and then lay back to collect his wits,
squinting at Amos in the shadows. He reached for his horn-
rimmed reading glasses and fit them to his skull.

"It's my back . . . hurts most of the time, sometimes worse."

"Does she ever give you anything for the pain?" Amos said.

He settled on a ladder-back wooden chair, resting his fore-
arms on the high bed.

"Once in a while, if I holler long enough."

"What does she give you? Is it a pill?"

"Nah, the needle. She thinks I'd ask for it when I didn't need
it if it was a pill," Elroy said. "I can sleep good when I get a shot,
but it takes a team of horses to get a shot out of her. I have to get
outta bed early; my back can't take being down so long. She
makes us stay in bed too much."

"Is that why she gives you a nip now and then?"

"Yeah." Elroy hesitated. "For the pain."

Marvin rolled over, swallowed, and continued snoring in a
new key.

"Smell that stinkin' man," Elroy said. "Sometimes I think I'll
go crazy living with him."

Elroy rolled on his side, with a muffled groan.

"How'd you wind up in here?" Amos said.

"I thought I was pretty smart, outliving my brother. Turns
out he's the smart one, just dropped dead one day as neat as a
pin. I was married twice, only one was worth it. My second

wife, Sally. I was selling insurance in St. Louis. Met Sally in an amusement park. She was twelve years younger than I. She was a wonder. I couldn't wait to get home at night, start thinking about quitting early as soon as I ate lunch. We had almost two years together, and it seemed like two weeks."

Elroy paused, thoughtful, and Amos noticed his grubby night-shirt as his eyes became accustomed to the dim surroundings.

"My first wife just left me. I don't blame her much, I guess; our life was pretty plain. I didn't have much hope for anything until I met Sally. With her, everything was different, you know what I mean? She brought out the man in me I'd have never known was there. Jesus! I've often wondered if our whole life would have been like that. Would it ever have gotten old between us and soured? But life doesn't give you the chance to find out those things before it pisses on you. It smells just like Marvin's bed, and it isn't ever going to be different."

"What happened to Sally?"

"She died in childbirth, no . . . childdeath. They both died. It was a little girl. The doctor couldn't explain it; they just died. It's probably a good thing the baby died 'cause I'd have been one lousy father in those days. I emptied a lot of liquor bottles after that. You could say I was one helluva drunk. I guess I still would be if I could have afforded it."

They both noticed at once that Marvin was up on one elbow, listening.

"You peed all over your bed again, damn it!" Elroy said.

"Only a little."

"Only a little!" Elroy said. "Jesus, they could smell you in Missoula."

Marvin ignored his tormentor and spoke to Amos, who turned in the chair to acknowledge Marvin as part of the conversation.

"Are you scared to jump Roland?" Marvin said out of the shadows enshrouding his bed.

"Yes, some," Amos said. He smiled. "But we'll be together."

"I'm scared," Marvin said. "If we don't get the job done, it'll be our ass in the sling."

"Are you afraid of dying?" Elroy asked Amos intently.

"Tell him about the Gypsies," Marvin said.

"Let me be," Elroy said. "Amos, are you afraid of dying?"

"Tell him." Marvin wouldn't be put off.

"What about the Gypsies?" Amos said as he ducked Elroy's question for the moment.

"It scares the hell out of me," Elroy said.

"But . . . you . . . the bleeding from your nose," Amos said.

"He picks his goddamn nose," Marvin said.

"I know, I know," Elroy said with a quiet desperation in his voice. "I'm so damn afraid I can't just sit here in this hellhole and wait for it. I can't stand just thinking about it. I don't know what to do. It's like when you'd done something terrible and you were going to get whaled when your father came home. It's that terrible time of waiting before he comes home."

"Tell him about the Gypsies," Marvin said.

"To hell with the Gypsies," Elroy half shouted.

"Tell me what the Gypsies have to do with anything," Amos said, his curiosity riled.

"All right, all right," Elroy said with a false reluctance, belying his own obsession with the story. He took a deep breath and began.

"There's a family of Gypsies living in a big city in Poland during the war, circus people, acrobats and such. The Germans are trying to kill 'em off right along with the Jews, exterminate them. They're living in a big tenement, hiding out, but the Nazis spot them. Well, it just so happens that when the Nazis move in to grab them and haul 'em off to get gassed, the Gypsies were out in some food line, hoping to get some bread or something, all except their little girl."

Elroy coughed and glanced at the doorway. They all paused, listening. Nothing. Elroy went on.

"The little girl is playing across the hall with some other kids, Polish kids, not Gypsies. Well, this other family sees what's going on with the Germans running all over, so they hide the girl, and the man of the house goes to warn the Gypsies. He finds them and tells them they can't go back to their room for nothing, that they had to leave everything or they'd be murdered. The Nazis are watching the building, front and back, checking everyone going in and out. The family has to take off out of there, but the father won't leave without his little girl. So he sends a plan back with the man."

Marvin broke in excitedly. "They was carnival people—"

"Do you want me to tell it or not?" Elroy said.

"Okay, okay, you tell it," Marvin said.

"The Polish man goes back to the building with the plan. At two in the morning the little girl is to go out on the roof and walk over to a side that overlooks a courtyard. She should stand at the edge and count to fifty, to allow her father to get in position below her. Then she's supposed to jump, and, like he'd done so many times in carnivals and circuses, he'd catch her. But she couldn't make a sound, not a blinking word, or the Germans would hear her and be on to them."

The ex-insurance salesman with the characteristics of a toad had started the story halfheartedly, but now his voice quickened, turned serious in tone. As if he were hearing the tale for the first time, Marvin was like an attentive child, spellbound, with his mouth hanging open. Amos found himself engrossed as well.

"So, at two in the morning the little girl goes out on the roof alone and walks over to the edge, eager to see her father. It was the dead of winter; a cold wind is blasting her. She looks down into the courtyard and it's pitch black; she can't see a blooming thing. She's shivering, and she starts counting, but while she counts, she starts to think. What if her father isn't even down there? He could be late. He could have been caught on the way, the Nazis could have him. The icy wind is tearing at her, standing on the edge, counting, and she wants to holler down into the darkness."

Elroy cupped his hands and called over the edge of his bed, "Father, are you there?"

Marvin got out of his bed and sat on the edge. Amos edged closer on his chair, caught up in this story that Elroy retold with a spellbinding vividness and urgency.

"But the little girl knows she can't make a sound, she can't call out to her father or the Nazis will hear her. She can't see her father, the courtyard is totally dark. The wind is howling. She reaches fifty. Can her father see her? She's paralyzed. She hesitates. She'd never know if he was down there unless she jumped."

Elroy paused. He glanced at Amos.

"Tell 'em, tell 'em," Marvin said with the impatience of a child.

Elroy spoke so softly Amos could hardly hear.

"The little girl whispered quietly down into the dark court-yard, 'Father, are you there?'"

Elroy stopped.

"Go on, what did she do?" Amos said, fully captivated.

"Are you afraid to die?" Elroy said to Amos.

"What's that got to do—"

"We're standing on that edge," Elroy said, "and we've got to jump into the darkness. Now some sweet souls tell us that God is there to catch us in his big loving arms. How in the hell do we know?"

Elroy's voice broke for a moment. He took a deep breath.

"I mean, I want to shout with that goddamn skinny little Gypsy girl, *Father, are you there?* Are you there, goddamn it, and if you are, why the hell won't you let us see you? But there's nothing there, no one. There doesn't have to be a hell with fire and brimstone and all that crap. All that's necessary is for no one to catch us, don't you see? We fall forever into nothing."

Elroy lay back in his bed and went silent. Amos and Marvin waited without speaking. Then, after a minute of gathering himself, Elroy gazed at the ceiling and spoke softly.

"In the morning they found the little girl's body, broken and frozen in the courtyard."

"No! no they never!" Marvin said, about to cry. "That ain't the way the story ends. He's lying, he's telling it wrong, in the morning the courtyard was empty."

"Shhh, not so loud," Amos said, perplexed by Elroy's devastating conclusion.

He sensed Elroy was taunting him, yet he identified with that Gypsy girl to his nerve endings.

"Amos, are you afraid to jump?" Marvin said.

"Yes, I suppose I am."

Amos thought about it and went them one better. They were all like that little girl, out on the windswept edge every day of their lives, not just at the end. And the choice they make each day determines the nature of their living, joyful, or in terror. Gypsy's choice is to live never doubting that the father will catch you. Otherwise, you had to believe you were fatherless, absolutely alone, falling through the darkness to nowhere.

"It doesn't seem fair," Marvin said.

"What?" Amos said.

Amos stood stiffly, all at once aware of dawn's light seeping into the room.

"We don't have any choice," Marvin said. "We have to jump . . . sometime."

"Oh, but we do. Gypsy's choice," Amos whispered.

"Do you think he's there to catch us?" Marvin said with a hopeful urgency.

Elroy propped himself up, anticipating Amos's reply. Amos thought, watching the distant mountains from the window in the predawn glow.

"The answer is in the jumping," Amos said.
"What the hell does that mean?" Marvin said.

"Elroy's right," Amos said. "No sweet soul can do your believing for you."

"Look around you," Elroy said, "and then tell me to believe. There's only a scream from the courtyard."

Elroy spoke with such a heaviness of heart, such desolation, that Amos was touched by his woe. He wanted to speak, but a sob caught in his throat. How could he tell them what he felt in his heart; that the words don't fall on an empty courtyard. Yes, there's the sadness, the scream, and always the darkness, the unknown that we try to placate, try not to acknowledge. But there is a knowing that lifts all of life away from the scream and toward the laughing, the warmth, the light. There is One in the courtyard we cannot fall through. Amos could find no way to share this brightness, struck dumb before his companions' anguish. Amos touched Elroy's arm.

"I'm going now. Are you all right?"

"Sure, as long as I can laugh and shit I'm OK."

Elroy tried to laugh but couldn't manage much.

"Don't tell anyone I was here," Amos said.

"Aw, Amos, I wouldn't. I just feed her bullshit."

Amos nodded at Marvin and sneaked back to his bed, gripped with a pang of grief for his hurting friends, for his voiceless, unuttered hope, his stupid inability to speak to their wretched despair. He lay down in his bed of sorrow and with the little Gypsy girl he whispered into the darkness.

"Father, are you there?"

CHAPTER 15

AFTER HIS NIGHTLY ROUNDS—checking the infirmary door, a visit with one of the men, his time with Fern—Amos spent some of his night life reading. The lavatory was the only place available with enough light and some safety. He could get a book from Robert's shelf, go next door to the bathroom, and read in the pale light for as long as his eyes held out or until dawn chased him to bed. With a renewed craving for an insight into life, Amos valued several of Robert's volumes: novels, philosophy, theology. Sitting there under the bare light bulb on the porcelain thunder mug, developing a wide red ring on his rump, Amos chuckled at himself and wondered how some of these authors would write from that point of view and if it would alter their outlook on things.

While reading one night he heard the floorboards squeaking in the hall too late. He set the book on end behind the toilet stool, under the tank, just as Daisy came through the curtain.

"Constipated tonight, Amos? We're not getting enough exercise."

Smiling out of a soft yellow robe and fur-lined slippers, she was more relaxed than he had ever seen her; sleepy, mellow, all pretense set aside at this hour of the morning. He attempted to imitate having a legitimate bowel movement, and in panic, almost did when he realized he'd forgotten the walker. Without the usual artificial pastry she dished up with sweet condescension, he hardly recognized her voice.

"How is my sterling little witness doing these days?"

"Getting tarnished," Amos said.

"Aren't you afraid I'll put you to sleep one of these nights like Johnny?"

She smirked slightly with her handsome face, now free of foundation and other cosmetics, exposing minor blemishes. Through the opening in her robe one leg showed bare to the middle of the thigh. Startled by the ease of her words, he caught himself tracing the curve of her leg.

"No, I'm worth more to you alive."

He pulled his pajama top as far over his knees as it would stretch.

"Why do you do it?" he said quietly, taken by his own melancholic mood and sensing a minor truce.

"It's very simple. They don't pay enough for what I do in this dungeon," she said calmly. "I deserve something extra for the dirty work. You couldn't pay most people enough to put up with it. Anything I can get I have coming. You think this is some sort of privilege taking care of you maggoty old people, cleaning up your drool and vomit and putrid beds, living in the same building with you? I deserve much more than the stinking county will pay."

She gathered one hand to her breast as she spoke.

"I deserve some reward, some tribute. So a few of you die sooner. God, you ought to *beg* me. It's my gift to you; you're better off."

"Are your parents still alive?" Amos said.

"What's that supposed to mean?" she said with a defensive note in her voice.

"You don't believe what you've just fed me," Amos said.

"Of course I do, I deserve anything I can squeeze out of this rathole. I don't intend to scrounge around here the rest of my life. I deserve a long vacation after this tour of duty. You think you're a smart old coot. You're not smart; you're stupid. If you're dumb enough to end up in here, I don't have to worry about you."

"Even smart people turn into old people," Amos said, feeling a strange compatibility with her.

"You just don't get the picture, do you?"

She sat on the edge of the tub as though they were having a family discussion.

"Listen, I could drop you off downtown and let you blab to everyone in the county. You know what they'd do. They'd back away from you and your wild stories, uneasy, frightened, pointing you out to others. You know what I tell them when I'm in town, the banker, the guy who fills my tank, the salesgirl where I shop, the waitress where I eat? I tell them little stories about this place, and they shake their heads and click their tongues. I tell them enough of the truth so when you complain to the preacher or some other visitor, they recognize your senile condition and give you their blessing."

She pulled her silken robe over her knees where one of her thighs had been exposed.

"You know what I told my hairdresser a week ago? I told her that old Amos Lasher was going around telling everyone that I kill the patients. You know what she said? She wondered how I could put up with it after all I do, and then *those people* go around saying terrible things like that."

She laughed with self-indulgent mirth, her head thrown back, hanging onto the edge of the tub with both hands. She swung her head to gather her loose hair and looked back at Amos.

"Try this, just for the fun of it. Tell the next Holy Joe that comes out here that I squeeze your balls from time to time."

She cackled, stood abruptly, and turned off a dripping faucet, scanning the washroom quickly with a trained eye. Amos slid his feet around toward her, blocking her line of sight to the book.

"Does the sheriff know what you're doing?"

"Honest John Thomas? Hell, no. I've got him right here."

She held out a cupped hand and slowly closed the fist.

"You can control any man if you can just reach his balls. My grip on the sheriff's is a little different from my grip on yours, but it works out the same."

She smiled sensuously, arrogantly. He felt his groin twitching instinctively from the certainty in her voice. She started for the curtained doorway, indicating that the true confessions were over.

"Do you really think you'll get away with it?"

"I already have. Yours wasn't the first letter. That's part of my story, the letters you buzzards are always writing. I let some of them go. I bring Sadie into town and show her around. You're a sideshow for them, the old cripples they don't want to be reminded of. Why do you think this dump is out here in the hills? People don't want to see where they're all headed."

"We must scare the hell out of you, then, seeing so clearly where you're headed."

He scored. She winced from the blow and tried to fight it off.

"What do you get out of Winston?" Amos said, attempting to keep her talking with this openness.

"The mailman? Government pension. It's not much. He has a government insurance policy for a few thousand. I may be greedy, but I think I'll just let that one go."

"A mailman?" Amos was taken by surprise.

"Yep, our house pet used to carry the mail."

"Did you kill Harold the way you killed Johnny?" Amos said, finding it hard to believe this conversation was taking place.

"Don't smart-ass with me, old man. I see the wheels turning in your wrinkled little head, trying to trip up old Daisy. Listen, better than you have tried. You might just as well forget it. I'm your final refuge."

"Maybe you're right."

Amos studied the tile floor, her words boasting an assurance that smacked of the truth.

"I've got to get some sleep," she said. "If you're that constipated I'll have Roland give you an enema, but I've warned you about just lying around."

She slipped through the curtain and disappeared. She never noticed that he didn't have the walker. He reached back and retrieved his book, pondering this strange meeting, an unexpected cease-fire in the middle of the battlefield, white flags momentarily aflutter. He always knew she hid behind a hypocritical nurse's guise, but he caught a glimpse of the real person tonight, just a fleeting glimpse, and he knew her in a different way. He would fight her no more or less for that vision. He opened his book and read.

Amos slept fitfully during the day, trying to avoid Daisy's blatant revelations, but they stuck in his mind, invading his dreaming, jabbing, annoying. She was right, and she knew it, and that's what nettled him. He had thought of escaping and reaching town to tell the people about what went on here. It would be terrifying. Everything he told them would be true, and they would smile uncomfortably, edging away from him so they could call the Home to come and pick up this runaway lunatic.

He had considered making it to a phone and calling Scott in Ohio, but his faith was shaken. After all these years, who's to say that his grandson wouldn't believe he was just another disoriented old man, like those you see on TV. Depression covered him like an afghan. He refused to relent to it with the conviction that there was no one else who could beat her, and somehow he'd got it into his stubborn craw that he could.

Robert was sitting in the tub, motionless, a quixotic figure that brought a catch to Amos's heart. Amos paused a moment at the curtain, wondering whose carelessness had left this man so pathetically marooned in this desert place. He pushed the walker through and approached the professor, who was facing the far wall.

"Hello, how's the bath going?"

Amos saw that he was shivering.

"Could you give me a hand?" the bald man said politely.

The water already cold, he was waiting for someone to return and help him out of the tub. Amos set the walker next to the tub.

"Here, take my hand."

Amos gripped his bony arm and lifted the best he could while Robert used the walker to steady himself. Together they managed to get him standing and out of the tub.

"Who put you in the bath?" Amos said loudly.

"I don't remember."

The schoolteacher dried his lower body, the only part that was wet, and Amos helped him into his robe.

"It's mighty kind of you," Robert said.

He looked at Amos through heavy glass lenses, his eyes magnified goldfish swimming in synchrony.

"This reminds me of the time the President visited my class. I took a bath that morning, wore my best suit. I was pretty nervous. But it wasn't as difficult as I imagined. The President was a down-to-earth fellow. I was the Outstanding Teacher of the State of Kansas that year. Yes sir, President Roosevelt himself."

Robert smiled with his memory.

"Did we have breakfast yet?" Robert said.

"Yes, about two hours ago," Amos said. "Cream of Wheat, applesauce, remember?"

"Oh, yes." His polished marble head shook gently.

Amos could tell he probably didn't remember.

"Thank you kindly for your help," Robert said.

He pushed past the doorway curtain and Amos figured Robert would forget all about the cold bath in five minutes.

Curled in bed under his blanket, Amos felt drained, and he knew he had to get his daytime sleep. He was becoming aware of a newborn feeling for his fellow residents, growing within him in spite of himself. Caught up in his own self-pity and rage, he hadn't cared about them, considered them a personal annoyance that disrupted his private and tragic drama.

But somehow, imperceptibly, it had turned around. No longer seeing them as stumbling incompetent old men and women, he began recognizing the people they still were in the adventure of life they continued living. Like slides on the screen of his mind, he could see Elroy happily hurrying home from work to be with his wife, Sally. He could see Johnny, dragging a bellowing calf with rope and horse, a peaceful satisfaction in his face. Mick, sharing a campfire with other tramps and drifters in a life of carefree acquaintances and inviting horizons. He could see Emil, shingling a sturdy barn in the western sun, a pride in craftsmanship reflecting on his tanned unswerving face; Robert, walking impressively into a classroom and commanding sincere respect; Winston, greeting friends along his mail route; and Sadie, happy raising a family that was now ashamed of her senility.

Falling asleep, he was surprised by the thought: He loved them. And almost as if in a dream, he saw it in a moment. No one died of old age. We have the wrong culprit. It isn't old age at all. Neglect, violence, heartache, yes. Loneliness, disappointment, despair, giving up; these were the pallbearers that carry us to the grave. And leading the procession is carelessness.

Marvin shook Amos from his nodding state.

"I got a blackjack," he whispered loudly and ducked away.

Amos blushed with anger when he thought about Marvin, living without a set of teeth because no one gave a damn, walking his last days destitute of a shred of dignity, ashamed to be wetting his bed, and worse, having everyone around him knowing he does.

That would do it, damn it! Amos sat up in bed with the eye-opener. He would wake Marvin and send him to the bathroom. If Amos did that every night, maybe he would have a dry bed in the morning. Amos lay back, pleased with himself for thinking of it. It would be one small victory against this place. He fell asleep.

It worked. Marvin was no longer a bed wetter, walking in the daylight with a renewed self-esteem. Amos would wake him no later than midnight, and that's all it took. The faithful sensor that wakes us when the bladder is full had gone dead on Marvin. Amos would be his sensor. Roland, somewhat baffled, rewarded him with hard candy he could suck, anything to have one less rank bed to deal with. As a matter of pride, Marvin would never let on that Amos was behind his renewed control. Daisy did nothing about the teeth.

"Winston! Where did that wacko go this time?" Roland shouted as he stormed through the building. No one paid any attention except Amos. It woke him from an afternoon nap. He slid out of bed and traced the view from the window with drowsy eyes, noticing the sun was moving north, proclaiming the certain end to winter as well as the end of this day.

"Nice sunset?" Spencer said as he gazed over his shoulder from the rocker.

"Lovely," Amos said.

He settled in his chair, hungry for supper. Roland burst into the room, searching its corners with an angry eye.

"Have you seen Winston?" Roland was pissed.

"Not since this morning," Spencer said meekly.

Roland smacked a fist into his open palm and blew out of the room.

"Has Winston run away?" Spencer turned quickly to Amos.

"He seems to be missing," Amos said.

Amos came fully awake, his mind bristling with expectancy. Had that goofy mailman done it? Scuttlebutt rolled up and down the hall, and Amos tried not to reveal the excitement racing through his hardening veins, step for step with Winston. Emil paused at the door and turned his bulldogged head.

"Winston didn't think much of Operation Gulliver," Emil said. "He left without us. Ha!"

Nell dispersed the men loitering along her route with her relentless dispensation of the evening meal. She had sneaked a scoop of pudding alongside the mashed potatoes on Amos's plate. Roland came swiftly behind her.

"Nell, did Winston eat his lunch?" he said.

"Ah . . . no." She looked at the ward ruffian blankly.

"Damn it, you retard, you're supposed to tell us if someone misses a meal."

He stood staring past her, trying to figure how long Winston had been AWOL.

"I thought he was just walking so—"

"Don't think, you idiot! You're not hired to think. You're doing this job because you *can't* think, so just do what we tell you to do. Don't confuse things by thinking."

The grizzly hurried away, muttering to himself, and Nell glanced at Amos, as if she hoped he hadn't heard. Amos attempted to give her a smile, to uphold her, but she didn't look long enough to receive his offering. She went on her appointed course, a dummy pushing a dummy cart, never letting on if Roland had hurt her.

Amos's thoughts jumped back to Winston, that crazy windup man out in the world somewhere. Just when Amos needed him as a vital cog in his newborn conspiracy, the post-man runs away. Of two minds, Amos wanted Winston to escape but knew that if he did his own plan would be sabotaged. It was really Daisy's plan, a carbon copy of her modus operandi, coming to him out of the blue, a pigeon alighting on the head of an unsuspecting statue. He examined it in the stark light of day. It would work, if Winston returned, and if Amos could muster the courage to see it through.

The evening passed and Winston wasn't found. He was running free, or more likely, stumbling around in the brush, lost and disoriented, calling in the dark for his dog. You could detect a low murmur from the rooms, men talking about his chances and fantasizing his adventure with elaborate detail. Was it possible Daisy had helped him get loose, to allow him to wander around town awhile? Look, there goes another lunatic from out at Sunset. She was shrewd enough, but Roland seemed genuinely upset, and so did she.

The men were enjoying Roland's and Daisy's anxiety, coupled with their own excitement, and they'd parlayed it all into a celebration. Winston was free. They were all out there with him vicariously, talking in hushed voices of what they would be doing in a similar situation. Talking as if it were thirty years ago, their boasting far outdistanced their physical strength and wherewithal. But they were having a lively old time, thanks to Winston's daring, and some of them started to believe that Gulliver, their own plan of escape, would actually work too.

That night Amos decided he'd better not roam, with people keeping an eye out for Winston. He sneaked across and jostled Marvin out of bed, but that was it. He wrote a note to Fern. He dozed during the night, and when he couldn't sleep he reminisced through the keepsakes in his mind. He remembered when he used to give Gregory his haircuts. That was fine until around the fourth or fifth grade when Greg started to protest. He didn't want his hair cut. After one stalling argument Amos wanted to know why.

"Because they all slap your head when you come to school with a new hair cut."

Amos asked if that was so bad, and the boy told him it was, especially hurting when the big kids took a swipe at him. Amos compromised, telling his son that he'd only trim his hair. Then the kids at school couldn't tell.

"Oh yeah!" The boy huffed. "They know if *one hair* is missing."

Amos smiled with the memory that kept him company in the early morning hours, recalling how sincerely Greg believed that. It was a long way from that grade school playground to the world Amos knew, but as he thought of Winston out there in the night, he wanted to believe there was someone else who knew when one hair was missing.

Surprised by the light and bustle, Amos woke to the new day. Everything seemed normal: Roland on his rounds, Nell with breakfast, Daisy back and forth. The odds went up all day in the betting.

"Have they found him yet?" Amos called to Emil.

"Nope. They figure he's out in the hills. Got down to twenty-one degrees last night. He could end up a *frozen* vegetable."

Briefly entertaining the hope that Winston's exploit might expose her treachery, extricating him from his reckless intention, Amos dismissed the premise quickly and gave it no credence. Wishful thinking.

The following afternoon Spencer looked up from his Bible.

"Do you think he's dead?" Spencer said.

"I don't know," Amos said. "He's been gone two days. He could be a pretty distance from here in two days."

Strange voices filtered down from the dayroom, drawing Amos quickly up to the lavatory from where he could better eavesdrop. When he pushed the walker through the curtain, he almost knocked Emil over, the grouch already in position, listening.

"I knew you'd find him, John."

Daisy's voice dripped with cheerful relief and applause.

"Just lucky," Sheriff Thomas said. "He'd have been out of the state in another few minutes. The highway patrol spotted him mooching at a truck stop in St.Regis, clear over on the western border."

Winston came stiffly into the lavatory, bumping into the two of them with their ears glued to the curtain. He had on a baggy winter coat and a cap much too large. He looked at them for a second and then went to the urinal.

"The only thing I can figure," Daisy said, "is he slipped out when the bread truck was here."

The sheriff's and Daisy's voices were fading. Amos strained to hear, but he could only catch something about a dog and then laughter. Emil and Amos crept up the corridor as far as Robert's doorway, ready to bolt at the wink of an eyelash.

"Well, John," Daisy said, "now you see why I don't encourage visitors. It's hard enough keeping them in this relic of a building without a lot of people coming and going."

"It still beats me how far that old geezer got," Sheriff Thomas said. Winston had impressed the lawman.

"Thank you so-o-o much, John."

Daisy was in good spirits, all the inmates accounted for, apparently no damage done and maybe some good; Winston adding to the Home's infamous reputation. Emil and Amos beat it to their rooms, dreading the time when Roland arrived for work.

Just before supper Roland thundered down the hallway. Amos and Spencer listened tensely with the rest of the wing.

"You trying to make Roland look bad, huh, monkey?" Roland said in a malicious voice.

"RIDE A COCK-HORSE TO BANBURY CROSS," Winston sang.

"Taking ol' Roland's coat, huh? You'll have to learn not to mess with Roland, you moron."

Winston cried out, the building held its breath, tension crackling around doorjambs and backbones. Winston grunted and the men guessed: a kick in the shin, a punch in the stomach, a knee to the groin. Roland was careful about the face, afraid to leave marks. Winston was sobbing loudly.

"Please don't hit me, please don't."

Amos shook with outrage. He prayed for his old Winchester, and one bullet, and he'd lodge it in that grizzly's brain pan.

Roland stomped up the hallway. The wing sighed relief with the passing of one more act of violence, the men agonizing through the fear that it might reach them and were temporarily soothed when it hadn't.

Waiting until well after midnight, Amos went quietly to Winston's bed. The runaway mailman was awake.

"Don't hit me," Winston said out of the shadows.

"Shhh, it's Amos. I won't hurt you, are you all right?"

"I went looking for Ginger, but I couldn't find her."

Winston spoke softly, saying the most he'd ever said to Amos.

"We were all pulling for you."

Amos touched his cold thin hand. Winston didn't reply, quietly weeping, turning his head into the pillow and silently shaking with disappointment, with failure. Amos put his hand on Winston's shoulder and squeezed his bony frame, making an effort to give him comfort. Winston was eighty-four years old. Did he realize this was his last punch, his final gasp, before settling into the dust. Damn it, he tried, displaying courage and intelligence and guts in his splendid run. To the world, only the erratic stumbling of a foolish old man; to Amos, a heroic venture. Winston turned his head from the pillow and raised it slightly.

"I couldn't find her, she's lost."

"I'm damn proud of you, Winston. We all are. Hell, you should have seen them around here. You had them going up the walls. For two days you had Daisy and Roland by the ass."

Amos hooted faintly and shook the mailman's shoulder with glee, sure he caught a faint smile streak across his houndish face in the dim hall light.

Amos sat with him until Winston fell into a deep sleep. What spark of life burned brightly in his sunken chest these past two days, a woeful, comic old-timer in an oversized coat and hat, running for his freedom, his sanity, his human dignity, or was he just searching for his never-to-be-forgotten dog?

Amos returned to his bed. He didn't know how he could ever explain it to Winston. They were all looking for what they had lost.

CHAPTER 16

Banging into the doorjamb, Mick fumbled with the wheelchair, learning all over again to propel himself in the world. After jumping freights for a lifetime, his legs were giving out on him, and Daisy dug up an old wooden wheelchair.

"You got a license for that machine?" Amos said.

"Damnedest contraption I ever rode," Mick said.

He fumbled to maneuver the creaking invention, peering from under the bill of his denim cap. He paused and lowered his voice.

"You still need my cane?"

"Yes, we need both of you," Amos said.

"You won't leave me in the dust?"

"You'll be riding with us down the freedom road," Amos said.

Putting his fear of being left behind to rest for the moment, the stooped little tramp beamed, backing the chair away from the door and getting it started up the hall. The rig—groaning and wobbling on untrue wheels—looked older than its driver.

"It's Clara Channing here."

She stood beaming in the doorway like a happy child.

"I have a big surprise for you today, Amos."

She stepped forward with pomp and occasion, giggling inwardly with her marvelous secret. Amos welcomed her with his warm smile, his own inner feelings tingling with an excited fear.

"Would you like to guess what it is?"

She tilted her head with the little game, her gray cap clinging to her white hair, his unsuspecting collaborator. Amos played the game.

"A pack of gum?" he said with sincerity.

"Ooooh nooo, my goodness, much better than that."

She couldn't wait to tell him, pulling a letter out of her bag.

"Daisy kept it until I came out. She knew I'd want to bring it to you."

She handed him the obviously opened and resealed letter.

"Open it, open it, it's from your grandson in Ohio. Remember the letter we wrote?"

Clara was more excited than Amos over this one. It was the next one that gave Amos pause. He read the reply aloud, a nice, newsy report from down home in Ohio. They were glad to hear from him. How was he getting along without grandma? Everyone there was fine, and they sent a recent snapshot of the family.

"Oh, look. These little ones must be your great grandchildren," Clara said. "Look at that. You'll have to visit them real soon."

She stabbed Amos unawares, ecstatic with the results of her good deed, a setup for his next request. He ignored the wound and went on, fanning the flames.

"This is the best surprise I've ever had," Amos said. "It was so nice of you to go to all that trouble, Clara."

He squeezed her arm. She ducked her head in a coy little display of embarrassment. He disliked using her, but he had no other choice. Clara roosted in Spencer's rocker, absorbing his gratitude like a dry sponge.

"Listen," Amos whispered in a secretive tone, "the men and I have been thinking. We'd like to do something nice for Daisy in return for all she does for us. A big surprise. But since she sees all our mail, we can't ever surprise her. We took a vote and we all picked you to help us do it."

"Me?"

Clara sang the word. Amos leaned close and held her arm.

"Would you like to do it?"

"Ooooh, yes, if I can."

"Wonderful. I knew you would. I told the men you would. I have a letter to my good friend in Denver. He works for this big company. We're going to have him get a real fine present for Daisy. We wrote the letter so Daisy wouldn't come by and see you writing one. Then she'd expect to see it, like usual. We scribbled it out the best we could."

Amos produced the letter from under his mattress and whispered to her.

"What's your address?"

"Four hundred and eight Lewis Street," she whispered, peeking toward the doorway.

Amos wrote her address in the letter, stuffed it into the envelope, and sealed it.

"Put this in your bag," he said. Clara ducked the clandestine message. "Don't let Daisy know you've got it."

"This will be so exciting," she said.

She actually squirmed in the rocker, wiggling her hips from side to side in anticipation.

"Can I be there when Daisy gets her surprise?" she said.

"You sure can, Clara."

Visualizing that scene, Amos laughed and wondered if Clara would ever figure it all out.

"Now listen, Clara. My friend will send his answer to your house in town. It will be addressed to me. You'll have to smuggle it out to me when it comes."

"Smuggle?" Clara repeated the word slowly.

"Yes. He'll send me a list of gifts we might pick, like maybe a color TV or one of those new fancy cameras. I'll tell him which one we'd like for Daisy, and then you'll have to take that letter out and mail it. That's all. The gift will come and Daisy will have her surprise."

"Ooooh, I'll do it, I'll do it. Daisy will be so happy that you men did this for her. I just know how much it will mean to her."

So did Amos. He hoped Clara wouldn't overdo it and act so giddy that Daisy's suspicions would be aroused. Clara had to pass Daisy three times with a concealed letter burning a hole in her satchel.

"You'll have to stamp the envelope before you mail it. I didn't have one and of course I couldn't ask Daisy for one. I'll owe you."

Amos grinned his elation, grateful for this kind, simple woman, her gullibility at this point her most precious asset. This was it, Amos realized, and he couldn't do it without her. Like Winston's run, this was his last punch and everything would be riding on unsuspecting Clara. He thought it was too bad that she couldn't be in on the real drama and compelling significance of her own actions, but the truth would be unduly terrifying for this domestic woman, the strain exorbitantly severe. Clara could never know what she was about or the whole structure would come apart and collapse.

"When the letter arrives, don't come right out with it. Bring it on your regular day," Amos said.

He attempted to calm her, to keep it light, helping her do this without any change in her routine patterns.

"I will, I will. I'll hide it in my bag and just come out on my usual day."

She was taking mental notes like an agent for the CIA, making this little surprise for Daisy into a matter of life and death. Amos imagined how she'd act if she knew it was.

"I'd better visit the other men now," she said, "so Daisy doesn't get suspicious."

She covered a snicker with her hand and picked right up on this new game they would play.

"Not a word to the other men either," Amos said, "or anyone at home. You know how someone slips and secrets get spread around."

She nodded as Amos attempted to foresee every possible failing in his intrigue, always fearing he'd overlooked something obvious. Clara went on to visit the other wonderful men who were going to do this nice thing for their head nurse, something so wondrous that none of them knew anything about it. Amos tried to keep tabs on Clara while she lingered on the men's wing, his heart in his throat until he knew she was safely out of the building. Then the exhilaration swept over him, and the razor-edged dread that he could never see it through.

The mobile post-office box on Sadie's dress appeared with her in the late afternoon. A few times she had shown up only in underwear. Amos managed to exchange notes without Spencer's notice.

Fern's: I MISS YOUR WONDERFUL VOICE AND BEAUTIFUL BROWN EYES. YOU ARE A SWEETHEART. BE MY VALENTINE.

Amos's: FAIRY TALES CAN COME TRUE, IT CAN HAPPEN TO YOU, WHEN YOU'RE YOUNG AT HEART.

Amos woke Marvin after midnight and sent him to the latrine. Then he pulled a button from one of his shirts and wandered around the building, stalling. He procrastinated until he was convinced he could delay no longer, putting it off as long as possible for two reasons. First, he was afraid that this mysterious man would simply kick over the milk bucket and reveal Amos's plot to Daisy. Because he was a much greater risk than Clara, allowing him to participate for the shortest possible time was an important safety factor. The second fear was Amos's doubt that the mailman could learn and perform the simple but tricky maneuver without Daisy catching him at it and—like a child under threat—would tattle on the one who put him up to it. Playing one more card in his hand, he woke Winston and gambled, his innards knotted like rope. They would have to practice it over and over until Winston could do it without hesitation.

"Remember, Winston, this will help us get away from Roland and Daisy," Amos said. "They're mean to us and if you do this, we'll get away for good."

Amos held the glass and coached. Winston practiced willingly, seeming to enjoy the game.

"That's pretty good," Amos said. "Let's do it again. Take the button. Have a drink. Good. Let's see. Oh."

They lost the button.

"That's all right," Amos said.

Amos pulled another button from his shirt.

"Let's do it again."

Winston seemed to understand, encouraging Amos, inflating his hope.

"It's like Button, Button, Who's Got the Button?" Winston said.

The mail carrier recognized something from his childhood.

"Yes, that's right," Amos said, "it's just like Button, Button and we don't want Daisy to know who's got the button."

Amos intended to go over it with him for several nights before turning him loose, until he could do it smoothly, without a change in expression, without blinking. A few more tries and it was enough for now. Winston crawled back into bed while

Amos thanked and reassured him. Aware that the scheme was fraught with peril, Amos came away daring to believe it might just work, daring to believe in this strange and haunting man who must play the game in dead earnest.

"I got your note. It was lovely," Fern said as she looked down at him in the dark corner between wall and bed. "Can you sing?"

"Let's leave that to Sinatra."

"Did you wake Marvin?"

"Yes. Roland can't figure it out," Amos said.

He laughed lightly. Fern and he were becoming attached, Amos looking forward to seeing her, skipping around to different men each night, but always making his way to Fern's bedside. Not wishing to bring any new hurt into her life, it troubled him, their growing affection, because he needed her love and compassion now. They held hands.

"Your hands are so strong and manly they give me a feeling of security."

She cradled his hand in both of hers.

"Louise McDonald died today, pour soul," Fern said softly. "She's been here longer than I." She paused. "You know, not one person ever came to see her."

Fern was angry in her delicate way. She intertwined her fingers with his.

"Maybe that's the hardest part," Amos said. "Life just keeps going on out there and no one notices that you're gone. You always suspect that you're not too important, but to be tossed away like an empty beer can with never another thought, that's hard."

He spoke without bitterness.

"We're important to our loved ones," Fern said, "but there always has to be the last one. That's us. It's very strange, isn't it? We all try to live as long as we can. We're the successful ones. We felt sorry for those who died first. But they were spared this."

Fern's voice trembled. Ruth stirred in her bed and started a blubbering snore.

"I sometimes wonder if there's any reason for us to go on living," she said. "Isn't that terrible?"

Amos wanted to tell her that he had found one, but he couldn't. He had to be very careful. No one must be held accountable because of his hazardous gamble. She answered her own question.

"Maybe we have the same purpose we've always had."

Fern tugged on his hand.

"What's that?" Amos said.

"To care about each other, to help each other. We ought to be good at it by now. We're all done stepping on one another to make a living and get ahead. Land sakes, we should be experts by now. All of us empty beer cans can still love each other."

Amos could see her seasoned smile in spite of the dark. He pried himself off the floor, grunting with the effort, and put an arm around her fragile frame.

"Can I kiss you?" he said.

"If you don't, I'm going to kiss you."

He kissed her, softly, fully, and felt a warmth arise within him he thought was long dead. He went to stand straight but she prevented him, clinging to him. He kissed her face, her thin sweet lips.

"You're a fine lady, Fern. I don't want you to take all this too seriously. We're all players in some grand comedy and I suspect it's going to turn out with a happy ending."

How could he tell her he was still going to get his chance to be a hero. He wished her a good night and went out into the dim hallway. He looked in on Sadie and Effie. He had toyed with the idea of using Sadie in his attempt, but as he looked in on her, heaped in a disheveled bed like a beached whale, breathing deeply in an intoxicated sleep, he knew he had been right to exclude her.

He crossed the dayroom and checked the infirmary door. It was locked, no! *the knob was turning!* Amos took two steps to the left and crouched along the wall, praying his bones wouldn't snap with the sound of a misplaced footstep in the woods. Daisy materialized through the door. She paused for a moment, her eyes adjusting to the murky light, surveying the room. Amos was out in the open, unprotected, in plain view if she glanced back to her right. She listened attentively for a minute and then went down the women's hallway. Amos scurried to the safety of his bed, relieved to have escaped a careless mistake on his part. He wanted to give Daisy every impression that he was beaten, his flag in the manure, her warfare ended. He tried to find some sleep alongside the now roaring river; his mind and stomach churned; the pressure grew.

Amos dug into his daytime bed, scrounging for small parcels of sleep. Spencer, with his Santa silhouette, kept him from finding any, pacing the room, his potbelly in his hands, complaining about the agony within, as Roland went by in the wing with Marvin.

"You're taking a bath right now. Wheeew, you're getting' ripe," Roland said, pushing Marvin along.

"I had a dry bed," Marvin said.

"You sure as hell did," Roland said. "The way you stink, I'm starting to think you're just absorbing it."

Emil and Carlos, playing checkers in the hall, leaned against the wall when Roland passed; the men always gave the grizzly wide latitude when he moved about the building. Carlos bent low over the board, figuring his next move. Mick came by in his Civil War wheelchair, attempted to pass, and jarred their board enough to rearrange the position of the checkers.

"Get that damn chair away from here!" Emil said.

You could tell who was winning by the reactions: Carlos giggled, the game ruined. Mick, with his soiled red bandana knotted around his neck, tried to steer out of the area, working the wheelchair, outrunning the curses, a frightened man struggling with his last means of moving himself around, understanding that the basket was next. All day he worked—until his arms ached limp—to replace his legs with wooden wheels, holding back that dreaded final chapter in a bed: the bedpans and urinals, the dirty sheets, the numb limbs and open sores, asking and waiting for every simple need. He'd seen enough of it. Maybe he could work himself to death while he was still free to control the movement of his body, before someone else would have to move him around like a stump.

"Mick, roll that contraption in here," Amos said.

Mick wangled his carrier through the doorway and bumped up against Spencer's chair. Spencer pulled him back a space and sat in his rocker, making a pathetic display of his boundaries.

"Listen," Amos whispered loudly, "your chair will make a perfect blockade for Roland when we want to set him up. You can come down the hall and pretend you're having trouble, making a roadblock just past the bathroom curtains. When he stops there and starts bitching at you, we can take him by surprise. That wheelchair is just the thing we needed."

"Yeah?" Mick glowed. "I'll practice so I can do it perfect. Ya still need my cane?"

"Yes. You're turning out to be the most important person in the plan," Amos said.

"When we gonna do it?" Mick pulled his engineer's cap snug.

"As soon as we're all ready," Amos said.

Daisy appeared in the doorway looking nasty.

"We're not socializing with Amos are we, gentlemen?"

"I'm just showin' Spencer my chair," Mick said timidly.

"I've warned you, Amos." She glowered. "We don't want to be putting foolish ideas into anyone's head, do we?"

"No."

Amos closed his eyes. Daisy turned on Spencer who was hiding in his Bible. With his little round spectacles he peeked out from behind the large book.

"Miss Daws, could I have some Pepto-Bismol. My stomach is killing me."

"All right, Spencer, come with me."

She paused at the door and noticed Amos's shirt.

"Amos, what on earth happened to all your buttons? Don't tell me we have a button thief now." She laughed. "Just don't forget the score."

She left with Spencer at heel and Mick struggled to get his chair out of the room. Amos wouldn't forget. Not one blow, one indignity, one life snuffed out for her personal profit. He only prayed that in the shocking moment of truth she would have to remember him and every injustice and cruelty she had heaped on his friends.

Depression avalanched over him without warning, catching him completely off guard. When his heart felt like wax, his plans like dust in the hurricane, Carlos, in his weathered adobe skin, came steadily to his bedside, pulled the bedpan from under the bed, and held it up to the sunlight. The plant had doubled in size; it filled the pan, blooming, prospering. Amos cheered somewhere inside.

Everything wasn't dying here. Some things were coming alive.

CHAPTER 17

Handicapped with shuddering apprehension, Amos set Winston in motion, becoming completely unnerved during the two minutes the whole thing took. He castigated himself for risking the whole kettle of fish on Winston's eccentric behavior and convinced himself that he had to find another way. The postman had come through with high marks that first time, but it could have been dumb luck. With that in mind, Amos left his bed earlier than usual. The Buick squatted under the cottonwood and some of the men played cards at Emil's casino.

It had been over a week since Clara packed the mail and he knew he had to press on in the belief that everything would fall in place. He would make a quick check of the door to the infirmary and return to his bunk for a while. He grasped the knob and turned, momentarily stunned to find it unlocked. She had forgotten, as he predicted, on a night when the Buick driver filled her mind with other things. He turned the knob as far as it would go before putting any pressure on the door, then pushed slowly for fear of a hinge lamenting in the dark. The door's hardware gave no protest and Amos slipped in and quietly shut the door behind him. His heart tap-danced on his rib cage and dread showed up in his belly like a crowd at a fire. The door leading to Daisy's apartment was slightly ajar, a shaft of light dimly illuminating the infirmary, making it possible for Amos to move about without knocking things around.

He could hear their muffled voices. He opened a small closet door and found only one white smock hanging there among several empty hangers. He carefully shut it and moved to a glass cabinet, more likely to contain what he was after. Suddenly the apartment door partially opened, throwing more light into the small white room and terror into Amos's breathing apparatus. The man stood with his hand on the doorknob, talking to Daisy, about to come eyeball to eyeball with one Amos Lasher. Knowing he'd never make it to the dayroom door, Amos slipped up inside the narrow closet and pulled the door shut within an inch. There was nothing to get a hold of to close it tightly from the inside.

Instantly the light in the room snapped on. The unseen lover was in the infirmary and Amos was in a coffin too confining either to stand straight or sit down. He leaned against the back with his bent knees facing the slightly cracked door, his head tilted to prevent disturbing the unused hangers. He realized immediately that he couldn't remain in that position for long, afraid to breathe, hoping the Buick driver would get what he wanted and get the hell out of there. If she caught him here, now, her anger might outweigh her reason and there'd be no telling what she might do.

He gathered his wits and made an effort to calm himself while Romeo bumped around the room, sliding the table, opening and closing drawers, clinking glass, until finally he was gone. He'd left the light on, but Amos had to risk that and escape as quickly as possible. With the instinct to flee driving him, he peeked through the crack and caught himself just before he touched the door. Standing inches from the closet, the mysterious lover leaned against the counter and clicked ice cubes in a glass he held. Clad only in a towel, he was waiting for her!

"Come on, honey, it's time for your doctor's appointment," he called, startling Amos.

They were so close it was hard to believe the man didn't sense there was someone counting the hairs in his left ear. Amos had a strange feeling he'd heard that voice before. He could only see a sliver of the man, revealing that he was large, had dark brown hair on his body as well as his head, and seemed in the neighborhood of Daisy's age. Amos froze in place, unable to slip back against the wall for fear that any slight rustle would prompt the man to open the door.

"You shouldn't keep me waiting," the man said and Amos could tell that Daisy had come into the room.

Faint strains of classical music came from her apartment. Amos couldn't see her yet, but the man put down his drink and reached out to her.

"Is the doctor getting horny?"

Her voice was warm and playful. Amos could partially see her when she came into his arms. They were kissing. She wore a light blue terry-cloth robe and a blue ribbon holding her pony-tail. The man helped her step onto a small wooden platform at the foot of the examining table. She was facing the unlatched closet door, her lover with his back to Amos. The Buick driver unfastened the sash on her robe while the music increased in volume.

"Aren't you going to put on your coat, Doctor?" Daisy said with a sensual inflection.

Amos swallowed, held his breath. She was talking about the white doctor's smock hanging with him in that tomb. He prepared to bolt when the playboy's words gave him a reprieve.

"It's too warm in here," he said.

That voice again. Amos knew it, but where?

Her robe hung open. Amos tried to catch a glimpse of his face. The Buick driver slowly slid the robe down over one shoulder, kissing her, only the back of his head visible from the closet. She allowed him his way as he freed her other shoulder and let the robe crumple to the platform. Amos was taken with how vulnerable she seemed now, delicately feminine, virginal, as she stood nakedly exposed to his brawny touch, displayed before his hot-breathed appetite.

The broad-shouldered man filled most of Amos's view, but he could see her face and part of her body. Her figure was stunning for any age, lush. The symphony continued to fill the room in greater measure. Amos tried to swallow but his throat was so dry his Adam's apple sounded like a plunger and he was sure they could hear him. With pain in every joint, he slid back into the corner where he could no longer witness their intimacy.

They went on playing, Daisy and her . . . Damn! Amos was jolted by the impact of recognition. It was John Thomas, the sheriff! Honest John Thomas, that son of a bitch.

Routed by this curious night, Amos couldn't sort it out. What surprised him more than anything, he was sexually aroused. Tortured from the position this grave imposed upon him, scared to death for his life, discovering the county's Lone Ranger was balling Daisy—something that threw all kinds of uncertainty into his carefully conceived plan—and still he was hard. He braced his hands against his thighs and shut his eyes while the torment continued, and the music, and the growing intensity of their lovemaking. He could hear their voices over the swelling symphony but couldn't decipher most of what they uttered, coming now in animated groans and sighs, short, urgent cries. He noticed that under the circumstances it was difficult to distinguish if the human sounds were those of pleasure or pain.

Amos felt the sweat trickle down his face; his back and legs beseeched him to move. The orchestra was playing softly now, a piece Amos recognized but couldn't name. Daisy began to moan and cry out, gasping, flinging her guttural expressions of ecstasy over the room as violins dominated the infirmary.

When would they be done? Amos had to look. He changed his position minimally with little relief from the pain. He tried to shift his weight. In all his years he'd never witnessed a man and woman making love. It must be what those pornographic movies are like and he joked with himself out of desperation. He figured a candid shot of the lawman's bare ass bending over the nude head nurse at the county poor farm just might make the front page if he only had a camera and a .357 magnum to protect himself after he snapped it.

Who'd believe he'd have his sexual education advanced at Sunset Home. But he was in serious trouble and he knew it, the suffering far outweighing his prurient interest. His backbone demanded to straighten out or it would wail without his consent. His legs were gripped with increasing bands of torture, each passing moment raw misery. He allowed the weight of his bony frame to wedge itself against the sides of the cramped cell, knees against one side, the small of his curved spine jammed hard against the other.

Only a few feet away they were noisily back to their lustful game, reminding Amos of some ancient carnal ceremony. The symphony orchestra was moving toward the resounding finish, all instruments joining in crescendo, the two lovers keeping pace with a growing frenzy of guttural notes and chords of gratification. His shrieking body proved that their mating had gone on for centuries and Amos wanted to time his cries with theirs to release some of his torment. He could not last ten more seconds. He felt his sweat mingling with theirs, his pain merging with their pleasure. He was in bed with them, tangled in their heat, feeling the throb and heave of their passion, carried along on the rising tide of their sex.

Restraining himself no longer, he leaned forward to his slice of vision, the empty hangers chiming a little tune when he grazed them with his head. They never noticed. Daisy had her body bent forward over the table and Honest John Thomas entered her from behind, a snorting, stomping stallion, stalled with a young mare in heat. Amos could feel the power of his craving, the energy with which she received him, her hunger accepting and consuming his every thrust.

Amos was wet, his face, his armpits, the back of his neck and shirt where the knives pierced his sanity. He knew he couldn't stand the shrieking in his bones a second longer. The drums roared, the musicians pulled all stops, the cannons . . . the *cannons!* Amos remembered, it was the *1812 Overture* and now it seemed so fitting, so appropriate in its climactic fury. The cannons booming, the frenzied stallion exploding deep within the loins of the mare, yet it was the stallion who was killed, not she; shot down by the guns of 1812, crying out in that moment like a man dying, his life flowing from him, unable to save it, to call it back, wanting to cling to it fiercely, forever, at the same instant he urgently hurled it into her.

The stud had finished with his breeding, slumped across Daisy's back, muttering something affectionately in her ear, the orchestra finished and retired for the evening without applause. Amos had consented to surrender to his body's demands and fall out of the pigeonhole onto the floor and let them do whatever they wished with him, shot down by the cannons of their fornication. The sheriff saved him, saying something Amos couldn't understand and shuffling off to the apartment. Amos hung on, persuading himself he would wait another heartbeat or two but afraid he would collapse and spill out at her feet. Daisy was slipping sleepily into her robe and with a symbolic shake of her ponytail, moved out of Amos's view. He heard the door close and latch.

Hanging onto the closet door, Amos stepped out on wobbly legs, breathing deeply for the first time in his life it seemed. He tested his legs, taking a halting step with each, his muscles afflicted with excruciating cramps. Then the door from Daisy's apartment opened, catching him helplessly unprotected. He just stood there, completely played out, unable to respond, watching curiously as Daisy's hand reached in, rubbed along the wall, and snapped out the light. The door closed and a deadbolt slammed into place.

His eyes strained to adjust to the total darkness. He paused for a moment. Their odors lingered, her perfume, a lotion, the scent of their mingled bodies. In the still darkness he stretched his body, bracing himself on the table, but relief came slowly. Still frightened, he looked fleetingly for the glass cabinet in the pitch dark but he knew he had to flee instantly. He moved stiffly to the door, opened it quietly, and slipped through like a crippled ghost.

He gathered his forces in the shadowy dayroom, his breathing and heartbeat gradually returning to normal after going through the valley of terror. He wiped his face with the back of his sleeve, scanned the now familiar shadows of the large room, and then hurried to the security of his blankets, thoroughly done in.

The card game had dispersed and Spencer sputtered in a peaceful slumber, unaware of the night's goings-on. Amos laid his aching body gingerly to rest and studied the plaster ceiling, the lath revealed in a darkened pattern like the room's rib cage. He had to think. His plan was based on the process of law, depended on an unimpeded routine execution of that blind process to justice. Would the sheriff's liaison with Daisy short-circuit that trust and destroy his last chance to topple her? Would he simply bury the evidence? Would John Thomas knowingly and willingly circumvent the law to protect not only his lover but his reputation as well as his position?

Another brick was mortared in Amos's mind, walling off all conviction that it might actually work. One point in his favor: the sheriff might not be able to plug the bursting dam even if he tried. Somehow, in the quiet place of his heart where hope and

147

optimism still burned, he couldn't believe that the lawman would be a partner to murder just to pay the tab for his frivolous fornication—unless he loved Daisy. That would be a new game. Now Amos was forced to rely solely on Winston's ability to provide the dynamite that would blow the dam, start the avalanche. He admitted he'd probably never luck on to another chance like the one he'd botched that night.

He couldn't sleep. He thought of Sarah Stark. Why, now, did he recall the time he and Sarah Stark went into Hansen's horse barn. Remember with such vivid detail, the sounds and sights and warm scented air of that Sunday afternoon. She didn't want to; said the barn was too dirty, it was too light, people might come. They both knew there wasn't a soul around for miles, everyone who could move off to the county fair. He persuaded her up the ladder into the hayloft, fussing and balking all the way. He recalled he about gave it up.

Way at the back under the rafters he laid a blanket on the hay. She wanted to leave. He went over and took her by the hand and convinced her to just sit on the blanket with him. They talked. He kissed her, gently. After a while they were lying in the hay, she in his arms, he kissing her until he gathered enough courage to put his hand on her blouse and lightly touch her breast. He smiled now, so many years after, as he remembered his complete surprise and joyous delight when she reached over and started unbuttoning *his* shirt.

From there they fell together into an oceanic rapture. Shafts of sunlight slanted through cracks in the loft wall, illuminating little specks of hay dust drifting around their heads like the golden down of passion. He had already promised to marry Sarah and he wanted to. That winter she broke through the ice on the river and drowned. He could think about her now, without tears, but the scar tissue was there somewhere in his heart. Or soul. It would go with him to his grave. Damn! He forgot Marvin.

He hurried out of bed, painfully reminded of his ordeal in the closet, and haltingly went into Marvin's room, too late. He could smell his forgetfulness over Marvin's bed. Figuring it was useless to wake him, he would apologize later, knowing that the toothless man with the blackjack would catch hell from Roland in the morning. Helpless to prevent it, Amos was sorry. He wanted to see Fern, but didn't have the steam and knew it. He returned to his bunk and tried to sleep. Had Daisy made love before she killed Johnny? Or did she return to the sheriff and play with him in the clinic after she put Johnny to death? What an alibi. To see Daisy as a vulnerable loving woman hadn't changed his resolve by a hair. He knew her in her street clothes and that was the woman he'd smash. He had to look ahead. Maybe Clara would come with the letter in the morning.

Drained physically and emotionally, he slid into a numbing stupor, hovering between consciousness and sleep. He felt like he'd been to bed with a woman himself: Daisy, or Sarah Stark? He thought of the little Gypsy girl on the rooftop, and down in the courtyard he could see Sarah's face, frantic under the clear river ice.

CHAPTER 18

THE HOME BUMPED AND SHOVED and bitched through another day. Amos slept on and off, contemplating ruefully the new turn of events. The sheriff's affair with Daisy only muddied the picture further and Amos's breakfast felt as though it stuck halfway down. It all looked so futile, so impossible. Yet in spite of the murky outlook, Amos chanced upon a crazy notion germinating in his head: that all that had gone before, his entire history, led to and prepared him for this course he would take, giving a renewed purpose to his life. He vacillated between the utter nonsense of that premise and the spine-tingling acceptance.

Sadie unknowingly delivered a note from Fern.

I MISSED YOU. ARE YOU SEEING ANOTHER WOMAN?

Amos relished her humor on this dismal day. He wrote his answer on her note and slipped it back in Sadie's pocket.

YES.

If Fern only knew what woman he *had seen.*

Daisy looked in on them during the day and he felt no uneasiness at facing her after the night's expose´. She'd never know he was like an aging Superman with X-ray eyes who could see right through her sexy underwear.

When he slid out of bed to roam that night, he promised himself that he'd never get himself into a grinder like the infirmary closet again. He slipped into Winston's room first, found the pill where Winston had hidden it, and quietly left without disturbing Winston's composed slumber. Marvin was next on his scheduled rounds, catching him before his bladder let go in some contented dream. Marvin had taken a blow from Roland that morning when Roland found the stinking bed.

Marvin had learned not to drink much after noon to try to cut down on his nightly flooding. But since Amos had been waking him, he drank all he wanted, right up to the time he

retired. It was a disaster when Amos hadn't arrived to jar him out
of sleep. He really unloaded and, in his fury, Roland unloaded
on Marvin. Amos didn't see the blow. But he'd heard Marvin's
outcry and tried to block it out with other thoughts. The accustomed waves of fear rolled down the hall like the incoming surf,
lapping at the door of each room, like a salty brine, leaving little
pieces of bone and skin and blood on the sills, small chunks of
terror.

Marvin stumbled back to his bed a sleepy child after
emptying his tank.

"Did he hurt you bad?" Amos whispered.

Elroy slept evenly in the other bed like a great toad.

"You know what I wish, Amos? I wish I could be my old self
for ten minutes, just ten minutes."

Marvin lay on his bed and looked at the flaking ceiling.

"You don't know it but I used to fight."

"Box? Professionally?" Amos said. He slid a wooden chair up
to the bed and settled on it.

"Nah, just fight. But we'd match up just like the profession-
als. You know, they'd be planned a week ahead of time. I was
good. I never practiced or trained, but I was fast. I fought a lot
as a kid. I could look 'em right in the eye, take their best punch,
and give 'em mine in the wink of a lash. You know, I felt
important then. I was around twenty-five, twenty-six, working
up on the Iron Range in northern Minnesota."

Marvin spoke with a warmth and joy that Amos had never
imagined in him.

"It started with some challenges between different crews. A
loudmouth in our crew, Harper Hunnicutt, was going to do the
fightin'. Hell, a little Polack from Hibbing coldcocked him the
first time he fought. Well, the crew felt like givin' the idea up
when I told them I could've killed that kid from Hibbing. So I
fought a couple of guys and won. I kept winning. Pretty soon
the crew was believin' in me. They thought I could beat anyone
in the world. I fought lumberjacks, fishermen from the Lake,
dock men, railroad workers. About once a week, usually Satur-
day night, someone would show up to fight me. The betting got
pretty high. There would be as much as a hundred dollars goin'

around in bets. My crew loved me, watched over me like I was somethin' special, treated me like a king. I knew a lot of it was just 'cause they was makin' some money off me, but they liked me. I won every fight."

Amos sat spellbound. He'd forgotten they had all lived a full life before they landed at Sunset. He had a hard time understanding some of Marvin's words with his toothless mouth flapping with the excitement of memory.

"Then one day I was to fight a Finn from Duluth. He worked the docks. It was spring, but still lots of snow around. My whole crew rode an ore train over to Duluth with me. The fight was in a warehouse right down on the docks. We had to keep the fights quiet; it was against the law. Lots of flour sacks and wooden crates in this building. The light wasn't too good. The floor was wood, but slippery smooth. When I saw the Finn I got scared. He was way over six foot an' musta weighed two hundred and fifty if he weighed a pound. I was just over six foot but I had long arms."

Marvin stretched out his scraggly arm in the shadowy space above his bed, measuring it against that day in Duluth.

"I was scared shitless. Everyone bet their money and we fought. No time limit. No gloves, not even working gloves."

Marvin wheezed, catching his breath. Amos was trying to project this hard-of-hearing, toothless, bed-wetting old man onto the screen of the 1920's in a waterfront warehouse in Duluth, facing a huge Finnish dockworker.

"What did you do?"

"I fought him. There was nowhere to run." Marvin laughed. "Besides, I couldn't let my crew down, after the way they'd boasted about me. I found out real fast that I couldn't get too close to him and that he was slower than me. I'd hit him and step back, hit him and step back . . ."

Marvin was sitting up in his bed, fighting the fight again.

"He'd swing wildly. I was pestering him more than hurtin' him. I didn't understand what he was saying to me, but I figured it wasn't very friendly. I couldn't hit him in the head. It was like iron, hurt my hands too much. I tried to get at his gut. He caught me once with an uppercut, lifted me right off my feet. I got off the floor as fast as I could and kept moving, but I was all fuzzy for a minute. But, you know, I remember, I wasn't afraid anymore."

Marvin began shadow boxing, snapping his long bony arms out in front of him against that mythical Finn.

"I could hear my crew shouting for me, egging me on. I felt good. My mouth was bleeding. He tried to trip me once. The sweat was pouring off both of us. We fought for fifteen or twenty minutes without a stop. We were both tired, startin' to stumble around, missin' a lot of our punches. He was more worn down than I was. I think he was used to puttin' guys away lots quicker. My crew was hoarse from shoutin'. I got his hands down around his stomach with two or three hard shots, and then I went for his head. I never hit anything so hard in my life, like sluggin' the trunk of an oak. He staggered, his knees was bucklin'. My crew was yelling crazy, and I went a little wild, seein' this big man giving in. I went after his unprotected head. I couldn't feel my hands no longer. He crumpled like a sawed-off fir. God, did he hit that wood floor.

"My crew went wild. The Finn never moved. His boys turned mean. They kept lookin' at each other as if they's wonderin' if they should pay us or kill us. My crew had all it could handle to get the money, get me, and back out of the warehouse. We walked a long way up the shore before we went into a saloon. I think my crew wanted to make sure we didn't run into any of them dock boys. Both my hands was busted up. My nose was broken, a couple ribs, I think. They wrapped up my hands and fed me and took care of me. Bought me all I could drink. We had a wonderful night. And you know, not one of them left for the whorehouse. We had some time together."

Marvin stopped talking. He was back there, in that tavern along Lake Superior with his crew, feeling and smelling and tasting it all again. Amos didn't break in on them. He waited.

"We rode an empty ore train back early Sunday morning. It was cold as a witch's tit. As we huddled together, them all around me, I felt good, like this whole train was running just to take me back to the mine. I was important to them. I made them into something. We was more'n just a diggin' crew. I never felt like that again."

Marvin's face was obscured in the murky room and Amos searched to catch a glimpse of the gladness in it. Marvin had savored that joy through the years, calling on it now in this cheerless night to lift him up once again. They were both quiet for a long time.

"I never had anything quite like that," Amos said, breaking the overbearing silence. "It must be something."

"It is," Marvin said softly. "You're their heart for a little while."

"You must have been a helluva fighter." Amos grinned.

"In my day, in my day . . . That's why it pisses me so to have to sit here and let that fat-assed Roland take free shots at me. Hell, I'd have kicked his ass right up to his jawbone!"

Marvin laughed happily, picturing Roland against him in his fighting days on the Iron Range. He turned to Amos, feeling his nose as if for evidence of the brutal punishment that Finn dealt him.

"Maybe that's all any of us gets," Marvin said. "One time, even if it's only for a few hours, to do something, when we can be important to someone."

"Well, you're going to get another one. Do you still have your pennies, your blackjack?"

"Damn tootin', they're hangin' in a sock inside the sleeve of my coat," he whispered, nodding at the closet and checking to see if Elroy was sleeping. "When we goin' to jump that bastard?"

"Soon. We have to pick the right time so we can get a long way from here before they start after us."

"Emil says he gets the first crack at him when we drag him through the curtain," Marvin said.

"We'll work it out. You take a swing at him the first chance you get. We'll have to get him quickly."

"I'm afraid Elroy will spill the beans to Daisy," Marvin whispered. "We shouldn't have let him in on it."

"It'll be all right," Amos said. "Did you fight much longer after the Finn?"

"Never again. My hands took a long time healing up. I got fired, couldn't work. I hung around awhile, but that was no good. My crew thought they owed me caring-for. I came west.

I guess the Finn won something too. He stopped my fightin'
days for good. But you know, it's kind of funny, but I'm still glad
he never knew that. It would be like he'd beat me."

Marvin lay back into his odorous bed.

"I'm sorry about last night," Amos said. "I was in a bind."

Amos smiled at the understatement, wishing he could
describe to Marvin where he'd been and what he'd seen.

"It's all right. Roland's a goddamn pussycat."

Marvin was comparing Roland to the Finnish dockworker
from out of that vivid past and Roland came up wanting.

"Good night," Amos said.

He crept to the doorway and peeked up the tarnished hall. It
was empty, except for the ghosts who walked there. No, there
was a live one. Winston came scuttling out of his room, up the
hall, sailing into the dayroom to the chorus of "THE COW
JUMPED OVER THE MOON, THE COW JUMPED OVER THE MOON,"
his thin pale legs scissoring under a short bulky nightshirt,
giving more the impression of a stork than a cow. He was shouting the nursery rhyme, waking the house. Amos grabbed his
walker and carried it to the bathroom, waiting to see what this
would bring. It occurred to him in a sudden flush of cold sweat
that he could very well be the cause of Winston's exuberance.
He'd never thought of it before, that his tampering with
Winston's chemistry, as he was, could have obvious side effects
and expose his plot at its root.

Damn, he suspected there would be unforeseen snags, but
nothing this critical. He would have to be more patient, returning a portion to Winston, knowing Winston couldn't be expected
to alternate without screwing it up. It would just take a little
longer. He could hear Winston clearly and figured he was
circling in the dayroom. Should he chance going to retrieve him
before Daisy was aroused? That decision was made for him. He
heard a door bang and Daisy's voice, chewing Winston out. It
was quiet for a minute, a door slammed, then he heard them
coming down the hall. Amos hopped on a toilet.

"THE DISH RAN AWAY—"

"Shut up! I don't want all the crackers up and running
around this hour of the morning. You've been wound up ever

since your little trip down the highway. Now get in your bed and stay there."

Amos couldn't hear the rest, as they marched into Winston's quarters. Amos watched her slippers go by under the curtain, hurrying to catch lost sleep. He waited, to be sure, and in the waiting was entertained by the presumptuous speculation that Winston knew exactly what he was doing. Then he accepted the fact that he was just a silly old fool—sitting on the toilet in the company of his knobby knees—attributing to the indifferent world some magical purposes and meanings that just weren't there. He waited ten minutes, warding off recurring visions of Mildred, twisted and torn in the wreckage of their lives. He held back unsuspected sobs still lurking in his memory, heard the word *killer* whispered somewhere in the shadows of his mind and that finally prompted him to flee to Winston's room.

That son of a gun! He'd done it again. Amos hoped it wouldn't derail the mental track in Winston's shrouded mind by convincing him to accept this button, and any others Amos offered.

"You're doing good, but we don't want to get Daisy mad," Amos said, putting his hand on Winston's forehead and running his fingers through the thin hair on his head, something Amos's father used to do when he was putting Amos to sleep. It still worked, Winston fell asleep in minutes, soothed by Amos's gentle touch. Amos returned to his room hoping that sleep would quiet his own mind and that the sunrise would bring the beaming face of Clara Channing. He got both.

It was midafternoon and Clara was playing her role with the relish of a housewife picked for the lead in the local amateur playhouse. She was lollygagging in Emil's quarters, going on and on about nothing, entertaining Emil with gossip from the outside and swooning over his observations. Amos paced the few square feet of floor space, to the window, around Spencer in his rocker to the door, and back to the window, restraining the impulse to go across and take Clara by the arm and ask her. Did she have the letter? Had she done anything to tip her hand to Daisy? Not knowing was worse than knowing the worst. Amos paced. Clara tittered like a happy bird, while Spencer raised his eyelids, interrupting his dozing with his big Bible resting on his tummy. He wondered what Amos was up to and unconsciously turned up his hearing aid. Finally, Clara left her perch and flew across the hall, alighting at Amos's doorstep.

"Good afternoon, gentlemen. Clara Channing here."

She sang her greeting and gave Amos a mischievous wink. Spencer opened his eyes, nodded groggily, and closed them again, his hands folded over the Bible. Amos sat on his bed, leaving the chair for this coquettish Gray Lady.

"How have things been going for you, Clara?" Amos said.

He smiled nervously and nodded at her bag, unable to join in the fun Clara seemed to be having until he knew where he was at.

"Ooooh, splendidly, just splendidly."

She enjoyed the excitement of the game and they began visiting about insignificant things, chitchat, until Amos was convinced that Spencer had dropped off with his hearing aid turned down. Amos nodded. Clara took the envelope from her bag and slipped it quickly under his blanket. Mick passed by in his unglued wheelchair.

"I didn't know your friend worked for an insurance company," she whispered.

"Yes." Amos held a finger over his lips and whispered, "he gets a good deal on TV's and things through his company. I'll pick something from his letter and the next time you're here you can mail it back to him. Then Daisy will get her surprise."

"Ooooh, this will be such fun." She was giddy with delight.

"One thing," Amos said gravely. "You must never tell anyone—even *after* the surprise—that you did any of this. Only you and I can ever know, promise!"

Amos looked into that trusting face, offering to mother the world, and waited for her thoughtful reply. It didn't come for almost a minute.

"I promise," she spoke solemnly. "Cross my heart."

And she did, as if taking the sacrament. They both eased back and raised their voices in pretense.

"It was good of you to come," Amos said.

"It's so nice to have the snow gone. I can come more regular now."

Clara was beautiful. She took it all so seriously, gullible, sincere, thinking she was cooperating in a cute little surprise for the head nurse from all the men, when she was in fact providing the possibility for their ultimate escape. Amos leaned toward the stout woman and whispered.

"You better go visit someone else, now. It's best if Daisy doesn't see you in here with me at all."

Clara scooped up her bag and departed too quickly, but not even Spencer woke to notice. Amos felt the letter under his blanket and sensed a warm rush of excitement course through his veins. He was closer than he wanted to be.

Marvin had been watered. A variety of snores and whistles drifted through the wing, much like the sounds from a slough on a summer's night: crickets, frogs, nighthawks, owls. He woke Emil.

"Will you do it?" Amos said.

"I will."

"You will have to lie. You will have to swear under oath that Daisy forced you to sign it. That she threatened to hurt you physically if you wouldn't."

Amos tried to impress each word into Emil's memory. There could be so many slipups—more and more people involved, greater and greater the chance for discovery—that at times he almost lost hope. Somewhere in the back of his head he had fostered the strong suspicion that if he didn't stop Daisy, she would go on unheeded for as long as she chose.

"I understand. I will do it," Emil said.

He got out of bed and put on his wire-rimmed glasses. He put his fireless pipe in his mouth, like some historic signing on a victorious field of battle, and he signed the change of beneficiary form in the semidarkness of his stale-aired room. He slid the paper to Amos.

"Thank you, Emil. I'm counting on you."

Amos took the paper and folded it carefully.

"You still think you can ride a dead horse?" Emil said.

"That's exactly what I want her to believe, that I don't have a chance."

"What if I believe it, too?" Emil said and he squinted at Amos over his thick gray mustache.

"No matter, just do what I've asked if you get the chance."

"I don't know what you're up to, but if it will stop her, I will do it with much satisfaction."

The determination in Emil's voice reassured Amos, who was fighting his own second thoughts and ghostlike doubts. He crossed the hall and hid the envelope under the paper liner at the bottom of one of his dresser drawers.

He was very tired when he returned from seeing Fern. He knew she was falling in love with him, and he with her, but he fought it. He knew he might do her more harm than whatever good their tenderness and love would bring. Yet, at this point in life, he knew the moment they had was enough, was everything. They had talked for over an hour and held hands and kissed and snuggled like two kids, forgetting themselves, laughing and sharing moments of joy, oblivious to their surroundings and predicament for a time.

He slipped into bed, knowing it would be a long wait until Clara returned to carry out the mail. A week, ten days, an eternity fraught with indecision, failing resolve and possible bungling. Yet it would come too swiftly, bringing him closer to the time when his courage and backbone would be tested. He would have to be stronger than he had ever been, and he wouldn't know his own fortitude until that time came. For now he must go on with his strategy as though he would be able to carry it out, that nothing would go wrong. Winston, Clara, and now Emil, were being drawn into the ever broadening plot, each with a separate task, each contributing to the whole without knowing what it was. He was afraid.

He listened to the night noises of his companions and imagined he was camping by a mountain lake. He could hear the insects, the frogs, his aching heart, telling him what he didn't want to hear. That he was caught at the edge of the raging current for only a moment, a twig hung up on the brush along the bank, the water pulling and sucking at him, fleetingly held from the certain plunge over the falls just ahead, into the misty chasm, the chaos. And the terror of life gripped him anew: how he was completely helpless and always had been to do anything about his own destiny or the destiny of his loved ones, impotent to protect them in any way from the fickle turn of destruction and death. That after all the bravado and bluster, he was unable to keep them from the kamikaze, the malignant tumor, the icy river, or a wayward bumblebee on a pleasant fall afternoon.

CHAPTER 19

AFTER CONSIDERING MANY, Amos found a safe place to hide Winston's buttons. The posts on Amos's bed frame were round hollow metal with an ornate cap on top. Amos worked the cap off one at the foot of the bed and dropped the capsules down the pipe. Accumulating there, concealed and protected, he could retrieve them simply by pulling the caster and cap off the bottom of the post.

Daisy burst into the room around midmorning, looking more ruffled than Amos had ever seen her.

"Everyone into the dayroom, the TV is on, play games, enjoy each other. Even you, Amos."

She fled to other rooms and Spencer and Amos regarded each other for the explanation that neither of them had. It wasn't Sunday. The traffic began up the hall, Daisy cracking the whip. Spencer wasn't about to be left out. The men shuffled and wobbled and limped to take advantage of this unexpected privilege. Mick, restricting the flow in his antediluvian wheelchair and denim cap, hollered in to Amos.

"Maybe it's bingo."

Winston was trying to go the wrong way in a temporarily one-way corridor. Daisy sidestepped her way, outrunning the field, in a rush to be elsewhere. Amos tucked in his shirt and shoved the walker behind the jouncing procession. Emil stepped out of the lavatory.

"It's the commissioners," Emil said. "They have an unannounced inspection once a year to go over the place, but Daisy has someone on the inside call and warn her. It gives her about a twenty-minute edge."

Amos arrived at the swarming room with the ladies streaming in from the other wing. Like bumper cars at the carnival, Mick and Ruth in wheelchairs were dueling for a spot in front of the television. Ruth was lost in a conversation with some unseen character from her past and Mick was trying to grab her attention. When Fern spotted Amos, she revealed her pleasure with a wide grin and held a spot on the bench next to her for him.

"Isn't this something?" she said.

She nudged him with her shoulder when he settled beside her.

"Have you been through this before?" Amos said.

She nodded and they both watched the circus parade, marching from the railroad yards, Daisy as the baton twirler, high-stepping out in front, and Roland, like an elephant, pushing from behind. Most of the residents were present. Daisy was trying to get them settled, as though they were in the places where they normally spent each day. Emil and Carlos fell right in with it and started a checker game. Effie was hanging onto Mrs. Swanson on the donated sofa, facing the TV. Mrs. Swanson was trying to watch the game show around Ruth, who sat in her wheelchair with her nose on the TV screen. Effie was watching the blackness dance in her mind.

Grace kept calling for bingo, trying to get a ground swell of support for her campaign. She warned anyone who would listen about chewing their food well. Sadie stood in the cotton dress with the flower print that she'd worn forever. It was unbuttoned for a space in the middle, her coarse wool underwear peering out like unwanted children from behind the drapes. She appeared confused by this unscheduled assembly, one of her support socks slumped in a heap around the top of her tennis shoe. Robert sat in the soiled stuffed chair with the book that Amos was reading nights, ignoring Roland's hurried touch-up with a mop and Mae's straightening the piles of dog-eared *Reader's Digests,* frayed paperbacks and finger-worn jigsaw puzzle boxes. Sadie took off down the men's hall, passing Winston coming the other way. They didn't seem to notice each other, like runners in a cross-country race, one of them going in the wrong direction.

The commissioners didn't knock. They were in the building quickly, scattering in all directions. Two peeled off into the kitchen.

"Must have clean wholesome food for the folks," a potbellied man said.

One went down the men's wing, poking his head into rooms. The first, of course, was Robert's, the next Owen's, and Owen could discourage the best-intentioned from going further. One of the officials, a short ruddy-complexioned man, came in and talked with the people. Daisy tried, unobtrusively, to stay within earshot of this one. Amos felt his pulse quicken, his mind leap at the unexpected opportunity. Maybe there would be another way! If he could find a minute to talk with this man, without Daisy's interference, he might convince him about Johnny's death, about this whole cesspool the commissioners were allowing right under their politically expedient noses. Amos's mind raced as he weighed the risk against the consequences. There was so little time to decide. The affable man stopped in front of Robert.

"Do you read a lot?"

Robert looked up with magnified eyes.

"Yes, as long as my eyes hold out."

Robert couldn't remember who this man was but thought he should know and therefore didn't ask.

"Do you have plenty of good things to read?" the commissioner said with genuine interest.

"Oh, yes, plenty. Miss Daws is very helpful when I need a book, very helpful."

Daisy beamed in the background, mingling with the old folks in a pretense of concern and helpfulness. The commissioner, in tailored western suit and polished cowboy boots, moved on to Spencer.

"How do you like it here at Sunset?" He spoke loudly over the game show Spencer was watching.

"Hello. Who are you?" Spencer said as he looked up between his glasses and woolly eyebrows, unconsciously reaching in his shirt pocket and turning up his hearing aid.

"I'm Burt Daniels. I'm a county commissioner. We're just out looking around to see how things are going here, to see how you folks are coming along."

Amos was quickly trying to assess the character of this local politician. Was he the archangel coming on a bolt of lightning to rescue Amos from his desperate plan, a glad-handing charlatan who wanted to be a commissioner to get the road paved to his ranch, or was he among the great majority somewhere in between? Amos knew instantly he was somewhere in between.

Maybe Amos could touch a chord in him, arouse a sense of justice, awaken a sleeping yearning for doing what is right. The man seemed sincere, but he talked down to Spencer, like to a grade-schooler or a simpleton. He probably didn't realize he was doing what everyone did; treating them as though age was synonymous with dementia.

"I'm Spencer Pace. Nice to meet you."

Spencer held out his hand and the two men shook hands politely.

"How do you like it here at Sunset, Spencer?"

Daisy moved around behind Burt Daniels where Spencer could see her eyes riveted on him. He looked at the floor to answer.

"Oh . . . it's all right. I'd rather be home."

Spencer wanted to say more but couldn't muster the courage.

"Yes, I'm sure you would," Burt Daniels said. "How's the food?"

"Not enough salt," Spencer said. "Everything's flat."

Amos sensed that the commissioner was honestly concerned with his responsibility for these people. If he got the chance, he would risk talking to him, though it seemed unlikely with Daisy hovering like his shadow. What should he tell him? The penny ante stuff or the killing? How much could this man believe?

Sadie drifted up to the stranger, black hair bristling out of one of her armpits, her dress threatening to break free from the few buttons that held it.

"I'm going home today," Sadie said, standing like a stump and crowding the man.

"Oh . . . you are?" Burt Daniels said, stepping back a pace. "Where is your home?"

He was trapped against Spencer's chair, ill at ease and searching for an escape. Would Sadie destroy his good intentions and send him looking over the physical plant like the others, instead of visiting with the people who had to endure within it?

"They'll be here soon," Sadie said. "Have you seen them?"

She moved closer, her face in his face. Burt Daniels didn't know what to do with himself. Daisy came to his rescue, leading Sadie away by the arm.

"Come on, sweetheart, we're not dressed properly this morning."

Daisy spoke so warmly to her that Sadie was startled. They disappeared down the women's wing. Amos had his chance.

"Commissioner." Amos waved his hand as to a waiter. "Could we have a word with you?"

Slightly hesitant, the man stepped over to Amos and Fern. What a bust. Sadie shakes him up and then they tell him their preposterous story and try to convince him they're not two melons off the same vine.

"I'm Amos Lasher, this is Fern Knutson. We don't have much time. We'd like to tell you about this place, but we're afraid to."

It sounded sane so far.

"Afraid?" Burt Daniels said and raised his eyebrows.

"Yes. This isn't the sweet old home it appears to be. Your Miss Daws punishes us physically. She allows the male orderly, Roland, to punish the men, kicking them, punching them, whatever he feels like doing."

Amos watched the women's hallway and spoke quickly.

"That's terrible!" Burt Daniels looked shocked.

"No, that's the truth and you should believe us," Fern said in her down-to-earth manner.

"Why haven't you told someone about it?" the commissioner said.

"We have, they don't believe us. They believe her, just like you will."

Amos was angry. He tried to control himself.

"Wait a minute, just a minute here. I'm going to talk with these other folks and if what you say is true, I'll do something about it, you can be *sure of that.*"

Amos had offended him, put him on the defensive, indignation in his voice.

"They won't tell you anything," Fern said.

Daisy sailed back into the dayroom.

"Why not?" Burt Daniels said.

"They're afraid, I'm afraid," Amos said and he took a deep breath. "I saw her kill an old man in his bed, for the insurance money."

Amos held Burt Daniels's sleeve with Daisy four strides away and closing fast.

"She'll punish us for telling you. She'll *kill* me!"

"Are they giving you any trouble, Burt?" Daisy stepped between them and the commissioner. "Did Amos tell you that I'm going to kill him or that we beat him up regularly?"

She smiled, turning loose her captivating charm.

"Well, ah . . ."

"It's all right," Daisy said. "He tells all our visitors that. They're both harmless."

Amos and Fern could hear no more of the conversation over the racket of the TV. They looked at each other and slipped into the quagmire of despair, neither able to hold up the other after this futile, half-witted, miserable mistake. Amos was incensed with himself for implicating Fern.

"I'm sorry I got you into this," Amos said. "I wasn't using my head. I should've talked to him alone."

He knew he had no right to involve her when he had no way of protecting her.

"I'll be all right, Amos, don't fret over it."

She twisted her hands anxiously in her lap.

"I'm getting away from you right now." Amos stood and gripped the walker. "I can only bring you danger and harm."

He shuffled over and settled next to the checker players, stunned by his own stupidity. Daisy led the conscientious commissioner to other, less dangerous, residents. First he chatted with Mrs. Swanson and Effie. Then he spent a few minutes with Marvin and Elroy. If not one other resident of Sunset verifies their accusations, the commissioner will write them off as the screwballs that Daisy suggested they were. Amos prayed that one of them would have the courage to tell him the truth. Daisy roamed, ignoring Fern and Amos, adjusting the television, moving Ruth's wheelchair so that others could see, and introducing Winston—her trump card—to Burt Daniels, interrupting his conversation with Carlos and Emil.

The other commissioners were moseying around the building, appearing and disappearing. One was looking at the infirmary. Amos wondered what the man would think of the wild copulation that went on in there a few nights ago. The building, as antiquated as it was, would always pass inspection. She kept it clean enough and most of the inadequacies could be blamed on the old structure. The commissioners wouldn't press the point, opening the barn door for talk about a new home and where the money would come from, taking it from more popular projects. Daisy's only fear was the truth about how residents were treated, and only Burt Daniels seemed curious about that. One of them looked at his watch, indicating he had more important things to do. They gathered at the end of the room by the kitchen.

"Miss Daws, could we see you a minute?" one of them called.

Daisy hurried gracefully through the room, her bright white uniform proclaiming her command of things. The men swarmed around her like bees with their queen and she led the swarm into the kitchen. Amos slid the walker over to the wall next to the serving window where he couldn't be seen from the kitchen. From there he could catch a few of the words being served up amid the cooking paraphernalia: budget, hours, kitchen help, per capita, rising costs, boiler, annual report. He didn't hear any of the words he had hoped for: abuse, cruelty, boredom, larceny, neglect, oppression, and murder. They gave their salutations and in a flurry were out the door.

A moment later Daisy appeared from the kitchen, a relieved satisfaction on her handsome face. She'd survived the inspection—if you could call it that—for another year. Another year of free reign in Daisy's kingdom. Amos shuddered somewhere deep inside. Burt Daniels would never give mind to what they'd told him, it being only a small fraction of the gibberish he had encountered in his attempt to communicate with the "folks."

"You all just enjoy yourselves for a while," Daisy said.

She ducked into her quarters, probably playing it safe in case one of the commissioners stopped back. Carlos bent down and scavenged a chunk of dirt from one of the commissioner's shoes, Roland left for home, and Fern and Amos looked across the room at each other and exchanged their utter despondency and dread. Fern managed a slight wave; Amos turned for his room.

Supper and the evening went without incident. When it was dark, Amos checked the letter under the liner at the bottom of the drawer. It was still there. He dozed, waiting for the time when it was safe to make his nightly visits. He awoke suddenly, as though he had heard something. He sat up and listened, a cry of pain from some distant place. Holding his breath, he tried to find it again along the shore of the slough in the night air. He couldn't. He breathed again, lay back, and closed his eyes.

He dropped off into a light snooze, then jumped again, sure he'd heard something. He sat up, wide-eyed. Did he imagine it? Was it a call for help from someone out of his memory, someone he had passed by in life? He couldn't discern if it was somewhere in the Home or just somewhere in his head. It was like the shriek of a woman, Ruth or Ida. Oh, God, Fern! Amos threw off the covers and hurried to the hall, listening, craning his senses. Only the frogs and crickets from the neighborhood swamp. He stood there, motionless, for a long time, shivering with the cold. Maybe it was out of his past, far down the road, some human cry that he couldn't name, its sound permanently embedded in his brain cells. It wasn't time to be up and roaming. He went back to bed and dozed fitfully, unconsciously holding back this unseen apprehension.

When he came stealthily into her room, he sensed immediately that Fern was in pain. She was sobbing quietly, squirming slowly under the bedding.

"What's the matter, Fern, are you hurt?" Amos whispered.

"She burned me, she burned me real bad. I didn't know what to do, I couldn't stand it."

Fern tried to whisper, but she broke down and sobbed loudly as Amos took her hands in his.

"She said I had a rash. She put something on me. It was all right at first. Then it started to burn. Oh, Amos, it wouldn't stop. It kept burning, no matter what I did, like my hand was on the burner and I couldn't take it off. I thought I'd die."

He could see the perspiration glistening on her wrinkled forehead; her hair soaking wet. He was incensed. The goddamn turpentine! He held on to his rage, reining a snorting horse that wanted to gallop through Daisy's door and stomp her to death in her own bed. He had considered killing her back in his concocting days but ruled it out for fear he couldn't do it, lacking the strength, and for the rage it would take. At this moment he knew he had the rage but still lacked the strength.

"Go sit in the tub. Fill it with cold water."

"I did. I've been in there for hours. I'm so cold."

Her words rattled on her teeth like icicles that shook out of her mouth.

"Have you any Vaseline?" Amos said.

"No . . . but I think Effie does, for her mouth."

Amos hurried to Effie's room, finding the two women asleep and an uncovered jar of Vaseline on the dresser. He brought the jar to Fern.

"Take a handful of this and rub it on the burn. It will help some."

Amos held the jar. Fern smeared her fingers and reached under the sheet. Amos knew well the searing torment she was going through. She winced, holding back any outcry. She took more Vaseline and covered her tender wound.

"I'm so sorry Fern. I got you into this and I promise you she'll never hurt you again."

Amos was unsuccessfully attempting to restrain his own tears, watching Fern curl up in the bed, shaking violently. He went around to the other side of the bed and kicked off his slippers. He dropped his pants and shirt on the floor, lifted the covers, and slipped in beside her.

"I don't have the warmth I could have given you once, but I still have a little," he said.

He pulled up her flannel nightie and folded his body to hers, his knees against the back of hers, his arms around her fragile, wispy body. He held her firmly, tenderly, and fought back his tears with anger. She wept softly, until there was no more. She whimpered now and then, her shaking subsided, and she fell asleep in his arms, feeling warm and protected and secure. Ruth piped a jagged melody, Ida cursed sporadically down the yellowed hall, and Sadie murmured from her bed.

Amos went over his plan time after time, to scratch and claw for every flaw, driven by his renewed outrage. He knew there were two risks. It would fail if people were careless, and it would fail if people didn't care. But it was the best he could do. He had ransacked his mind for some other scheme, but to his growing dismay, this was always the best he could come up with. When he considered killing her, one other consideration always haunted him. If he succeeded, the truth would never be known about what she was doing here, Daisy would be a martyr, killed by one of the crazies she did so much for, and this place could go on much the way it was now with Daisy's replacement. His way would prevent all of that, if it worked, and that depended mostly on Amos. After the baptism of their tears he felt strong and even brave.

He didn't dare stay any longer, figuring it must be close to dawn. He couldn't afford to get caught now. Trying not to disturb her, he slid out of bed and pulled on his clothing.

"Are you leaving?" she whispered.

"I have to go, I'm sorry. I'll see you soon."

"Thank you, Amos, I'm better now. You know . . ." She took his hand. "I had a very nice figure, once. Now I'm more like dehydrated fruit."

"You're just right, honey. We'll do that again."

He kissed her cheek and tried to stay frivolous, but she pulled him to her lips and kissed him urgently, her instincts instructing her beyond her understanding.

"I love you, Amos. You are a noble man, kind and good and generous."

"Shhh, you lay quiet now. You're just a silly old lady who wouldn't know a noble man from a horse trader like me." He laughed out loud. "I must go now."

"Thank you," Fern said softly.

"For what?"

"For calling me honey."

Amos wasn't aware that he had. He slipped away to the accompaniment of Ruth's symphonic snoring and returned the Vaseline on the way to his bed.

Amos tried to sleep but his mind wouldn't lie down. In theory he had always believed that the seeds of atrocity lie deep in every human heart, but in practice it appalled and sickened him. How did Daisy first nurture those seeds? Did she bilk one of these old people out of a twenty on some shopping trip only to discover how helpless they were? Did she then try for fifty, a small bank account, then a pension check, until she was willing to kill them? Did she justify it in her own heart by rationalizing that they would all die soon anyway? What difference did a week or a month make? She might even be doing the poor wretches a favor.

Maybe someone she had set up for murder actually died of natural causes before she got around to him, saving her the trouble. What frightened Amos the most was this thought: If they knew the truth, would the people on the outside *care?* Would they believe it didn't make a whole lot of difference as well? After all, what have old people got left to do but to die?

He thought of Fern and Carlos and Winston and Grace and Emil, all of them, as dawn blinked its eyelids. He vowed to himself that he would do it, if it only saved these people for a few weeks or months of decent living. Amos had pondered it for a long time. When justice fails, when do we take things into our own hands and act? And what means are forgiven if, in the end, justice is served?

CHAPTER 20

Roland DIDN'T BEAT AROUND THE BUSH when he heard of Amos's conversation with the commissioner. He caught Amos sitting in his chair and nearly split Amos's shin with a vicious kick.

"Look at you," he said, while Amos bent double, cradling his howling shin in his hands. "You're a shrivel-assed old man, dumb, weak, and penniless, and you think you can take us on. You got more spleen than brains."

Right at the moment Amos had more pain than brains and his agony caromed up and down the hall in one short grunt, freezing the men for an instant at whatever they were doing.

"You're a clown. Why don't you look in a mirror?"

Roland left him with those words and a growing lump on his shinbone.

The men were growing a lump of impatience, pushing and pleading to put Gulliver into immediate action.

"Just say the word, and we'll get him," Marvin said as he stood in the doorway to Amos's room. "If I'm dragging Roland under the curtain, how am I going to get the first whack at him?" he whispered.

Daisy held off her impatience, cautious that no more than one be hurting at a time, just in case. Several nights later, shortly after lights-out, she caught Amos in his bed, vulnerable in a nightshirt. She entered the room quietly and was on Amos before he realized what was happening. A shark under the sea of sheets, her hand moved swiftly and struck, seizing his testicles before he could roll away. Amos grabbed her arm to hold off her attack as she squeezed with a crunching force, opening Amos's mouth like a cave, releasing cries of agony from the Stone Age. He popped up, as if he'd been hit with high voltage, and fell back into the mattress, releasing her arm. The pain draining all strength from his body. He screamed, unable to breathe; her torturous grip slammed into the back of his skull. He fainted.

"There, there, Amos," Daisy said with her motherly voice. "It must be your gallbladder. Probably stones. Be patient, it will pass."

Spencer, rigid in the neighboring bed, sensed it wasn't any gallbladder attack, but in the dark he was unable to see what *was* going on. Daisy kept a tight grip with her right hand under the covers, unseen, while she rubbed Amos's wet forehead with her left. Amos came around, trying to remember what was happening, remember where he was.

"Is it getting better?" she said.

Daisy bore down again. Amos shrieked as he folded like a jackknife. He sat right up and fell forward. She wouldn't relent. He couldn't contain the agony and took flight on his piercing wail. The men's wing was awake and breathless, unavoidably partaking in Amos's castration. He saw lights flashing behind his eyeballs, no longer able to suck any breath into his dying body. He fainted again.

"Another attack? Oh, what a shame. It must be stones. Daisy knows how painful that can be. I'll have to put this in your file. I hope you don't have them often."

Amos came back to the present, wishing he hadn't, her face in the wash over his bed. He fought for short gulps of air, his body a hot coal, consuming his sanity. She still held one testicle in her strong right hand. He sat up and fell back dizzily, fighting against the torment shooting through his legs and mainlining into his brain. Daisy leaned close to his face, in case Spencer might have put his hearing aid in.

"You're going to have these nasty little attacks regularly, old man, until Daisy knows you're through stirring up trouble."

"Please, please," he said, "no more, no more."

She removed her hand from under the covers.

"Any more trouble from you, *ever?*"

"No, never, God, no, please. I've had enough. I give up."

He curled like a snail to fight against the remaining screams from his nerve endings, coming at him in waves. She was standing beside the bed as one broke on the shore of his violated groin, slamming his eyes shut with its ferocity, and when he opened them again, as it receded out to sea, she had been carried away by the tide.

Amos didn't dare move; small shooting stars and Roman candles of misery were still going off within. In shock, he had no strength, no energy, no will. His body and mind had been crushed with the testicle, defeated, nearly destroyed. The throbbing ache kept him awake for hours, long after the other men slipped under their blankets of terror and found sleep, each thankful it hadn't been him.

Amos woke, surprised he had slept, fearing he might have gone past Marvin's limit. He got out of bed carefully, unable to straighten up, and walked on shaky legs, feeling as if he'd been hit in the balls with a hockey puck. He reached Marvin in time, then to Winston's room. He was too weak to go any further, doubting that he could make it back to bed. She had crippled him. He knew the physical portion would pass, but would the terror ever be erased from his mind? He pulled himself back into the sweat-soaked sheets, his forces too scattered to fight. He was crushed, a fool to ever think he could beat her. Roland was right. He was a decrepit old geezer without the strength or the cunning to take her on. Who was he kidding? He was no different from the rest of these men, wanting to think that he was, trying to impress himself and these final peers, but she could easily whip him with simple, brutal terror and all its henchmen. No hero after all, he was as scared and helpless and human as any of them. He ran up his white flag and fell asleep under its flutter in the solitary darkness of his night.

The following afternoon Daisy came into the room, catching Amos dozing in his chair.

"There's some mail for you, Amos."

She smiled insidiously, presenting him with the envelope. He recoiled slightly at her appearing, instinctively pulling up his legs and then remembering it was Roland who did the kicking. He accepted the letter and from the return address realized it was from the bank in West Stover. He was petrified, sliding to his doom on the icy slope with nothing to grab hold of to stop his fall. It was over. She would find out everything.

"Open it," she said.

He could see that she already had.

"It's just a bill," he said.

He tried to sound calm with this semi-annual billing for his safe deposit box.

"It looks like we have a safe deposit box, doesn't it," she said with a smugness in her voice.

"They put a few things in it for me when I was laid up in the hospital."

He hadn't successfully covered the trembling in his voice.

"Well, I'm going to run into town in a few minutes. You get dressed up, and we'll just go see what's in our little box."

She took the pink statement with her. Amos didn't know what to do. He could stand no more gallbladder attacks. He had to keep calm. Think. Maybe they wouldn't allow her into the vault with him; maybe he could find a moment to duck it away. He had to find a way to keep her from seeing it. He searched the rioting confusion in his mind as he put on his good suit. It was getting baggy on him. When you're a child, you outgrow your clothes. When you're old, your clothes outgrow you. He'd always feared that some fluke would pull the plug on his shaky ship, and now the fluke had shown its face.

He took the safe deposit key he'd concealed behind the cardboard of a photo in his cigar box and dropped it into his empty pocket. He was knotting his tie when she appeared in the door looking vivacious, a pink spring coat over her uniform.

"Come on, Amos, we don't want the bank to be closed. Do you have your key?"

Amos nodded and followed her up the hall with the walker. The men gawked from their doorways. Just as they turned into the dayroom, Amos's stomach knotted, heaving under his rib cage. Clara was coming out of the women's wing and heading their way. She looked at Amos without any sign of excitement or preference, passing on her way to the men's ward.

"Can you wait just one minute, I want to get a sweater," Amos said.

"It's nice out today," Daisy said.

"I'll hurry, I'm cold."

Amos started down the hall, dreading the negative command he was sure would come. It didn't. He ducked into his room, took the envelope from under the paper liner, and waited. Clara was lingering in Robert's doorway and she sensed the dilemma accurately. She glanced back up the hall and glided into the room. Amos slipped the letter down into her bag, blocking Spencer's view, and kissed her on the cheek. He pushed her gently, and she scurried to Emil's room, tittering. Amos started back. The sweater! He turned and grabbed his gray button-up and hurried toward his certain doom. Daisy was waiting at the open door, rapping her fingers on the hardwood, itching to look into Amos's treasure chest.

Amos stepped out into the March sunshine and it over-whelmed him: the fresh air, the view, just to be outside. He had forgotten what a joyful thing it was to be alive at a moment like this. Daisy put the walker in the trunk, and they dashed for town in her shining red Mustang, blowing slush off the road and exploding through puddles. He guessed she found enjoy-ment in driving very fast. So overcome with the experience, Amos almost forgot where they were headed. He feasted on the mundane sights that people on the outside never seem to notice. His spirit soared. Maybe this would all work for the best. Clara had the letter. The last step was under way. It would be in the mail today. Yes, the more he thought about it the more he realized that this might turn out better than he had planned.

Crows and magpies still swarmed over the dump. He won-dered what kind of a winter they had had. He remembered how he felt the last time he passed here, and now he was living out a drama he never dreamt possible. It was totally inexplicable. As he absorbed the daily life around him on the road, he examined this fantastic pilgrimage he found himself undertaking. Riding along in the sunshine it seemed too remote to believe. He thought about growing old. Things cool down: ambition, aggression, sexual drives. But one thing seems to remain constant, never changing: the temptation to the heroic.

They moved through the suburban traffic of West Stover as normally as if it were eternity. Amos was refreshed to see people of all ages: walking, shopping, visiting, children running, dogs yapping, a beer truck honking. It was fresh air blowing into his spirit. The world was alive, and he wanted to be a part of it for whatever days remained, to rejoin the human fellowship he'd always taken for granted. It was incredible, absurd, the Home so close to this, yet galaxies away. His comrades could be living like this, in the mainstream of life, for a while longer.

Daisy found a space near the front of the bank and parked. Amos stepped out and stood by the trunk. She came around and offered her arm.

"The walker?" he said.

"You can just hold on to me," she said.

Shrewd. Helping him walk was her ticket into the vault.

"Hello, Daisy, beautiful day," an employee at the bank greeted her as they crossed the high-ceilinged lobby.

"Hello, Fred."

Daisy guided Amos back to the vault.

"Hi, Jane. Amos Lasher would like to get into his safe deposit."

"Sure . . . Amos Lasher . . . Amos Lasher."

The bank clerk thumbed through a small file drawer. Amos brought the key from his pocket and slid it across the oak desk. She pulled the card.

"Would you sign this, please?" the young girl said.

Amos signed, noticing how scribbled his signature had become. The clerk marked the time, and the three of them went into the huge round vaulted door. When she had opened the small steel door and pulled the thin drawer partially out, she left Daisy and Amos to whatever mystery the green metal held. And of course, it was no mystery at all. It was Amos's life insurance policy.

"Well, well, well. Look what we have here," Daisy said. "I wonder why we didn't tell Daisy about this." She allowed a satisfied smile to take root and grow on her face. "We'll just take this along with us."

Daisy slid the policy into her purse, flipping through the other papers in the box: Amos's will, government documents from Greg's war years, several newspaper clippings of historical moments in their lives, including one of the accident, birth certificates, a marriage license. Amos smiled on the backside of his face. She was helping him, unwittingly adding a piece to the evidence that he hadn't counted on. She locked the little door, removed the key, and they started out of the bank.

"I'll hold onto the key for you," she said.

"Why don't you sign the card? Then you could get things for me," Amos said.

She paused and looked at him, suspiciously, he thought.

"Good idea. I've done that with several of the residents."

They walked back to the safe deposit desk and Amos put his weight on her to contribute further to her belief that he needed a walker.

"I'd like to have Daisy . . . er, Miss Daws, sign my card so she can get into my box for me." Amos smiled at the girl.

"All right, Mr. Lasher."

She found the card, handed Daisy a pen, and pointed out where she should sign. Now he had *Daisy* doing the signing.

"You sure do a lot for your people, Daisy," the bank clerk said. "I think it's terrific."

"Oh, it's nothing. Someone has to take care of the poor darlings."

Daisy tossed her hair back and headed for the door, Amos dragging along beside her, both of them delighted with the outing to the bank. Amos stopped on the sidewalk and looked up Main.

"Could we walk around for a minute?" he said.

"I have to get back."

"Just for a few minutes?"

"I have to get back," she said and led him to the car.

Amos slid in with his aching heart. To taste this scene and then have to leave it, to go back to that bleak captivity, was pulling him apart. He hadn't chosen this fight with her, any of it. He wanted to jump out of the car and run on his scrawny little legs, faster than Daisy, back into life, and grasp it while he had the chance. Amos sagged in his seat—as the town disappeared in the rearview mirror—riding the red sports car back to the dump. He felt tattered, torn, shredded.

"Twenty-eight thousand, huh?" Daisy said. "You're worth more than I thought. Who's the beneficiary?"

"Mildred."

"But she's dead. That money should go to the living."

"My grandson in Ohio," Amos said quickly.

"Amos, Amos, you surely don't want any more of those nasty gallbladder attacks. We'll take care of the beneficiary one of these days. Remember, Amos, it's your gallstones."

She pulled around a pickup overloaded with hay bales and laughed with self-assurance.

"Speaking of your gallstones, what's this I hear about the clever little plot you're brewing?"

She glanced over at Amos as he gulped for words.

"Plot?"

"Yeah, you know? How you and the men are going to overpower Roland and escape. Something with the quaint name of Gulliver."

They were passing the dump. Some gulls were in, fighting the magpies and crows for the daily servings. A red-tailed hawk sat in a cottonwood, watching them squabble over the bits of garbage, deciding which was the plumpest for his taking.

"Oh, that," Amos said with intense relief. "You certainly don't take that seriously, do you? Roland could handle the whole men's wing with one hand tied behind him."

"The men seem to take it seriously," she said.

"That's the whole point," Amos said. "They needed something to think about. Something to invest their time in, to look forward to."

"And you provided them with something," she said.

"It's harmless. They needn't know it's only a fantasy."

"You don't think Roland is in danger then?"

She turned to him and smiled.

"Hardly."

"I wonder what Roland would do if he knew you were plotting against him with the men. Maybe I'll inform on you the next time you get out of line."

She rode her confidence with conceit. The gravel flew out behind the sleek machine as she poured the gas to its powerful eight-cylinder engine. She had everything going for her. Like the powerful hawk in that tree, she could take Amos whenever she chose. But deep within himself he stood firm. Amidst the tempest that was raging around him and within, he found a small center of peace. There he smiled, he leaped with joy. *He would do it.*

With his back to the town, the Sunset sign hanging cockeyed just ahead, he resolved that he would not look in the rearview mirror again. He watched Daisy until she caught him at it and the smile on his face seemed to bring a brief cloud to the bright sky that was hers.

He got out of the car and she took the walker from the trunk. Toward that awful building, his step did not falter.

CHAPTER 21

Winston was doing his part cleverly and with dedication, only losing the button a few times. It had been almost a week since Clara mailed the letter. Amos sensed he was close. He also knew he was showing the strain. His emotions pulled in so many directions, overwhelmed his body and flooded his brain. He had a newfound love for life and a fresh compassion for those people who, through some coincidence of fate, walked this last journey beside him. He fought to keep the lostness and fear out of his face and voice.

"You have a visitor, Amos," Roland called on his way past the door. "Daisy wants you in the dayroom. She's pissed."

Amos couldn't function for a minute. A visitor? It couldn't be Clara; they'd let her come to the room. Someone from the company! Oh, God, he never thought they'd be that efficient, not for his piddling policy. Now Daisy would figure it out. Reluctantly Amos stood with defeat in his saddlebags and pushed his way up the corridor. He didn't notice the men along the way, overwhelmed by this turn of events that seemed too harsh to accept.

He slogged into the dayroom to find Daisy visiting serenely with a young man. They turned as he approached; the young man stood, beaming.

"Grandpa?"

The stranger's face struggled to conceal his shock at the change in Amos since their last meeting. Amos pushed the metal frame closer and looked searchingly into his youthful face.

"Scott?"

"It's me, Grandpa. It's been a long time."

"Amos is a model patient," Daisy said, "though he gets a little mixed up at times."

Daisy sat there like a stump with no indication of leaving.

"Sit down, Grandpa, here."

Scott held Mrs. Swanson's favorite chair for him. Amos sat carefully, stunned by Scott's miraculous appearance.

"Miss Daws doesn't want me to stay too long. I guess you have a lot of flu going around, but I have a surprise for you, Grandpa."

With sandy hair, a boyish face and a fair complexion, young Scott turned to Daisy.

"Could I talk to my grandfather alone for a minute, Miss Daws?"

"Oh, yes. Excuse me. I was—"

"That's all right," Scott said, "I appreciate your help."

Daisy glided off into the kitchen with what Amos recognized as a gripping attack of utter panic. Like an angel out of heaven, Scott had broken into this boot camp to the gallows, and there wasn't a damn thing Daisy could do about it without causing grave suspicion. The unheard of had happened. Daisy's plaguing nightmare, the unknown relative who suddenly appears at the door. As the possibilities dawned on him, Amos began to awaken to the miracle.

"I tried to call you several times, Grandpa, but they said you couldn't come to the phone. So, I decided to fly out and tell you. I'd have to come anyway."

Scott was uneasy yet happy, his freckles shining planets in the sunlight of his wide smile.

"There isn't any flu going around here," Amos said.

"There isn't?"

"She doesn't cotton to having visitors."

Daisy came back through the dayroom and went into her quarters, trying to appear preoccupied. Amos considered telling Scott about Johnny and the rest but felt it would be futile. How could he believe such a story, and even if he did, what could Scott do about it?

"I don't know how to say this, Grandpa, but Ellie and I have talked about it a lot. I know I haven't kept track of you and Grandma like I should have, with living so far away and the job and the kids and all. I was always going to write and would never seem to get around to it."

"No need to apologize, Scott. I know how it is."

"I realize I don't even know you, living back in Ohio since I was a small boy, but Ellie and I were talking. You're our family, and leaving you in this place all alone, well, it just isn't right."

Scott was losing control, tears welling in his eyes.

"What I'm trying to say, Grandpa, is that we've just moved into a nice big old house in the country. We have plenty of room, I'm doing great with the company, and we want you to come and live with us."

Scott spoke rapidly, padding the offer.

"There are fruit trees and a huge garden and birds and the kids would love to have you there. Ellie's a great cook. What do you say? How would you like to come back to Ohio with me *right now?*"

Scott watched Amos's face intently for every hint of the response to come. Amos was flabbergasted. He turned and looked out the window at the coming spring, trying not to flinch from the thunderclap Scott had just delivered. His mind was awash, his legs quaking, and he had to be steady now. An alternative he thought was forever gone to him fell into his lap. Scott could take him, that minute, out of that place for good, and Daisy would be unable to stop them. It was too much, this gigantic choice that seemed to be no choice, only the getting up and going. Winston strode into the room with his camellike step and his tennis racket, wearing only boxer shorts. He stopped and looked at the stranger and Scott withdrew slightly. Then Winston slogged on down the women's wing.

"You play tennis here?" Scott said.

"I can't go with you," Amos said. "It's mighty fine of you and Ellie; you don't know what it means to me that you want me, but I can't go."

"Why not, Grandpa?"

Scott was crushed. All the way from Ohio he could hear Grandpa's whoop! over the invitation.

"I have something I have to do."

"Can't you do it in Ohio?" Scott said with naked disappointment in his voice.

"No."

"Can't someone else do it for you?"

"No," Amos said softly, "I don't think so."

"What is it, Grandpa, that you have to do?"

"I can't explain it."

"I don't understand. I thought—"

"Neither do I," Amos said, shaking his head slightly.

"Gosh, Ellie and the kids will be so disappointed. They're already fixing up your room, even your own bath."

The scene ripped at Amos's heart, visualizing what had become only a far-fetched fantasy, now held out to him for the taking.

"I'm sorry to disappoint all of you, Scott."

Daisy emerged from her apartment and crossed to the men's wing.

"Are you sure, Grandpa, absolutely sure. You could come with me right now. We'd be home tonight."

"I'm sure."

Amos fought off the voices within, clinging to his resolve until Scott went out the door and Amos would be unable to call him back. Inside, he was scattered like dead leaves in November's wind: whirling, failing, trying to find footage. They visited about the family, old times, the accident, Grandma, Amos's hip and slow recovery, where Scott's children were in school, who broke an arm riding her bicycle, and Amos held onto his heart like fragile crumbling pastry.

"Listen, Grandpa, maybe you need more time. I could stay over. Maybe tomorrow you'd feel differently."

"No, nothing would change by tomorrow."

"I shouldn't have surprised you with it like this. We could come back in the summer and get you, on our vacation. That would be fun for the whole family. A trip to get Grandpa. What do you think?"

"Yes, that sounds good. Maybe next summer."

"Listen, I didn't bring you anything because I thought you'd be coming back with me. Is there anything you need? How about money, or something I could get for you in town?"

"No, thank you, Scott. It's nice of you to ask. Just having you come and being able to see you is wonderful. I think you look more like your dad than your mother. But I see the Lasher in you, your eyes, the set of your chin. It's nice to know that some of the Lasher goes on."

"I think she wants me to go now, Grandpa. We'll write. And you let us know about summer. I can get off just about any time with a couple weeks' notice. It would be a wonderful trip for all of us. Can you ride in a car all right?"

"Just fine. I was in town with Miss Daws just the other day."

"Good."

Scott stood. He hesitated awkwardly for an instant, then bent and hugged Amos firmly. Amos held onto him for a moment, imploring his arms to refuse to let go, begging his stubborn heroism to forfeit the game and just cling to his grandson all the way to Ohio. Scott released him and Amos followed suit.

"Take care of yourself, Grandpa."

"I will, I will, and you take care of that family. Bring them my love, and thank them for wanting me."

"I will," Scott said and he started to back away.

"Scott. Did you tell Miss Daws that you were going to offer to take me home?"

"Yes, I did."

"What did she say?"

"Nothing. I think she was kind of surprised."

"Please tell me. What did she say?"

Amos stood by the walker, looking into his grandson's eyes.

"Well, she said it would be very difficult to take care of you, that you needed . . . ah, watching or something."

"I can imagine what she told you. And you were still willing to take me?"

"Of course, Grandpa."

Amos looked down quickly and set his jaw against the flood welling within him. He only had to hold on a minute longer, then the options would be gone. He took several short breaths and looked back at his grandson.

"Thank you, you're a good one. Don't forget to take a fat kid with you."

"Yeah, Grandpa, you too. Mom told us about that. She was always saying that, and I didn't know what she meant for a long time. You too, Grandpa, take a fat kid with you."

As Scott's image faded behind the outside door, Amos sagged into the chair and sat motionless, listening to something from within condemning him for his stupidity. Daisy came into the room immediately.

"Is he coming back?" she said with an uncharacteristic note of fear.

"No."

"I thought he wanted to take you with him?"

"He must have changed his mind. Didn't say anything about it to me."

Amos swallowed the heartache that was choking him.

"Oh." A mild satisfaction arose in her voice. "Maybe I misunderstood. He's going back to Ohio?"

"Yep."

"How nice of him to come and see you."

Daisy headed for the kitchen, relieved and pleased with her subtle persuasion of another do-gooder relative. Their concern wilts quickly when they see the picture she paints of what caring for these old people would be like. It's like having a two-month-old baby again, helpless, drooling food and messing its pants, only now it weighs a hundred and ten pounds or so.

"Yes, how nice it was of him to come," Amos said.

Amos closed his eyes. He could see a jetliner flying back to Ohio, Scott on his way home, with an empty seat beside him.

CHAPTER 22

Daisy gathered her children for bingo and another frivolous evening. She was smug, elated at the way things were turning out. Emil was the big winner, and you could smell Elroy's betrayal on his breath. After the party Amos sneaked into Fern's bed and they snuggled, imagining they were young again under the cloak of darkness. Though he left his clothes on the floor and took pleasure in Fern's warmth and touch, Amos couldn't completely eliminate the ambiguous dread rustling around in his mind. She unhesitatingly caressed him in the most intimate ways, embarrassing him that he couldn't get hard; but she made nothing of it and they talked, unable to consummate the love they both felt.

"That was the biggest surprise of my life," Fern said. "What a wonder it is between a man and woman. Never was taught a thing."

"The biggest surprise of my life was that I got old," Amos said.

He thought of Sarah Stark and recalled Mildred's cold attitude toward sex. They clung together for several hours and when he left, Fern told him that she loved him as much as she'd ever loved anyone, then added that at least they didn't have to worry about getting pregnant. Owen was laughing softly when Amos passed his room as if he heard Fern's joke.

Like a sailor who missed his shore leave, Roland swabbed out the room with a minimum of mercy and an extravagance of disinfectant. Amos and Spencer perched on their beds, giving him a wide berth, while he pulled Amos's suitcase from under the bed and swung the mop further than he usually bothered. Out popped the bedpan, greening with philodendron. He left his mop and dragged Carlos into the room, shoving the bedpan up under his nose.

"Now, how do you suppose the weeds got started in this crapper, wetback?"

Carlos held onto the bedpan to prevent Roland from shoving it into his face.

"You know what we do with the contents of a bedpan. We flush it. Let's go flush it together."

Roland pushed Gandy Dancer roughly toward the bathroom. Spencer and Amos remained on their beds, listening for the flushing water. Shoved roughly by the bully, Carlos stumbled back into the room with the wet, empty bedpan and, following Roland's command, slid it back under Amos's bed. Carlos stood meekly by the window while Roland finished mopping the room. The room was disinfected, all living forms eliminated. Roland stuck the mop in his bucket and rolled it out into the hall. Carlos waited a moment, then followed slowly toward the hall. Behind his back, gently held in the cup of one hand, a slip of philodendron.

Spencer pointed it out to Amos, who was already laughing, and they both whispered, for fear of betraying the mad-dog gardener. Amos rejoiced at the little man's dogged heart.

"He lifted that right from under Roland's nose," Spencer said, sliding off his bed and moving his rocker where he liked it. Spencer settled in his chair with his Holy Writ and shook his head. "Right under his bossy nose."

Spencer thumbed blankly through the pages. The pine scent was overpowering. Spencer began to weep. Amos waited. Spencer sobbed until there was no more. He looked at Amos.

"I get so depressed I can't go on. I always got down, but I went on. I could always tell myself that there was a chance things would change . . . get better. But now I know there's no chance and I can't breathe I'm so down. All my chances are *gone!* There isn't any reason for anything."

Spencer looked at the page without seeing. Amos didn't speak, but he knew Spencer had put his finger on it, the bleakness of their life here. There was no longer any chance, for anything. They had to have the hope that tomorrow could be different, better, changed; that there was still the remote possibility that something would break in on them, something happen that would redeem them. In this wasteland where miracles don't occur, their hope had been ground to ashes by the ironfisted hand of time and blown away in the arid winds of indifference.

But a miracle *did* happen. Amos had that miraculous chance that only angels could arrange. Scott appeared! And what did Amos do? He turned his back on it, this gift from God, cast it away. Was he insane!

Amos took his cigar box and rummaged through the bits and pieces of memory, stopping at the recent photo of the great-grandchildren in Ohio. It would be something to see these little people who carried his seed in their bodies into the future, on and on. Daisy popped into the room, cheerful and sunny.

"Here's your check, Amos."

Amos laid his box aside and signed the check without hesitation, handing it back to her promptly. She smiled and cocked her head, studying him a moment, this old man who had fought her stubbornly awhile.

"I think you're going to turn out smart," she said.

She was charming, he had to admit. She patted Spencer on the head on her way out, asking him how the Bible reading was going. Amos wished he could see into her mind as nakedly as he had seen her body. How long did she plan to keep him alive before cashing in on his life insurance? He had her where he wanted her. She was confident—with the gallbladder attacks and all—that he had quit. He grinned inside and trembled slightly at knowing how terribly misled she was.

Winston came striding into the room, as if on stilts.

". . . LADY UPON A WHITE HORSE."

He stopped abruptly at Spencer's chair and stared. Spencer glanced up at him and went back to the page. Winston stood motionless in his baggy attire, quiet, watching. Spencer's aggravation grew steadily.

"What do you want?" Spencer said. "Go on, get out of here."

Spencer waved his hand in a shooing gesture and went back to simulated reading. Winston shifted his weight from foot to foot, slowly swaying like a tall tree.

"Will you please get out of here!"

Spencer peered over his glasses and tipped the book against his round belly. Amos watched them carefully, trying to read the signs. Winston waited in his skeletal frame, his soiled trousers, one shoe untied. He bore down on Spencer with an unrelenting gape, pleading from behind his haunted eyes.

"He wants you to read something to him," Amos said.

"What? That's utter nonsense. He wouldn't understand a word of it. This isn't for children or the simpleminded."

"Are you sure?" Amos said.

"Look at him," Spencer said. "He has absolutely no idea of what's going on around here."

"How do you know?" Amos examined his own narrow-mindedness.

"Can't a man read his Bible in peace? This isn't some nursery rhyme, you know. Go away. Get outta here! Go look for Ginger."

Spencer was shouting. Amos came over and took the Bible from Spencer's lap, thumbing through it until he found what he was searching for. Spencer watched with astonishment, as Amos smiled into Winston's gaze.

"This is what Jesus said."

Amos read from the heavy book.

"ARE NOT SPARROWS TWO A PENNY? YET WITHOUT YOUR FATHER'S LEAVE NOT ONE OF THEM CAN FALL TO THE GROUND. AS FOR YOU, EVEN THE HAIRS OF YOUR HEAD HAVE ALL BEEN COUNTED. SO HAVE NO FEAR, YOU ARE WORTH MORE THAN ANY NUMBER OF SPARROWS."

Amos closed the Bible and regarded Winston. The mailman stood silently, with an abandoned countenance, thinking, as though he were still hearing the words. Then he turned and marched into the hall without a sound. Amos handed the book back to Spencer and went to the window. He couldn't catch sight of a sparrow anywhere.

Voices grew from a murmur to an uproar of shouts and laughing. Amos walked to the door and looked up the hall. Ruth had come down the wing in her wheelchair and Mick, going the other way, had tried to pass her in his. Somehow they met just right, jamming their inside wheels together, wedging the outside wheels against the walls. They were stuck, without the strength to back out of it. Robert watched from the far side, while Elroy and Carlos were hooting and deriding from the near side.

"Come on, Mick, gun it!" Elroy shouted.

Ruth was rapidly talking to herself, trying to ignore the predicament.

"He says if we don't get rain the whole crop will jes burn up and there ain't nothin'—"

"Get that rig outta my way," Mick shouted but she never even looked at him. Sadie came out of the dayroom and down to the logjam.

"I'm going home," Sadie said, "they're coming for me."

"Shut up, you goddamn cracker!" Mick shouted at her.

Marvin and Emil came up the hall to watch and Spencer leaned out around Amos with mild curiosity. Winston marched out of his room and up to the disabled wheelchairs. It was fast becoming the social event of the year. Arguments broke out as to who was at fault and how to solve the deadlock. Winston pushed on Mick's chair, trying to shove it through, only jamming it worse. Nell came around the corner with supper. She took Robert's tray into his room and pushed the cart up to the crowd.

"Move the wheelchairs," Nell said matter-of-factly, "I have to get through here." She looked at them with a vacuous expression.

At that instant, Ruth shrieked with an inhuman sound and attacked Mick. She clawed and scratched at his face and grabbed him by the throat. Mick tried to fend her off, but she was the stronger of the two.

Amos hurried to the jam without his walker and pulled and wiggled Mick's chair. Emil joined him immediately. Nell pulled on Ruth's chair, struggling to break it free. They came unwedged, but Ruth clung to Mick, coming out of her chair and dragging him to the floor with her. Ruth kept insanely attacking, clawing, howling with an unearthly wail. Emil and Nell each took one of her arms and hauled her back into her chair. The instant she settled in her chair, she started babbling to herself, as though nothing had happened. Mick's face was bleeding. Nell pushed her cart through, and the men dispersed to their rooms for supper. Amos fetched a wet washcloth and wiped Mick's torn face.

"She's a goddamn devil, a witch," Mick said. "She tried to kill me." Mick spit as he raved. "She's a goddamn batty freak. They ought to keep her in a cage."

"She's us, Mick," Amos said and he dabbed at Mick's torn skin. "And they do keep her in a cage."

"She almost scratched my eyes out," Mick said. "Do you think we should try that when we jump Roland? He'd never get by that roadblock."

"If you turn your wheelchair sideways, I'm sure that will be enough. Hold still."

Amos realized he'd need some tape.

"When are we going to do it?" Mick whispered. "The men think we should right away. They're afraid Elroy will rat on us. We're ready. There's no sense waiting any more."

"It will be soon, Mick, I promise you."

Daisy approached the scene of the accident, saw the victim, and did her nursely duty.

"I'll take care of him," she said. "I see you're getting along without your walker."

"I used the wall when I saw Mick was in trouble," Amos said.

Daisy turned and wheeled Mick up the hall, leaving Amos braced against the sullied plaster.

"You'd better get to your supper," she said.

Damn, he hoped she wouldn't make anything of him without the walker. He met Nell in the doorway of the room; Spencer was already eating. Their eyes met for a moment and Amos blocked her retreat.

"Do you know what's going on around here, Nell?"

She twisted her blotchy face with the question, her eyes darting as though the answer were written on the inside of her eyeballs.

"Yes . . . I'm bringing the suppers."

She stood thinking, her tongue watching at the side or her mouth.

"Do you like it here, Nell?"

Amos felt foolish, knowing his first question was totally inappropriate.

"No."

"Why do you work here then?"

"My ma makes me, sez it's the only work I can get. Sez I ain't good fer nuthin' else."

Nell didn't change her expression, no hurt showed through her enduring mask, but Amos sensed it was buried there somewhere.

"I'm glad you're here, Nell. You do a good job. You're a bright spot for all of us."

Amos reached out and squeezed her arm, and Nell followed his hand with her eyes as if no one had ever touched her before. Her expression didn't change much, a slightly larger smile than the one she perpetually wore, but her whole being lit up, took on an intangible glow. She returned to her cart, walking, it seemed, with a lighter step.

"Stewed tomatoes," Spencer said. "I remember when we had our garden down along the Snake. We grew tomatoes you wouldn't believe." Spencer filled his mouth. "We raised cucumbers that would pass for watermelon. Potatoes, gracious. You ever do any gardening, Amos?"

"Yes."

Amos's mind darted back to the garden on the ranch, Greg more interested in saving worms than weeding, having to finish a certain number of rows before he could go fishing. Amos held the image of him, a small tyke in baggy clothes, wearing one of Amos's old straw hats, fishing all day in that grubby outfit. The point in the river where Greg spent hours, like a figurine: wide-brim hat, pole projecting out, bare feet, still there on the screen of his memory. It was like a trigger to the nightmare.

Amos had dreamed the dream too many times. The Zero, diving at that point, a Japanese kamikaze. But the warplane was flown by a small Japanese boy with a fishing net. No matter how many times Amos tried to yell and warn Greg, he never heard, and the two little fishing boys were destroyed in the flames. Amos thought about that Japanese pilot, losing the war and taking the only option left for him. But what destiny brought Greg into the predestined arc of annihilation? Spencer was talking cantaloupe, Amos was struggling kamikaze. Amos ate the stewed tomatoes and wrestled to stay back there in his past with those he had loved and lived beside, the agony bittersweet, the nostalgia comforting, but life was ahead, and he turned to face the hard stone.

The day faithfully dissolved into night, and when it was safe, Amos sifted into Winston's room to collect the rejected capsule, then to rouse Marvin and point him toward the urinal, muttering and groggy. Marvin was Amos's choice to be the last piece of the puzzle, the final detail, if only he could convince Marvin to do it. Amos figured he had to have physical marks, bruises, something to trigger investigation.

Amos had tried, God knows, to find another way. Maybe it was his age, his mind no longer clear and sharp. Maybe there were dozens of better, easier ways of getting it done, but he couldn't imagine them. He wanted to ask Marvin tonight, relieving this last doubt in his mind, one way or the other. But he didn't dare, leaving Marvin too much time to think about it, to lose his nerve, or to spill the beans. Amos would wait until the last minute and just spring it on him, rehearsing what attempts at persuasion he would use on the old miner.

Marvin slogged back to bed in his socks and nightshirt, thanking Amos several times and nestling into his dry odorless bed, confident that he would receive no blow in the morning. Amos showered, standing under the hot water as long as he chose, then went to Fern's tender bed. He casually asked to borrow a needle and after convincing Fern he should do his own mending to protect her from Daisy, she gave him one, the last item for his fated errand.

"Poor Grace," Fern said, "she lost her husband two weeks after she was married. Choked to death on a piece of beef right at the dinner table."

"Oh, God, that's why—"

"Yes, that's why she annoys everyone, always warning them to chew their food."

Amos caught his breath.

"If we really knew a person's story," Amos said, "we'd probably give up all our judging and knocking each other."

"My Tom stuck by me all those years and I'd sometimes wonder why," Fern said. "I think he was lonely, hoping for something that'd never come, something I couldn't give him. He never let on, but I'd see a look in his eye, and I knew there were things missing for him. He'd be so far away I couldn't touch him, but he never said boo. He always was kind and considerate, tried to make life good for me. Then things got better our last years together, like it had passed, and he was content. Or he'd given up."

"There's always been something I couldn't give to those who were close to me," Amos said, "but I could never nail it down, never name it. I love to be with friends, family, to give and share and enjoy the company of those around me. But I withhold something. I don't understand what, but they feel it, or lack of it. I have a dark side, a crippling, a poison that prevents me from loving people the way they need. I think some people thought I was a cold bastard."

"Oh, Amos, why do we hurt ourselves so, cut our own hearts until there's only scars and crippling. Why can't we love each other without getting so fouled up?"

She paused; Ruth snored.

"I never could have children. I brought up adopting, but Tom would have none of it. Later on, he let me take a few foster children from time to time, but only temporary. I wanted to keep each one of them. Lord, when they'd go back I'd just die a little. Another would come and I'd have hope again. Then we had this scrubby little boy, Eddie Swisher, and I could see Tom breaking down. That boy would rather fish than eat, and Tom loved to fish. The two of them got to sneaking off together, and I was pleased as punch. The boy hooked Tom and tangled up his heartstrings."

They heard a sound in the hall. They held their breath and listened. Nothing. Fern went on in a whisper.

"Well, one morning, when Eddie was at school, Tom told me we could keep him. I was so happy, Amos, I screamed with delight and threw my arms around Tom. Then, after our hearts were set on it, the welfare people told us we couldn't keep him, that he had to go back to his mother. Eddie wanted to stay with us. The day he left, he and Tom cried something awful. It broke Tom's heart. When he could finally talk about it, he told me *never* to bring another child into the house. 'Look what it got us!' he said. He brooded over the boy for a year, wouldn't go fishing, wouldn't mention his name.

"It's strange when two people live so close together for so long and still can do so little for the other in their loneliness. I felt helpless. I jabbered and baked things and asked to go places, and Tom got through it. I didn't know if I could. But you know, worrying over Tom, I got through it too."

Fern looked into the shadows.

"I wonder sometimes how Mildred felt, if she was happy," Amos said, "if she ever just wanted to go away but was too frightened and dependent to make it. I knew sometimes that I didn't know her. I'd look at her and ask myself, 'Who is she?'"

"I thought that very thing when Tom died," Fern said. "I stood at the coffin, alone with him at the funeral home, and I told him he'd been a fine man, a good husband, but I didn't know who he was. In eternity I'll walk up to him and say 'Who are you, Tom Knutson? Please tell me.'"

Fern nestled in Amos's arms and he told her the story of the little Gypsy girl, omitting the brutal, pitiless conclusion that Elroy had hammered them with. Amos still wondered about the truth of Elroy's telling. Fern didn't speak for almost an hour, holding onto Amos tightly, covering his face and neck and shoulders with her kisses. Then she whispered in his ear. "I wish we could go off the roof together like this."

Amos didn't answer.

An hour before dawn, Amos stopped in Owen's room, trying to see his face in the blackness. As his vision adjusted, Amos could see that Owen's eyes were open, staring at the ceiling, blinking at nothing. In reality Amos knew that Owen was far away somewhere, in the past, in the future, on another planet. But he had to tell someone, another human. Amos sat next to the bed and explained his plan to Owen in every detail. He wished that Owen could tell him if it would work, if there were any flaws in its fabric, a single thread that would unravel and doom it.

Amos knew this freedom would mean nothing to Owen, caged as he was for as long as he was earthbound, stuck on the wintry roof, unable to jump to the father's arms. But Amos could share his plot with none of his friends, knowing that by its very nature it would only succeed in total secrecy. If one other rational person knew the truth, it would obligate him morally to speak up and save Daisy. Even if he didn't, it would mean the risk of telling others and in these environs rumor could spread. He would take no chance on leaving a crack for Daisy to slip through only to satisfy his deep human need to tell someone, to hear their response, their praise, their encouragement and support. If he would be certain, he must deny himself all human companionship in his quest. Owen was as close as he could come to human comfort.

And he told him everything, asked Owen if he thought it could succeed, fought back his tears, clung to Owen's cold unresponsive hand. Amos emptied himself before his mute confessor, admitting his misspent life, the unresolved certainty that he had killed Mildred with carelessness, that he lost all of those he loved with carelessness and neglect. He confessed that he had no idea how he'd arrived in that room on that night as lost and frightened as he was. There were no more tears.

No one answered him. No one reassured him. No voice in the stark silence of the coming morning save the insects and frogs, singing their night song. Amos sat silently with his companion of stone. Maybe Owen could hear it all and understand. Maybe, under that rigid flesh, inside that fossilized head, Owen was leaping with joy, celebrating Amos's victory, urging him on with all his spirit. Amos stood and looked into Owen's mummified face, longing for some sign of consent. Owen began laughing as if he'd just heard a wonderful joke, quietly cracking up.

Amos hid the needle in his cigar box.

CHAPTER 23

SPRING HAD COME TO THE MOUNTAINS, and with it as always, even to Sunset Home, a spirit of hope. When he mopped, Roland left the door at the end of the hallway open for a while. Amos gazed out the unbarred threshold and smelled new life in the air, charging into the cadaverous building with such robust proclamation that it pillaged Roland's disinfectant and over-powered it. The clean March breeze sent them all back into their memories of spring days in other places, other times, other people, a narcotic, rendering them all silent. It was a balm for their wounds, it was a stab in the heart. It cast its spell over Amos, a whiff on his memory of spring nights, a country road, boyhood days. He fought it with great energy, or he knew it would drag him down, turn him around. He wanted to give in to it, a warm, inviting but forbidden woman.

Clara visited in the afternoon, chirruping like a bird just returned from the South. She whispered to Amos only once, dying to know what it was they had chosen for Daisy's surprise. Amos had to think for a moment, then told her it would be one of those new color TV's. Clara flashed a delighted expression and went back to serious visiting.

Lights out finally came, too quickly. To everyone else it was another stifling monotonous day, except for the brief and hyp-notic fresh air. To Amos it had been the longest day of his life, and the shortest, longing for it to pass and at the same time pray-ing that it never would. Itching to take the final step that would throw Daisy into disarray and personal disaster, he desperately hoped that he would never have to, that some stroke of fate would intercede to change his course irrevocably. But with Scott gone back to Ohio, he knew he had forfeited his only miracle.

Amos struggled to remain calm and act normal. The irony reached ridiculous proportions and he was amused at his fear of the needle to come in light of the leap that followed. He always hated those damn needles. Struggling to keep his wavering scribble legible, he carefully printed a note for Fern. He had contemplated its contents for days: how much he could reveal to her, and with what subtlety, without putting her in jeopardy? If in fact it all turned out the way he'd schemed, he wanted Fern to at least suspect it was *he* who happily brought Daisy to ruin.

This was the time he always worried about. While his companions turned to sleep, Amos opened the cigar box and squinted to read the words he'd written on the back of the photograph, copied from one of Robert's books. The light was too poor and he could only recognize a few of the words. But it didn't matter, they were etched clearly in his mind. He procrastinated endlessly until, with little caution, he fled to Fern's warm affection. He wanted to hide in her, to escape, to return to his origins. Fern misread his urgency, but not the hardness that she gently caressed and guided into her seasoned body. Amos wanted to stay wedded like this to her, one with another human being, safe and warm. Unable to bridle his urgency, he spent himself within her sooner than he wished. They embraced silently for several minutes, then Amos whispered in her ear.

"Fern, we're all going to get free of this place real soon. Will that make you happy?"

"Oh, Amos, that would be something. But I don't want you getting into any more trouble with Daisy. If we can be together at night like this, we'll make it."

Amos wouldn't accept that. Surviving here, surprised at a crumb of kindness, any decent human act, spending the rest of their lives like this, no matter how long that might be. The rage within him was coming forth. Happy for it, he encouraged it, fanning its flames. He knew he needed the rage.

"That's not enough. You're a good, decent woman. For you to spend one more day cowering around here is wrong. Wake every morning only to have to remember where you are, go to bed every night frightened that she might come to hurt you, tremble with panic every time she walks the halls. It's not enough to merely survive. It has to end."

Amos didn't realize he was talking out loud.

"Shhh, she'll hear you," Fern said, laying her head on his chest. "Would you ever consider living with me when we get free?"

Amos didn't answer for a minute, picking the right words.

"Yes, I would be happy to," he said.

"Would Mildred mind, do you suppose?"

"No, I don't think she would mind at all."

"I don't think Tom would either," she said. "Shucks, I think he'd be happy for me, to have you now in my life."

Fern was quiet for a moment.

"Amos, did you ever imagine that you could fall in love when you were seventy-eight years old and that it would feel just like it did when you were seventeen?" She laughed in her fragile way.

"No, I can remember thinking that when I hit fifty my life would be over, even forty. But it isn't. It goes on, as long as we face up to it. In a way, the last few months have been the most demanding and meaningful of my entire life, not discounting all that went before. The adventure goes on. It surprises you when you least expect, if you don't give up on it."

He held her tightly.

"I want to tell you I'm proud of you, Amos Lasher. You're a strong, gentle man. I'm flabbergasted that you care for me, overjoyed. I want to tell you, here and now, how much I love you."

She kissed his lips lightly. Amos held his breath, trying not to cry. He didn't know if he could handle it if he broke down now. He wanted to say the words to her, but he knew that if he uttered one sound, every swelling emotion churning within him would pour through that gap. He held on, trying to swallow, ignoring the catch in his heart.

Suddenly a flashlight's beam traced erratic figures on the wall of the corridor. Amos slid to the floor beside the bed, naked, silently, trying not to bump anything or put his foot in the bedpan. Daisy came to the doorway, swished the light quickly across the two beds, and stood for a moment. Fern breathed heavily, trying to imitate sleep, lying still in her utter fright. She gave thanks that Ruth was warbling her usual sleeping clamor, covering any slight rustle Amos might make. Daisy made her sweep of the women's wing, and neither of them moved until she headed back toward the dayroom. Amos stood and pulled on his clothes.

"I forgot to lump my bed to look like I'm in it," he said.

"Oh, Amos, what'll you do?"

Fern's whisper was freighted with alarm.

"I'll follow behind her. By the time she goes in my room, maybe I can slip into the bathroom."

Amos buttoned his shirt and leaned to kiss her.

"I'm going now."

"Be careful, Amos."

"I will."

He disappeared quickly into the shadows of the wing, the shadows he'd become akin to these past months. Either Daisy had walked the men's wing first or she was cutting corners, because he caught her image just as she ducked through the infirmary door. He puffed up his bed to look as though he were in it, just in case, then went and woke Marvin. Amos was later than usual but luckily the plug had held. Marvin meandered sleepily to the toilet from a dry bed and Amos waited what seemed like half the night for his return. Marvin thanked Amos and started to crumble into bed.

"Wait, Marvin," he whispered, not to disturb Elroy, "I want you to help me."

"Now?"

"Yeah, now."

"What do you want me to do?" Marvin yawned.

"Remember when you fought the Finn in Duluth?"

"Yeah, I remember." His rubber mouth smiled.

"Do you want to get away from this place, from Daisy?"

Amos spoke slowly, close to Marvin's ear. Elroy rumbled some in a fitful sleep.

"Yeah, as far as I can, but I never will."

"If you do what I ask you, we'll get rid of her for good, honest," Amos said, fearing Marvin would never do it.

"What do I have to do?"

"I want you to wrap your hand in something and then hit me right in the face, as hard as you can."

"Nah . . . I can't do that, Amos. I like you."

Amos took him by the shoulders and shook him gently.

"Listen to me, damn it! I didn't say it would be easy. I know you like me. I like you. If you like me, if you want to help me get that son of a bitch Daisy, you've got to hit me. I probably won't feel it much, but if I get just a little black eye, I have a plan where Daisy will get blamed for it and they'll boot her out for good."

"I don't get it," Marvin said. "She'll just say you got it falling down."

"I have that figured out. Just do it, please. I promise you, if my face is bruised, Daisy will fall."

Elroy rolled over, slurping and muttering unconsciously. Amos picked up a dirty undershirt from the floor and started wrapping Marvin's right hand like a trainer. Marvin didn't protest. Amos was jubilant, almost forgetting it was *his* face that would be battered.

"You can't have any bruises on your hand, just in case."

They had the old fighter's hand ready for one more knockout punch, a punch that might cold-cock Daisy permanently. Amos sat on the bed.

"I'll sit here. If you knock me back, I'll just hit the mattress. Now, Marvin, hit me! Hit me hard!"

Marvin moved around in front of him, cocking his right arm, sparring in the dim light.

"Amos?"

"Yes," he whispered, fearing that Elroy would wake and ruin it all.

"Will you remember that I like you? You won't think—"

"No, no, the more you like me the harder you'll hit me."

Amos thought the contradiction was exactly like life; Marvin should easily understand.

"Now hit me!"

"OK. I hope this works."

Marvin stepped back slightly and wound up. He swung out of the darkness and missed, falling into Amos's lap. They both started laughing, desperately trying to muffle the comedy this ludicrous scene had aroused in them. Elroy threatened to wake, shifting restlessly under their giggles. Amos gathered his forces first and got Marvin back to business. His next try hit Amos in the left eye and cheek and nose. Amos had closed his eyes so he wouldn't flinch as the blow approached, and he found himself flat on the bed, the pain sharp through his head. Amazingly,

Marvin still had some of his punch. Amos had to go on quickly, before his instincts took over. He sat up, weakly.

"Are you sure you beat the Finn?" Amos said. "You're not lying are you? Hell, I didn't even feel that. Think of Roland, Marvin, kicking you, laughing at you. Hit Roland!"

Amos closed his eyes just as the blow came, hammering Amos back onto the bed. His head bounced. He was momentarily stunned.

"Are you all right?" Marvin said too loudly.

Amos groggily pushed himself up on his elbows.

"Shhh, yes, I'm all right. I was just funnin' you. You hit real hard."

Blood oozed from Amos's nose. With a hand on Marvin's shoulder he got to his feet. His knees buckled for an instant. He caught himself and stood, a reed in the wind. Marvin sat on the bed and Amos leaned close to Marvin's face, as if he were about to kiss him.

"One more thing, Marvin." Amos glanced at Elroy, seemingly asleep. "You must never tell anyone that you hit me. No matter what happens, *never* admit to anyone what you did. If you do, Daisy and Roland will get away scot-free."

Amos made an effort to speak gravely.

"If that's so, I'll never tell no one, not even the devil in hell."

"Good . . . go to sleep now, Marvin, and dream of being free again. I couldn't do this without you."

"I ain't lying, Amos, I really beat the Finn."

"I know, I know," Amos said.

Marvin flopped onto his pillow and Amos pulled the blanket over him the way he'd tuck in a small child.

"Goodbye, Marvin."

Amos went unsteadily for Winston's room, his face throbbed. So far so good.

Winston was awake, watching Amos's approach like an ancient seaman, high in the crow's nest, scanning the dark horizon. His nose jutted out from the bedding he had pulled up tight around his face.

"You can quit playing Button, Button now, Winston. Just do like you used to do. Don't fool Daisy any more."

Winston nodded that he understood, but Amos had a leaden foreboding that, when it was too late to turn back, Winston would give it all away. Amos touched his shoulder, knowing he had no other choice but to trust it all with this strange old man.

"You did a good job. You stopped Daisy more than anyone. No more button, just do what Daisy wants."

In the obscure light the postman spoke from his mummylike position, dumbfounding Amos.

"You shouldn't do it. She isn't worth it."

"I know . . . but we are."

The words came of their own accord without Amos ever thinking them, so taken by Winston's awareness. Did he understand what Amos was about to do, he more than any of the others at the heart of the conspiracy, or had he hit on a sequence of words that gave the impression he knew what he was talking about. Winston said no more.

Amos wiped the blood that was trickling down into his mouth, his face swelling on schedule. At that moment he was certain that this lanky prattler of nursery rhymes was a solid ally, that he would in no way aid Daisy when the time came. He gripped Winston's arm for a moment and turned for the hall on shaky legs. His head hurt, his face stung, his heart raced.

Sadie slept heavily when he crept into their room, Effie a spindly form in the other bed. Sadie's dress hung in the shadows of a doorless wardrobe. He tucked the note as far down in the pocket as possible and knew that Fern might never receive it. That might be better, and he realized how strongly he felt about Sadie, the outcast linebacker.

He sneaked quickly back to the men's wing and pushed himself mechanically through the motions, never allowing himself a second thought. He pulled the caster and base from the end of his bed post and the capsules spilled onto the floor. He replaced the bed parts and gathered up Winston's buttons. There were more than enough to do the job, but he couldn't leave one, not a trace. Robert was using the urinal when Amos filled his glass with water.

"Thirsty?" the teacher who had entertained the President said.

"Yeah, throat's kind of dry."

Amos hurried now, knowing Robert would never remember.

"Sleep well," Amos said.

"You too. Don't let the bedbugs bite," Robert said.

Amos sat on his bed and forced himself, allowing no hesitation, no second thought, kindling his rage and speaking aloud as he swallowed.

"Take that, you murdering bitch." He took several capsules at a crack. "Thought you beat me, you female bastard?" Another handful. "This is for Johnny," he paused. "Yeah, and for Sadie and Mick and Carlos." God, it was for all of them.

He ran out of water. He hurried to the lavatory for a refill and was unsure of how much time he had now, still with things to do. He finished off the capsules in fear that St. Tranquility would arrive too soon. He tidied up the room, left the glass over on the bureau, and put himself to bed.

He took Fern's needle from the cigar box and followed Daisy's technique to the letter. Angry now, well aware that he was butting up against indifferent carelessness, he shoved the needle into his arm where the damn nurses always did, deep enough to make a nice hole, again and again, flinching from the self-inflicted pain and cursing anyone blind enough to miss such evidence. Some of the punctures bled, some didn't. He switched over and did the right arm, speaking aloud while Spencer slept.

"We'll find out what you're made of while we're at it, Sheriff, grit or glands?"

He surveyed his riddled arms and felt confident their unfurled flags would be seen above the carelessness. He pulled his pajama sleeves down to cover the marks from Daisy's eye, then dropped the needle into the hollow bedpost and secured the ornate cap. He was finished.

He felt an uncommon happiness, certainly not as frightened as he imagined he would be, even as he had been an hour before. He thought of his friends, sleeping in their rooms around him, totally unaware of his guerrilla warfare, oblivious to their imminent deliverance. Winston made it possible, Emil signed the form, and Marvin had punched him with great reluctance. If she got the note, he hoped Fern would figure out enough to salvage some comfort or even peace.

He couldn't help but wonder what Clara would make of it all after faithfully bootlegging the mail. Now their future depended on him whether they knew it or not, whether they believed it or not. A helluva hero, *only Daisy* would know he did it, not his friends, not Fern, and the irony grated him. But Daisy'd know, by God, and that would have to be his satisfaction. Would she ever figure out Winston's hand in it? He wanted them all to know and was suddenly stricken by the demon that laughed in his face, telling him it would surely fail. That Daisy would dance on his grave unscathed, and everything he sacrificed was for nought.

The time went slowly at first. He neatened the bedding and lay quietly, listening for any signs of rebellion from his body. He wiped the small trickles of dried blood from his arms and caught a sob. He steeled himself, wanting no nonsense at this juncture. But he loved life, especially his own. He wanted to go on living, who knows, maybe five or ten more years allotted. But as he'd known from the beginning, his life was all he had to fight with, the only arrow in his quiver, the only weapon she would never suspect. He was a kamikaze, the divine wind that cast the enemy ships away from the shores of homeland Japan, strapped now in the cockpit of suicide, the one vehicle that would impale her on the rocks.

Images raced through his head, memories came in swells and tides, washing over him. He was cold and suddenly frightened, catching himself dozing and battling to stay alert. He could no longer comprehend how much time was slipping by, imagining he was sliding downhill across a wide, bright snowfield and he couldn't stop, the hill dropping steeper as he went with nothing to brake his descent. Breath came with difficulty, he gasped, rapidly, trying to sit up and failing. He was suffocating. He looked over at Spencer.

"Spencer, help me!"

His voice sounded strange, echoing in his skull, someone else's voice, weak and distant. He was terrified.

"Spencer, please, help—"

"Shut up! Your goddamn dog is dead," someone down the hall shouted.

Spencer slept peacefully, his hearing aid lying precisely where he'd placed it on his Bible. Amos tried to call once more, but he had no breath for it. He quit struggling. One star was visible through the narrow window and he wondered if it had a name.

He was boarding a train in a depot. It was the old Northern Pacific he rode to Chicago. The train was leaving, and there was a group of people arriving late to say goodbye to him. He saw them from his window, Marvin and Carlos and Mick; they were all there, standing beside the train. The train started to move slowly, and Amos waved. He had something to tell them, something happy, but he couldn't get the window open. They were keeping pace with the train as it pulled out, Robert and Elroy and Winston, looking up at him. He tugged on the window frantically as the train picked up speed. They were searching his face for what he had to tell them, running now the best they could, waving, some stumbling, Fern and Greg and Sarah and Johnny. He struggled with all his might but was unable to open the window. They began to falter, Mildred and Emil and Linebacker, tears streaming from their eyes, the train accelerating steadily with increasing noise. Amos was shouting, pounding on the glass with his fists, but they couldn't hear him over the train's roar, and their sweet expectant faces swiftly shrunk from view.

Amos was no longer breathing.

With the little Gypsy girl, he leaped off the wintry roof into the blackness below.

Down the hall Owen was laughing.

CHAPTER 24

NEVER UTTERING A SOUND, Nell dropped his tray and fled up the hall. Spencer jiggled him gently, thinking Amos was sleeping a little late. Daisy marched into the room in a morning-fresh uniform with Nell at her heels, stepping smartly over the splattered oatmeal and broken dishes.

"Come on, Amos, it's time to get up."

When he didn't respond she shook him, then rolled him over, knowing instantly that he was dead. Baffled by the colored swelling that covered the left side of his face, she turned to Spencer, her voice normal and calm, but her expression displaying a storm of confusion.

"Amos has left us, Spencer, poor soul. Do you know what happened to his face?"

"He was fine when he went to bed," Spencer said, shaken by death's fingerprint suddenly appearing so closely. Daisy pulled the sheet over Amos's face with an experienced disregard and turned on Nell.

"Clean this mess up. What's the matter with you? We have people dying here all the time."

Nell picked up the tray and shattered dishes, wiping the floor while her tears silently fell into the smeared applesauce and coffee. She delivered the rest of her trays, now cold, and the morning news. Amos had flown away. One by one the men peered into the room, seeing for themselves if the rumor could be true. Scuttlebutt ran rampant in the wing, small clusters buzzed. Thinking they were accustomed to death, the men were stabbed with a grief they never suspected.

Hatred for Daisy ran knee-deep in the hallway as Amos's colleagues were rocked by remorse, sadly aware of how thoroughly they had come to look to him for direction and hope. His sudden and unexpected death wrenched them to the heart. Their curses and vain threats were more therapeutic than any real danger to Daisy. They drifted in the corridor with scattered thoughts and confusion. Marvin believed he'd hit Amos too hard, afraid to share this sorrow with any of them. Elroy attempted to mooch liquor from Daisy at every opportunity, believing with several others that Daisy had killed Amos because Elroy had ratted about their plan of escape. Some thought Amos died naturally, Daisy among them. No one knew the truth. Sure that Daisy was guilty, Emil hid in his room, unwilling to admit to himself the bursting dam behind his eyes.

When the words exploded in her mind, Fern gasped as if all the air were sucked from her body. Her chest ached. She bit her lip and turned to the window, hanging onto her wits as best she could. Daisy had caught him at whatever it was he was up to and killed him. Who could Fern tell? She wept bitterly, knowing she would never see Amos again, never keep house with him when they'd get free of Sunset. Oh, she knew that was only a pipe dream, but how could she carry on without his nightly visits, his touch, his calm strong voice.

One by one they turned to face one more saltless day. Amos had given them flavor for a while, but now the morning came on starkly and their anger melted into fear when they reconsidered Daisy's unremitting power.

The coroner made his customary trip, with Daisy at his side. The body was examined superficially, the papers made out. The man didn't waste much time. Spencer questioned meekly from his rocker.

"What did he die from?"

"His heart just quit on him most likely," the county official said without glancing up from his work. "Do you know how he banged up his face?"

"It was fine when he went to bed," Spencer said.

"He probably fell in the bathroom last night," Daisy said. "He was always falling."

"Amos wasn't always—"

Spencer caught himself under Daisy's threatening glare. She attempted to explain his battered face to herself as well as the coroner.

"Are you finished, Harry?" Daisy said.

The men with the big bag waited in the doorway, fidgety.

"Take him away," the coroner said.

He stood, threw his things into a leather bag, and departed. The attendants threw Amos into their plastic bag, zipped it shut, and lugged him out to the jaded Cadillac. Daisy threw his things into the suitcase and a large garbage bag, a bit relieved to have the body gone, reluctant to have anyone else inquire about Amos's face. She uncovered the blooming bedpan, ordered Carlos to flush it in the toilet, and watched as he made no effort to salvage any of the philodendron. Gandy Dancer no longer seemed to care. Daisy stripped the bed to the mattress cover and had the room ready for another boarder without a clue that Amos had ever dwelt there.

Roland passed on his morning rounds, pausing in the doorway and surveying the naked bed.

"Amos kicked off, huh? Never did figure out that old bird. Well, he made baggee, like old Roland told him."

When he turned into the hall, the grizzly almost tripped over Mick in the wheelchair.

"Get that damned thing outta my way, you scrawny coot. It's April Fool's Day, go play a joke on yourself."

Roland's brawny threat bristled down the corridor, sending Mick skittering out of his way.

"April fool, April fool," Winston picked up the chant.

"God, you can say that again, Winston," Roland said, "if I ever saw one."

The ward bully tried to laugh to lift the drudgery of his life.

On the women's wing, Sadie wandered as usual, although she spent a great deal of time loitering in Fern's doorway. Fern noticed this new behavior but, in the thunderstorm of her own heartbreak, gave it no importance. Once during the afternoon, when Sadie's haunting annoyed her, she chased the linebacker up the hall. Sadie returned in a few minutes and took up her stand on Fern's front stoop.

Daisy moved Sadie away from the door as she delivered Ruth in her wheelchair back to the room. Unable to control her sorrow, Fern huddled in her chair. Daisy talked to herself while she manipulated Ruth into the bed.

"He just didn't wake up. Well, I guess he won't be giving Daisy any more trouble."

"How did you do it?" Fern said.

She looked Daisy straight in the eye, surprising herself with such boldness. Never in all her life had she been so brave. Daisy stopped short with Ruth and scowled back at Fern.

"You were around him too much, little woman. I see we'll have to straighten out your mind as well."

Fern turned away from Daisy's menacing stare, angry and helpless and overwhelmed with sadness. She spoke softly, but firmly.

"You can easily hurt me, but you can't touch my mind."

Sheriff Thomas phoned Daisy in the afternoon, semi-officially.

"You have any idea what happened to his face?" he asked.

"No, John. Probably a fall."

"Could Roland have done it?" John Thomas said.

"Of course not. I'm sure I saw Amos after Roland left. Why, John?"

"Oh, Harry thinks it looks like several blows. Could any of the men beat on him?" the sheriff said lightly.

"Heavens no." She laughed. "Those poor old scarecrows?"

"Well, he thinks there's reason enough for an autopsy, just to determine the real cause of death. He sent the body over to Bozeman, just routine. I hope you don't care."

"Hell no, John, if the county has money to burn."

She didn't care. In fact, it couldn't have worked out better. She was happy the boy scouts had picked Amos's body to play detective with instead of Johnny's. It would be another confirmation that she ran a just and proper home.

"See you tomorrow night?" the sheriff said warmly.

"I'm looking forward to your coming."

She laughed and hung up, calm and relaxed, imagining what they'd do together at play.

The day went slowly away. Winston walked his woeful path like a gaunt hound grieving for his departed master. Marvin stuck to his room, trying to figure out what went wrong. Amos said it would work, but it hadn't, and Marvin was scared stiff that Daisy would find out that *he* had killed Amos. Elroy bore the same guilt, that his snitching had caused Amos's death, but the toadlike stoolie said nothing to his roommate. They stewed together but in different juices. Emil said little to any of them, always expecting the worst, but he remembered that damn insurance form and he couldn't comprehend why Amos would aid Daisy before she killed him. Nell brought a tray for Amos that evening with dessert and all. She set it on the empty bed table, and their dreary heartsick day poured through the hourglass and was gone.

The second day went by without event. The men talked about Amos, seeking relief from their heartache and disappointment. Of course Marvin wet his bed and Roland shoved his face in it before rewarding him with some form of suffering. Fern quaked at every sound from the hall, sure that Daisy was on her way to punish her for those precipitous words. But it was usually Sadie, haunting Fern in her room, following her wherever she went.

"Do you want something, dear?" Fern finally confronted her.

"I'm going home today," was all she'd say.

During one of the conclaves, while four of them played whist with the dog-eared deck, the conversation went like this.

"At least he got outta here," Carlos said, squinting at his hand.

"Yeah, but we never got to jump Roland," Marvin said.

"We still can," Carlos said with a frown.

"Not without Amos," Marvin said.

"It never would have worked," Elroy said.

"It sure as hell would have," Marvin said.

"It doesn't make any difference," Emil said, "one way or the other." He stoically stroked his great scrub-brush mustache and sucked on his empty pipe. "Amos never intended to pull that foolhardy stunt."

"You mean all our plannin' was for nothin'?" Marvin said.

"You got it," Emil said. "Amos had as much of a chance against Daisy as a baboon fishing with a lug nut."

They continued their game in a subdued silence, all of them feeling cheated and defeated, not sure by what or by whom, but maybe by Amos.

John Thomas got Daisy to the phone again before noon. They visited for a minute, the sheriff awkwardly circling around to what he was calling about.

"About Amos Lasher, were you giving him any shots?"

"Shots?" Daisy thought fast for anything she had to cover. "No, John, not Amos. Why do you ask?"

"Oh, nothing." He was hesitant, grasping for words. "Just routine. Harry's still fooling around with cause of death."

"See you tonight?" she said.

"Oh, I'm sorry, Daisy. I have to check out this horse rustling that's going on up the valley. I've got to go on a stake-out tonight. I won't be able to come out."

"Come late. I'll wake up for you," she said invitingly.

"I'm afraid this will take all night. Sorry."

When Daisy hung up, apprehension had conceived in her belly, a small stone in the pit of her stomach. Something wasn't right.

The next day was different. Daisy answered the ring at the door while the residents were eating breakfast.

"John, what a nice surprise. How did the stake-out go? Would you like coffee, rolls?"

She backed away from the door and ushered her uniformed lover into the narrow foyer. She looked smashing this morning even though restricted to her nurse's whites. The sun found a cloudless sky when it rose from behind the mountains.

"No . . . no thanks, Daisy. I have to ask you some questions."

The big man was tentative, somber, clearing his throat uneasily. Daisy was puzzled by his seriousness, usually so openly slickered by her glamor. They moved into the dayroom on their mutual discomfort.

"I missed you last night," she said.

"I'd like to see your medical file on Amos Lasher."

"Why, of course, John. Sit down, I'll get it."

She was calm, knowing she had nothing to hide concerning Amos, everything accounted for in the record, except for the marks on his face. *What the hell were they?* She brought the file and handed it to the sheriff along with her charm. Taking the file and ignoring the charm, he mulled over it for several minutes, raising her pulse rate several points.

"What's this?" He pointed to a scribbled entry.

"Oh, that was something like a gallbladder attack, the best I could diagnose."

She looked into the file over the sheriff's shoulder, becoming increasingly nervous and not knowing why. This was ridiculous. She hadn't done anything to Amos.

"I don't see any regular medication here," he said. "Am I reading that right?"

"Yes, Amos didn't receive any, I told you that on the phone. He fell a lot with his bad hip, poor man, always bruising himself. But he didn't need any medication."

Daisy forced a smile. Winston strode into the dayroom and stood staring out the window. Daisy ignored him, realizing the sheriff was dead serious, grimly questioning a suspect. Little streaks of panic raced through her body and gathered in her belly.

"What is this about, John?"

"We've worked on this for two days. I didn't want to come out here like this, but I'd hoped you'd have some explanation."

John Thomas was in a box, trying desperately to find some small passage out of it. Daisy's smile was packing its bags in a hurry.

"Worked on what, for God's sake!"

She was talking rapidly and she didn't know what she was defending. Her mind was blanking on her. Johnny and the others were rotting in the ground, she had nothing to hide, but her accumulated treachery wreaked confusion and disarray in the ranks of her reason.

"Do you give tranquilizers to any of the residents?"

"Yes . . . two of them regularly. Others get it as they need it."

Daisy's disorder was a windswept forest fire.

"What do you give them?"

"Right now we're using Elavil. Winston and Sadie get it. Winston at night, Sadie twice a day."

"Could anyone else get at it?" he asked.

"No one. I keep it tightly locked."

"Any missing lately?"

"No, not that I know of," she said, biting her lower lip.

Daisy couldn't cover her flanks when she didn't know which of them was exposed.

"Do you give it to them?" The sheriff came at her relentlessly.

"Yes, of course. They're not competent enough to trust with it. I put it right in their mouth and see that they swallow it. I can account for every capsule. Just what in the hell is this all about, John?"

"I'm sorry, Daisy, but you've given all the wrong answers. I'm afraid I'm going to have to take you into custody until this is cleared up."

The big lawman took a step toward her.

"What are you *talking* about, *custody?* This doesn't make any sense. Take *me* into custody?" Her voice rose and flushed with anger. "You'll have your ass in the wringer if you try to arrest *me.*"

"It's Amos Lasher."

He took her arm in one of his large hands.

"Amos Lasher? That old man died in his sleep. So what?"

She jerked her arm free and stepped back, almost stumbling over an upholstered chair.

"They sent some blood to Great Falls. Amos had enough Elavil in him to kill several men. Now you've just told me that you're the only one out here with access to the drug. I have no choice."

His words struck Daisy with a sledgehammer blow, knocking her back against the wall, her face flooded with shock, her mind running riot as she tried to understand what was happening. Her world was falling in on her and she couldn't catch any of the pieces.

"I didn't do it! John, you have to believe me."

The sheriff tried to grab one of her arms, but she swung them wildly, screaming.

"I didn't do it, damn it, I didn't do it!"

He had one of her arms, trying to restrain her.

"You know me, John, doesn't that count for anything?"

She tried to recapture an air of charm and composure, pleading sweetly.

"Would I kill that nice old man? It doesn't make any sense. There's no reason."

While he got one handcuff on her left wrist, both of them almost fell over the back of the sofa. Winston stood motionless, watching from across the room. Bertha and Nell peered from the serving window. Daisy felt the steel on her arm and began flaying her arms at her double-crossing lover.

"Goddamn it, I didn't do it! You're not taking me anywhere!"

The sheriff shielded his head and face with his arms and waded in to subdue her. His voice was official, humoring her.

"That's not for me to decide. I have to take you in until we clear it up. If you didn't do it, you'll be all right."

She was telling him the truth and he didn't believe her. She couldn't stand it and she went a little crazy, screamed at him, tried to beat him with her fists, her hair disheveled, uniform rumpled, makeup smeared.

"You'll go down with me, you bastard. The whole town will know whose bed you've been rutting in. Can your wife and family handle that?" she shouted.

"I guess they'll have to."

He wrestled her under control, cuffing both hands behind her.

"Don't make this any worse than it is, Daisy."

He was puffing from the exertion. She quit struggling and spoke calmly again, regaining a touch of class.

"Don't I mean *anything* to you, John?" she said with a note of sadness in her voice.

"That has no bearing on it."

He led her across the room toward the door.

"It'll be your job, you know," she said.

"You're probably right about that."

Bertha ducked back into the kitchen, but Nell just gaped at the two of them, trying to figure out what was going on.

"Amos Lasher," she said, shaking her head slowly. "I thought I'd seen the last of that old man."

When John Thomas opened the door, a waiting deputy took Daisy to a patrol car. It stood under the cottonwood tree, but it wasn't a secondhand Buick.

CHAPTER 25

Winston went roaring down the wing, "to see a fine lady fall off her white horse, fall off her white horse." He broadcast into every room, even Owen's, and a few of the men sensed the uncommon excitement in the mailman's proclamation. Emil hotfooted it for the dayroom, a giveaway that some spark of hope survived under his sullen pessimism. Marvin was moaning from a blow he'd just received from Roland when Winston reached his room. The grizzly stood with a menacing paw in the ore digger's cowering face.

"Every time you piss in the bed, that's what you'll get."

Winston threw caution to the wind and chanted his good news.

"ding, dong, the witch is dead."

Roland was in a nasty mood and he didn't get the message.

"Shut up, you imbecile, I've got enough shit without you."

Moving quickly to the door, he kicked the messenger in the shin. Winston leaped with the pain, spinning around like a top and falling hard against the wall and floor. Crumpled there, he noticed Emil slipping from one room to the other down the hall and the men, one by one, stealthily heading for the lavatory. Winston nursed his throbbing shin and watched Roland strip the saturated bedding down to the plastic mattress cover while Mick positioned his wheelchair just beyond the men's room door, blocking the hallway. Winston got up and limped to the roadblock and the men dragged him through the curtain into the bathroom where they whispered and plotted frantically. The old tile lavatory hummed like a hive. Mick alerted them that the bully was on his way and they went stone silent, except for Carlos, who was giggling.

Roland approached the wheelchair with an armload of reeking bedding and shouted.

"Get that chair outta my way or I'll kick your ass up to your eyeballs."

Mick's cane came out from under the curtain, hooked around one of Roland's ankles, and jerked him off his feet. The beer-bellied bully hit the floor dead weight, unable to free his arms in time to break the fall. His head drummed solidly against the far wall. They hadn't planned it that way, but it helped, and they dragged the grizzly into the bathroom already stunned. The whacking, stomping, kicking, and shouting began in a frenzy. The men shoved and shouldered one another for a shot at the prey. Shocked by the bushwhacking, Roland swung back as best he could and was beginning to overcome when Marvin showed up with his sock-and-pennies blackjack, finally realizing what all the commotion was. He got in a telling blow with his first swing, flattening his tormentor onto the tile floor.

They shouted and laughed and, when Roland caught them with an erratic swing, yelped. Mick was tangled in the curtain and couldn't get his balky wheelchair through the door. The caning and whacking and punching went on sporadically. Between swats the Sunset gang rested on the toilets and tub while one or two kept up the attack. Roland could no longer fight back. They cheered each other on and improvised creative aggression in their turn to give a bash, showing off with magnificent clouts and thumps. Robert didn't actually strike Roland, but he pinned one of his legs during the thrashing. Spencer fell back into the urinal during the scuffle and Winston gave Elroy a black eye with the backswing of his tennis racket.

They had pulled off Gulliver with a bang, and they had done it without Amos, or so they thought. They figured Amos would have been proud of them.

The battle noises had eventually reached the sheriff in the dayroom where he was talking with Mae and some of the women. He glanced down the men's wing, but made no immediate move toward the mugging, which sounded like a downtown gymnasium for eager young boxers fighting over the only punching bag available.

"You mean Daisy isn't going to take care of us anymore?" Fern asked the officer. With the disbelief in her voice it sounded as though she were disappointed.

"I'm afraid it looks bad for her, ma'am," the lawman said politely. "I'm not the one to say, but I don't think she'll be coming back."

All the women who had congregated began to smile as the consequence of his words sank in. They squealed little sounds of joy.

"Don't worry, we'll have someone out here in a little while to take over until this is all straightened out."

John Thomas still hadn't caught on to the true mood in the room. Fern grabbed Sadie, who was leaning on her, and twirled her stumpish body around, hooting and laughing. Effie danced up and down in place, singing "Buffalo gals, won't you come out tonight . . ." Grace began clapping, and the sheriff finally realized he was bringing glad tidings. The other ladies took their cue and began to celebrate, stepping and dancing the best they could with what they had. Grace kept hollering, "Bingo! bingo!" Fern stopped her jig with Sadie, suddenly realizing she could tell him without fear of reprisal. She took hold of the big man's arm.

"She killed Amos Lasher, you know."

"Yes, ma'am, it looks that way, but how did *you* know?"

"He told me she would. He told you, too, and how she killed his roommate, Johnny Sumers."

Fern looked him straight in the eye.

"Humph . . . ah, I don't remember . . ."

"Well, she didn't get away with it this time," Fern said.

"I'd better see to the men," the sheriff said.

He gracefully dodged Fern's bayonet, targeted for his embarrassment and shame. As he approached the men's room, the noise had settled into cheers and laughter and exuberant conversation. Elroy came out with a bruised face, exhausted but happy. Emil pushed through the frayed curtain with half a pipe in his mouth. He was smiling. Carlos held the curtain aside for the sheriff, his ear bloodied. Gandy Dancer squinted at the big man, trying to figure out who he was.

"He ain't gonna hurt no one today," Carlos said.

Roland was lying tangled in the soaked sheets, holding his crotch and groaning incoherently. Marvin sat on one of the toilets, his rubbery face spread with delight, his fists red and bruised as if he'd fought the Finn again. There were pennies scattered all over the room. Winston stood with his tennis racket in hand, breathing heavily from his workout on the court. Mick had finally maneuvered the wheelchair close enough to Roland and was standing wobbly, trying to get his fly open.

"That's enough, men. I'll take him now," the sheriff said.

"Shee-it," Mick said, "he's been pissing on me for years."

With disappointment he sat back in his chair. Sheriff Thomas took stock of the ludicrous scene and the motley bunch of offenders and attempted to keep a straight face.

"You boys know you're breaking the law?" he said.

"Jail us," Mick said. "Haul us all to jail."

"Yeah, haul us all to jail," Carlos said.

"This is just DEE-layed self-defense," Marvin said. "We's protecting ourselves. Ain't no law against that is there?"

"We're balancing the books," Robert said politely.

The officer ducked a laugh by sorting Roland out of the sheets, only to discover that the orderly's clothes were urinated as well. He looked as if he'd been hit by a truck—an old truck.

The wrinkled warriors joined the celebration in the dayroom where the television displayed a parade with full volume: floats and marching bands and Walt Disney characters providing the beat and atmosphere for their wingding. The anguish and sorrow and rage that had accumulated over the past three days, and well before, were awash with spring water gushing joyfully from some deep place.

Carlos danced a remembered step by himself, squatting low and attempting to kick out a leg. Nell and Effie marched in place to the drums. Spencer and Grace and Elroy had linked hands and were weaving through the traffic, cracking the whip in geriatric fashion. Winston latched on to the last hand and followed stiffly. Like a barnyard of startled turkeys, all those able enough were celebrating the change in power with the televised parade, stiff-limbed, crooked, crippled bodies, turning and bouncing and flapping in this burst of ecstasy.

Their endurance quickly dissipated, and they flopped into chairs and sofas, completely spent, the room ripe for cardiac arrest and stroke. They sat for a long time, some chattering, some with their private thoughts, and some rallying around John Thomas, a hero in shining armor who—though he accepted the praise of these grateful forgotten citizens—knew his armor was stained with blood. Sadie began another new quirk to add to her bizarre behavior of the past few days. She stood leaning on Fern, who was seated on a bench, and began bumping Fern with her hip like a very uncoordinated rumba dancer. Fern almost chased her, almost, but caught something in Sadie's expression that caused Fern to reconsider. Sadie continued doing the rumba until out of the blue Fern realized that this peculiar old woman was nudging her, not with a hip, but with a *pocket!*

Fern fumbled in the cotton mail pouch and came out with Amos's note. This irrational lady had continued to play the game that Amos and Fern assumed she had never noticed, and Fern had been too dense to catch on while Sadie waited impatiently for Fern to open her mailbox. With trembling hands Fern opened the note like a message from the grave. She read it slowly.

WORD FROM THE COURTYARD, I LOVE YOU
SOUNDS FROM THE COURTYARD, LAUGHTER

That's all it said. Fern relished the "I love you," but she didn't understand the rest, feeling there was something familiar there that would make itself known in time. She folded the note, gave Sadie a hug, and went to her room to be alone.

Emil sat off by himself, trying to fit the jagged pieces into his logical mind, wondering if they all hadn't missed the point. He couldn't completely shake the vague impression resting somewhere in the back of his head that Amos had something to do with all this. Daisy had underestimated that cunning old man, thinking she had broken him, and by God, just when he looked the weakest, and when even *they* had all given up on him, he had ridden that dead horse right over her. Emil shook the pipe dreams from his mind, he was trying to make something out of nothing. Daisy had simply become too greedy, made a mistake, and by coincidence been found out in the killing of Amos. But it stuck in his craw. Why did Amos have him sign that damned insurance paper?

Two women arrived from town, one of them a registered nurse, and the sheriff left with the suspects. They had to call for the two men with the old makeshift Cadillac ambulance to haul Roland to the hospital. He didn't quite make baggee. The two new authorities gave the inmates the run of the building against Mae's advice. Clara Channing arrived when things had settled back toward normal.

"My, my, good morning everyone. In the dayroom so early? Well it is a special day. Wait till you see what I've brought."

She beamed into the room with a large brown bag. Emil stood.

"Amos is dead, Clara," Emil said.

"What! Ooooh, nooo . . . Poor man. That's awful."

She set down her sack and sat on a bench to catch her breath.

"Now Daisy won't get her surprise," Clara said.

She at once put her hand over her mouth, remembering she wasn't supposed to say anything, ever. Emil paid no attention.

"Daisy has been arrested for killing Amos," he said.

"Ooooh, my goodness, that can't be," Clara said. "That just can't be. She loves all of you so much. Daisy couldn't have done anything like that. There must be some terrible mistake."

The kind, bewildered woman spoke to no one in particular, wandering among them for more than an hour, mumbling to herself, repeating herself to each of the residents she approached.

"I just know Daisy couldn't have done that."

She had forgotten about the chocolate bunnies she had brought for each of them. They'd melted into grotesque shapes on the radiator where she set her bag when she heard the shocking news.

The sheriff cared about Daisy in more than a carnal way until he realized what she had done. Then his coital relationship collided with his decent nature. Nevertheless, he was plagued more by his own treatment of Amos Lasher than by any fear of disgrace over his philandering. Amos had pleaded with him, pathetically, warning that Daisy would kill him, and all the lawman had done was humor the old man, laughing about it later with the head nurse over a generous slice of cherry pie. It had all been true. He had abandoned Amos, defenseless, when Amos had trusted him for help and protection, turned to him for justice. His conscience goaded him incessantly, and to soothe its ire, he saw to it that everyone at the Home who wanted to could be at the funeral.

It was a strange sight on that warm spring day. Most of the people around the grave looked as if they might be going in it. The wheelchairs, the canes, the stooped and rickety, with a preacher who looked innocently young among them. Nell was there, and Clara. Burt Daniels was the only county commissioner with the grit to show up, the story having spread through the small town like scandal. A handful of the curious appeared. Winston stood near the foot of the grave in a sagging gray wool suit that was too short for him. The casket was suspended over the earthen hole on nylon straps. The preacher was reading from the Bible.

A breeze ruffled the plastic grass they'd laid over the mound of soil. Marvin stood close to the coffin, grieving for this friend who had been kind to him and wondering how Amos's battered face had anything to do with what happened. Amos said she'd get blamed for it, but she must have gotten so mad she up and killed him. Clara scanned the faces around the grave, still unaware of her part in the whole drama, confused and upset with Daisy's arrest, never realizing that she *had* brought Daisy her surprise: the final piece of evidence not yet in. Spencer hadn't wanted to come, having avoided funerals all his life, but he had been swept along with the event. He listened to the words the preacher read, words that Amos used to underline in Spencer's Bible, irritating him no end.

Burt Daniels didn't lift his head, reeling under the weight of knowing he could have prevented Amos Lasher's death. Had he known the deeper agony, his torment would be intolerable. It is one thing to bear the burden of permitting a murder. Quite another to bear the burden of leaving a fellow human, who looked to you for justice, no alternative but to take his own life to achieve that justice. Burt Daniels would never know the real sorrow, or the triumph.

The preacher closed the Bible and led the gathering in a prayer. They sang one verse of the hymn "Amazing Grace" in several keys and melodies, and when they all stopped, Grace kept singing another verse in a sweet soft voice. Fern gently hushed her as the minister took a photo out of the book and turned it over. It was the photo of Amos and Mildred in Los Angeles.

"Mr. Pace told me that these words of Rainer Maria Rilke meant a great deal to Amos. I'll close by reading them for you."

He read slowly, the words that Amos had printed late one night in the bathroom, sitting on the toilet with his trousers down around his ankles.

> *"We are all falling. This hand's falling too—*
> *all have this falling sickness none withstands.*
> *And yet there's always One whose gentle hands*
> *this universal falling can't fall through."*

The clergyman slipped the photo back into his Bible and stepped away from the grave, confused about who should receive the special condolences he always gave to the immediate family. They were all his immediate family, but maybe Fern should receive the flag, if there'd been one. The casket was slowly lowered into the grave. It was too fancy for Amos; the commissioners' guilt made them splurge. The winches creaked; the casket swayed slightly and came to rest gently at the bottom. Each of them in turn threw a handful of earth into the grave, their final gesture of affection for their fallen companion.

Mick, his denim cap pulled tight, threw his farewell from the wheelchair. Winston slowly let the grains of soil trickle through his fingers, the truth of what happened falling forever into the ground. Fern first helped Effie throw a goodbye so that the sightless woman wouldn't miss the hole, and Grace reached into her pocket and threw a billow of confetti and missed the grave altogether. Her gift blew across the mourners and the cemetery lawn.

Fern paused, thankful for that lovely man who came into her life when she'd given up all hope of ever being loved again. She knew she shouldn't feel bitter or angry because that wretch had struck him down, but she did. She threw her handful of earth and turned away. Marvin stood for a moment, squinting into the grave as if looking down into the courtyard for the catching arms. He whispered, "Father, are you there?" his tears falling into the earth with his words. Emil, Robert, Carlos, all of them felt the strange confusion dwelling in their midst, their newly given freedom shrouded by the death of this friend.

They started back to the cars, walking, rolling, shuffling across the cemetery, helping each other through the sunshine. John Thomas had provided a van for the wheelchairs, Burt Daniels had lined up the cars. Fern led Effie over the greening grass, and Burt Daniels caught up to them, unable to look Fern in the eye.

"Mrs. Knutson, I wanted to speak to you before you left. I want you to know how sorry I am, how terribly sorry. And I'm going to do something about it."

He was breaking down, attempting to finish his say before he choked up.

"I'm going to see that we build that new home right off Main where we have the property. Some good will come out of this."

The sheriff came up and overheard the last part of the conversation. He wanted to add his penance while the confessional was still open.

"This was a terrible thing that happened, Fern. I promise you here and now, it'll never happen again."

"Oh, but it *is* happening," she said sadly, "right now . . . somewhere."

She led her blind companion to the car, leaving the two county officials standing quietly, trying to decide what to do with their hands. Clara walked along with Winston.

"Why, Winston, you're not looking for Ginger anymore."

She was pleased. The lanky old mailman looked down at her as he trudged along in his baggy suit.

"No, I'm not," he said.

The cars filled and pulled away, leaving the graveyard silent, but for its natural sounds. A small sparrow was singing wildly atop a marble tombstone. Soon his fellows would return from the South. It was spring. All the world was coming to life. Winter had passed. Everything was breaking free.

CHAPTER 26

WITH THE DUMB LUCK that desperation sometimes breeds, Amos had picked his co-conspirators shrewdly. Daisy's last ship sank when they discovered she was the new beneficiary of Amos's life insurance. Emil testified without batting an eye—to Daisy's creeping insanity—that she had forced him under threat of violence to sign as a witness to the change of beneficiary. She stood in the courtroom and shouted that he was a lying bastard. Emil gazed back at her over his Teddy Roosevelt mustache with cool indifference, finally striking a blow at those faceless dynamiters who had gone unpunished for so long. The closest Emil could come to the truth was that Amos set a trap that would snag her if she killed him.

While the trial continued, they had uncovered five insurance policies Daisy had collected on as the sole beneficiary, Johnny's being only one of them. They were just beginning to piece together the magnitude of her fringe benefits: pension checks, social security, insurance payments, savings accounts. None of the residents had much, but together it was an inviting sum.

Toward the end of the trial they had to gag Daisy in the courtroom because she kept yelling that she hadn't done it, that she had been framed, but everyone now figured she was mad. It helped the irate and embarrassed townspeople explain to themselves how anyone could do such terrible things in their good community. They were hard on Daisy and Roland, attempting to heap on them the public shame and guilt that had surfaced in the Sunset scandal. Daisy was convicted of first-degree murder. With her sentence of twenty-five years, it turned out that she wouldn't be eligible for parole until she was over sixty-five years old. She was sent to the state hospital for the criminally insane, an institution the public gave little attention to, allowing the administrator free rein.

Roland got five to ten for several assault charges and conspiracy. Marvin and Mick, in his tattered engineer's cap and red bandana, and even Carlos, squinting from the witness stand, testified against him with an air of solemnity and frivolity that delighted the courtroom. The judge had to whisper to Marvin to use the word "testicle" instead of "balls" when describing Daisy's methods. Carlos tried to explain about his philodendron in the bedpans and the one in Owen's shoe. They didn't call Winston, thereby forever missing their closest brush with the truth. Scott flew back from Ohio for the trial, never understanding why Amos hadn't gone home with him or what it was that Amos felt he had to do. Scott was awarded Amos's insurance, and Johnny's insurance company, after recovering their funds from Daisy's diverse accounts, was searching for Johnny's original beneficiary: a Jane Marie Clendenon, address unknown.

Clara was at the trial, finding it almost impossible to accept Daisy's guilt and wondering how she could have missed all the terrible things that went on. Nell testified to no one's hurt or aid. She didn't get any of it, but she worked at the new home just off Main Street in downtown West Stover. Burt Daniels kept his promise, coming perilously close to losing his chance. The ripples the trial made in the county rolled out in ever widening circles, engulfing some of the county commissioners when their time came for reelection.

Ironically, Burt Daniels was narrowly reelected on the campaign of confessing honestly and asking for a chance "To Make Things Right." They built the home right downtown where anyone could pop in the door at any hour and say hello. They were all there now, except Sadie. Sadie died a year after the trial. Several relatives from the valley showed up for her funeral with a generous display of flowers.

The new Convalescent Center was more like a boarding house for those who could get around. They sat in the dayroom and watched the children on the way to school, the shoppers, the traffic of the town, the ebb and flow of life. Marvin watched the fights on television and Elroy found ways to get a drink now and then. Carlos hung out with Emil at the game room in the Mint Bar, playing checkers and poker while Emil sucked contentedly on a tobaccoed pipe. Robert frequented the local library and often forgot his way back. Winston was given a job at the

Center, wiping up tables, stacking dishes, keeping the dayroom neat. He helped whoever might need assistance with some simple everyday chore, never again reciting nursery rhymes or calling for his lost dog. He did occasionally carry his tennis racket.

Sheriff John Thomas was defeated at the polls, not so much because of the stories that circulated about him and Daisy—the community took all claims that Daisy made with a great deal of suspicion—but he was returned to ranching because he was a deserving scapegoat. Fern testified that Amos had told the sheriff everything.

They were all part of the community again, a part of life. At the evening meal they often ended up at the same table, a handful of the Sunset gang, without excluding any of the many newcomers. There was something there between them one could sense. Each kept his private piece of the puzzle a secret to the grave, honoring their promise to Amos to never tell. Three years had gone fast in their new surroundings, and now they took their freedom and restored dignity for granted. They were old, their minds rusty, and they would forget.

Fern was visiting Marvin as she had done each day since he'd become bedridden. He was slipping fast.

"Is there anything I can do for you?" Fern said.

She always asked, and he always said there was nothing. But not this day.

"Get Elroy to tell me about the Gypsies, and the courtyard," Marvin said weakly.

Fern lost her train of thought.

"The what?" she said.

"The Gypsies."

"No, no, you said something about a courtyard," Fern said.

"Yeah, the courtyard in the story. I want him to tell me."

"Oh, I'm sure he will," she said and her heart fluttered in her chest.

"No, he won't. He won't never tell it right."

Fern found Elroy at Rosy's, visiting with others his age along the oaken bar. He was astonished at seeing Fern in Rosy's. She asked him if he would grant Marvin his wish. Elroy refused.

"I've told him that story a thousand times, that stinkin' man."

"Just once more," Fern said. "It means a lot to him. He may not be with us much longer."

"Hell, he'll be wettin' that bed for another ten years. Thank God I'm not his roommate anymore."

Then Fern took the note out of her coat pocket. She had gone to her room to fetch it right after talking with Marvin.

"I don't know if I should do this," she said, "but I want you to tell me what you think this means. Amos wrote this to me the night he died."

She opened it and laid it out next to his beer. Elroy leaned close and read the printed words.

WORD FROM THE COURTYARD, I LOVE YOU
SOUNDS FROM THE COURTYARD, LAUGHTER

"When did Amos write this?" he said excitedly.

"The night he was killed. What do you think it means?"

"*What does it mean!* You've had this all this time and you don't know what it means? My God, woman, I'll tell you what it means."

He slid off his stool and led Fern by the arm out onto Main Street where they could talk in private. He huddled close to her, his hands on her shoulders, smiling happily out of his wide flat face with an uncharacteristic hilarity, ignoring the shoppers who passed them on the sidewalk.

"It means, dear lady, that *Amos killed himself!*"

"Goodness gracious, are you sure?" she said.

"Don't you see? If he says the word is from the *courtyard,* it means he knew he was going to die. And if he knew he was going to die, it could only be because he was going to kill himself. That son of a gun. He did it! Daisy was telling the truth all along. Ha!"

Elroy let go of Fern and slapped his hands together. Fern stood on the sidewalk outside Rosy's Bar completely overwhelmed, a shivering elation coursing through her body as the meaning of Elroy's words crashed in on her.

"Do you really believe that's what it means?" she said.

"Without a doubt." Elroy beamed.

"We must never tell anyone," she said.

"It'll be hard," he said and he laughed and did a little jig.

"For Amos," she said. Then she remembered Marvin. "Will you tell Marvin the story once more?"

"I don't know. This doesn't change that, you know. Amos wrote the note *before* he jumped. He still didn't know," he said.

"If this could happen, for heaven's sake, trust him on the rest. Tell Marvin one more time."

"I'll see . . . when I get back."

Elroy returned to Rosy's to have another beer and celebrate Amos's triumph. "Hot damn!" He laughed as he pushed open the saloon door.

Fern wandered around town for over an hour, attempting to comprehend what Amos had done.

Fern stood in the doorway that evening and listened as Elroy told his old roommate the story of the Gypsy girl one more time. Fern remembered when Amos had told her, snuggled in her bed, and she wondered why she'd missed the significance of the courtyard for so long. Marvin lay childlike in the folds of his bed, catching Elroy's every word, anticipating, almost dreading the ending in the courtyard. Sitting in a chair beside Marvin's bed, Elroy spoke slowly, raising his voice so the dying man could hear.

"So at two in the morning the little girl goes out on the roof alone and walks over to the edge, eager to see her father. It was the dead of winter, a cold wind is blasting her. She looks down into the courtyard but it's pitch black; she can't see a blooming thing. She's shivering and she starts counting, but while she counts she starts to think. What if her father isn't even down there? He could be late. He could have been caught on the way, the Nazis could have him. The icy wind is tearing at her, standing on the edge, counting, and she wants to holler down into the darkness."

Elroy cupped his hands and called down to the floor.

"Father, are you there?"

Elroy paused.

"Don't stop," Marvin said, "please don't stop now."

"But the little girl knows she can't make a sound," Elroy said, "she can't call out to her father or the Nazis will hear her. She can't see her father, the courtyard is totally dark. The wind is howling. She finishes her count. Can her father see her? She's paralyzed. She hesitates. She'd never know if he was there unless she jumped. She whispers down into the dark courtyard, 'Father, are you there?' Then she takes a deep breath and leaps into the darkness."

Elroy paused.

"And in the morning, the courtyard?" Marvin said, struggling to raise his head from the pillow. Elroy glanced at Fern.

"And in the morning," Elroy said, "they found the courtyard *empty.*"

Marvin laid his head back on the pillow and grinned with his toothless mouth.

Fern turned and walked down the hallway. Her happiness was more than she could bear and tears blurred her vision. She stepped outside and watched the town's life flowing by. It was a gorgeous balmy night. Oh, Amos, he had known how it would turn out all along and had tried to tell her in his note. He had gone willingly, alone, into the jaws of the grizzly, laughing.

Stanley West was born in Saint Paul, grew up during the Depression and the World War II years, and attended Macalester College and the University of Minnesota, earning a degree in history and geology. He moved from the Midwest to Montana in 1964 where he raised a large family. He has lived there since. Though he has had a wide variety of "day jobs," he is currently writing full time and trying to keep up with his grandchildren. *Amos* was his first published novel.

Author's Note

The novel was written under the title *To Ride A Dead Horse.* During editing it was arbitrarily changed to *Amos.* I wanted to honor the original title with this revised reprint edition, but the book had taken on a reputation as *Amos,* and I didn't want to confuse the issue, therefore, the subtitle, *To Ride A Dead Horse.* The original title came out of the conversation between Amos and Emil when Amos had picked up the gauntlet to take on Daisy. Emil told Amos, "You'll be riding a dead horse."

Sunset Home was based on a county rest home in Montana in the midsixties where the residents were often treated in the manner depicted in the novel. Many of the characters are based on real people who, without family or friends or funds, were trapped there at the end of their lives. In the midseventies the place was bulldozed into the ground after the Daisylike head nurse had skipped town. No one was ever indicted or charged with any crime in connection with the operation of that institution.

Amos was produced as a CBS *Movie of the Week* and featured Kirk Douglas, Elizabeth Montgomery, Dorothy McGuire, Fred Coffin, Ray Ralston, and Pat Morita. It received four Emmy nominations.